TWO FAIRIES, ONE DESTINY

A PROPHECY OF WINGS

JANE MCGARRY

Published: 18 May 2021
Language: English
Paperback ISBN: 978-1-7365884-1-3
Ebook ISBN: 978-1-7365884-0-6
© Copyright 2021 by Jane McGarry

All rights reserved. No part of this publication may be reproduced, stored in a retrieval system or transmitted, in any form or by any means, electronic, mechanical, photocopying, recording or otherwise, without permission in writing from the author.

This book is licenced for your personal enjoyment only. This book may not be re-sold or given away to other people. If you would like to share this book with another person, please purchase an additional copy for each recipient. Thank you for respecting the hard work of this author.

This is a work of fiction. Name, characteristics, business, places, events and incidents are either the products of the author's imagination or used in a fictitious manner. Any resemblance to actual persons, living or dead, or actual events is purely coincidental.

For every Dahlia in the world—you are not alone.

PROLOGUE

The pains came more frequently now. Even with the help of Edwina, it was a struggle to run. In the cramped darkness of the tunnel, she tried to maintain her footing, an impossible task with the burgeoning weight of her belly. Time was of the essence. They must not be caught, but the spasms were nearly unbearable.

"I can't go on," she gasped, a sharp pang taking her breath away.

"Just a little bit further, Your Highness," the enchantress coaxed.

Every step down the seemingly endless passageway was sheer torment. Queen Ivy willed herself to continue. She was the last hope for her people, and she must not fail.

Edwina stopped so abruptly; the queen stumbled into her back. The enchantress pulled the weakened monarch through a narrow gap in the wall. They crossed the threshold of a doorway into the depths underneath the forest. A tangle of tree roots filled the cavern, their sinuous forms dwarfing the fairies. A robust scent infused the air with bark, stone, and earth. Queen Ivy, a Volant used to the skies, reeled at the unfamiliar smells and fell to her knees.

The enchantress, more experienced with Groundling habitats, remained unaffected and surveyed the area. She assisted the queen in a nook hidden between the sides of two large tree roots, which soared overhead out of sight to meet the tree's trunk somewhere way above.

"Wait here," she instructed, a moot directive to her incapacitated companion.

While Edwina disappeared the way they came, Ivy settled down her awkward frame. How had it come to this? The past few months had turned her world upside down. Having one's sister hunt you like prey was horrifying enough, but having her baby targeted for death, rocked Ivy to her very core. Instinctively, her hand flew to her stomach, the muscles again tightening with the tremors of labor.

Her friend returned, hair disheveled, wings drooping, and announced, "As far as I can tell, we may have lost them in the maze of tunnels. I have used cloaking measures along the way and put a spell on the door to keep others out. But your sister's powers are strong. If she were to find us…"

"She will find us. It is only a matter of time," the queen declared. Dahlia was learned enough in dark magic to track even a covered trail.

"Well, it is time for this baby, so here must do."

Queen Ivy sighed, resigned to the situation. When she discovered she was with child all those months ago, she had not envisioned giving birth in a dark hole underground. The enchantress spread a blanket on the earth for the queen to lie down. She checked the progress of the baby and nodded.

"It is time. You need to push."

Above all, the baby must survive. Otherwise, the prophecy would remain unfulfilled, and the kingdom would never be restored. The monarch braced herself against one sturdy root, its surface surprisingly warm and smooth. Under the calm direction of her lifelong friend, she delivered the child.

Edwina laid the baby girl into her arms. Ivy admired the feathery blond hair and the round little nose. Tears welled in her eyes at the sheer perfection of the infant. The enchantress finished tending to the mother and turned her attention to the newborn. After a quick examination, she ripped a length of fabric off Ivy's skirt to wrap her. "You could not have asked for a healthier daughter. Now, what shall her name be?"

"Her name?" the queen pondered. "I've not thought of one. All I have thought of is her safety."

Before Edwina responded, they heard it—the rattle of armor. Soldier's footsteps approached, their faint clinking unmistakable. Both women froze in terror.

"She has found us," Ivy whispered in dread, her arms tightening around the baby.

"Perhaps not. Perhaps it is King Theros on his way to tell us he defeated Dahlia."

The footsteps grew louder.

"No," the queen affirmed. "It is my sister. I feel her presence. You must take the baby to the other world and keep her safe until the time is right. Dahlia cannot follow you there."

The soldier's armor rang loudly in their ears. They came to a halt right outside the doorway.

"Come then," the enchantress conceded, holding out a hand to help her friend rise.

"No. I must stay and try to defeat Dahlia. Take her." She thrust the infant into Edwina's arms. "Go now."

Loud hammering filled the air with the enemy's attempt to break the door down.

"But My Queen, she will show you no mercy. I will not leave you here to die."

Queen Ivy leaned forward and placed her hands on her friend's, which cradled the child. She slipped the crystal-bound amulet inside the swaddling. "Yes, Edwina, you must. I command it. Take her now and keep her safe."

The enchantress desperately tried to think of another way. Axes and spears crashed upon the door, weakening her spell with every stroke. Sadly, she stepped back and conjured the words to transport her between the worlds, a power only she possessed in the entire kingdom.

The new mother watched the toss of the seeds, and Edwina's frantically whispered spell. A cloud of dust encircled her friend and her baby. Too weak to even stand, she blinked through her tears. Just before the two vanished, she said, "Lina. I want her to be named Lina."

Edwina nodded, the final wish heard, and with a poof, they were gone.

The door finally gave way, a multitude of soldiers pouring in, their armor dark as night. Queen Ivy turned to see her sister step through the broken threshold. Dahlia scrutinized the scene, the queen's deflated belly and the cloud of dust on the ground. Her eyes narrowed in malice.

The baby was beyond her reach—for now. She met Queen Ivy's eyes and despised the look of triumph in them.

"Kill her," Dahlia ordered.

The queen whispered one last anguished prayer for her daughter before an arrow pierced her heart.

CHAPTER 1

Lina pushed her hair out of her face and wrote her list with great care. She did not make as many trips to the healer's since her mother's health declined, and she wanted to make sure nothing was forgotten. Lina's parents were in their older years when they had adopted her, at an age when they were more likely to be grandparents. When a sudden illness took her father at the end of last fall, her mother's strength suffered. At sixteen, Lina took on the role of caretaker. She was determined to act with the same love and devotion they showed her.

"Don't forget to ask Winnie for more turmeric. My knee has been acting up," the older woman called weakly from her bed.

"All right," Lina replied. She scribbled another line onto her list.

In the darkened bedroom, she refilled a glass of water on the nightstand. The room brightened when she pulled open the curtains. "You should let some light in. It's not good to keep them closed all day."

Her mother smiled at her but said nothing. The winter stole much of the older woman's vitality, arriving right on the heels of her husband's death. Lina hoped the coming spring might lift her spirits. With one last glance to make sure all was in order, she fetched her shawl and headed out the door. Her snug cottage was nestled on the border of a rambling forest. The healer's cabin sat a good way into the woods.

On the path through the trees to old Winnie's house, Lina pulled her wrap tighter around her shoulders. The steel grey sky guarded against the sun's warmth. Though lovely signs of spring stirred in the forest, winter was loath to release its relenting grip. A few squirrels stirred in the underbrush, but there was still no birdsong in the trees. With a sigh, she reminded herself they would return soon— especially her favorite swallow. Her springtime friend's arrival was always a source of comfort for her.

According to the townsfolk, Winnie was not a healer but a witch. Lina's mother did not encourage using the word witch. Her mouth pursed into a small circle when someone used it. Yet, the girl could not think of a more appropriate word to describe the strange woman. With long grey hair and a hunched back hidden under long, black robes, she certainly looked the part. Though Lina had to concede, Winnie did not act it. She was odd but kind. Without her knowledge of herbs, Lina's mother would not have outlasted her illness this long. At this thought, Lina quickened her pace.

Eventually, the small cabin appeared, the brown structure blending seamlessly with the barren woods. The nearest town was a mile or so off. Lina's family did not get many visitors at the forest's edge. The townspeople ignored the cabin, save for the few who did take advantage of her healer's knowledge. In the warm months, a multitude of climbing flowers covered its walls and roof; today, their empty limbs wrapped the house in a skeletal grip.

The infamous wind chimes rang all year round despite the weather. Their tinkling could be heard long before the cabin came into view. Dozens of tiny bells clanked with every movement of air, a tannic iron smell drifting from them. They overwhelmed the low-lying branches outside the house like ripe fruit waiting to fall. Why Winnie had so many was anyone's guess. Absently, Lina twisted the amulet around her neck, a plain, clear stone she wore since she was too small to remember. Sometimes she swore it vibrated every time she came around the chimes. However, she knew this was a childish notion.

Once on the porch, chimes cluttered every available space. Lina ducked around several to find the front door. It stood ajar, so she leaned inside a bit. "Winnie?" she called out.

"Come in," the familiar voice answered.

She entered the large main room, its space aglow with the light of so many candles—small, thin, and white; they littered all surfaces like counterparts to the chimes outside. Lina took a few steps around the chaos of mismatched furniture and overflowing bookshelves. Bottles, papers, and unrecognizable trinkets covered every surface—most layered with a thick film of dust.

The witch shuffled into the room, her stooped posture slowing the process. In her hands was a tray of cookies. She motioned the girl to sit, the long black sleeve of her robe swaying softly. "How is Hazel feeling today?"

Lina perched on the edge of a ratty old chair; the fabric was worn to nothing in the seat and the arms. She found it difficult to relax in the woman's presence as if she was intensely scrutinized, but for what she did not know.

"She is still weak. Her appetite failed to increase despite the gentian you gave her last time," Lina answered with a frown between her brows.

"Oh, I had hoped the herb would help, but the death of Felix hit her hard. They were together for so many years," Winnie stated. She pushed the tray of cookies toward Lina, who took one.

"Yes," the girl agreed between nibbles, "she hasn't been herself since Papa passed. Hopefully, the warmer weather will perk her up."

The old woman nodded and went to her workbench, where she gathered some vials, her crooked body an awkward array of motions. The strong scent of herbs filled the air as she poured liquid and ground leaves into powder. After depositing the completed remedies into a burlap bag, she shuffled back and, with a smile, dropped two cookies inside before handing it to the girl.

Part of Lina wanted to stay and talk to the healer. After all, she must be lonely out here all by herself, yet she did not know what to say. While the woman's eyes studied her intently, she rose to leave, grasping the parcel close to her chest as she navigated her way to the door. Winnie hobbled slowly to see her out.

"You are a good daughter," the witch praised, watching her from the porch. "Remember, I am always here if you need me," she concluded and winked.

A gust of wind blew, and the cacophony of chimes drowned out Lina's reply of, "thanks." Once on the path home, she again pulled her shawl tight around her; though the air was fresh and crisp, Winnie's stare gave her the chills. When the chimes faded into the background, Lina shook off the eerie feeling Winnie always evoked in her.

The medicine helped ease her mother's pain but did little to restore her health. Day by day, as spring roused the earth, drawing forth the plants and animals, Hazel faded, her strength not improved by the awakening of life around her. Despite all her efforts, Lina could do nothing to stem the tide.

One afternoon, she bundled her mother up, though the air was warm and balmy, and assisted her to a rocker on the front porch. Side by side, they sat content in the silence of each other's company. Flowers bloomed all around, their aroma carrying softly through the air. The girl threw some seeds down so they could watch the birds flutter and peck in front of them.

"Look," Lina cried at the sight of a particular bird, "It's Knox. Our swallow has returned."

Swallows were not common in the area, but this one had been coming to roost every year since the girl could remember. So distinct were his markings, he was recognized immediately and celebrated as the true herald of warm weather's return. As with most swallows, his head and wings were blue and most of his body white, except for his red face. Yet, Knox was unique, with a spray of red feathers shaped like a heart on his chest. Never had Lina seen another swallow like him. When she was quite little, Winnie suggested the name Knox, which sounded as regal and handsome as the beautiful bird.

Knox landed on the porch rail in front of them, a happy song trilling from his beak. Hazel smiled, a relieved look crossing her face. Perhaps this would be the very thing to pull her back to health. He hopped around a bit before soaring to a nearby tree hollow where he always nested.

After a long silence, Hazel said, "Go inside, look under the bed and bring me the small purple bag from the chest."

"The small bag?" Lina repeated, disbelief in her tone.

Her mother nodded a firm assent.

The girl went to the bedroom and crept to the bed. She pulled a rowan box out from under it. With a certain amount of awe, she lifted the lid. To others, it would merely look like a jumble of papers, a few keepsakes, and a small velvet bag. Still, they were precious relics to their family—a marriage license, adoption papers, a tiny handprint stamped in clay, a drawing Felix made of his beloved wife, and the bag. These items told the story of their lives.

Lina picked up the bag, a slight shudder passing through her. What lay inside was a mystery to her. When she was younger, on a rare occasion when the box was opened, she picked it up, fascinated by the luxurious fabric and shiny golden cord. Both her parents called out in fright for her to put it down, which she did without question. It was the only time she remembered either of them raising a voice to her. And now, her mother asked for this very thing.

Back on the porch, she carefully handed it over. Hazel took it hesitantly. Again, they sat in silence, Lina too nervous to ask any questions. For a long while, the only sounds were the old rockers and Knox's bird song while he happily built his nest.

"Lina, when I am gone, you must promise me something," Hazel finally said.

"Yes, Mother, anything," Lina agreed readily.

"You must take this bag and give it, Winnie. Do you understand?"

"Winnie?" Lina replied, confusion in her tone mixed with unease.

"Yes, promise me you will do this," her mother said sternly.

"Of course. I promise."

"Good, sweetheart. Now put it back where it is safe," she requested in a now softer tone.

Though bewildered, Lina did as her mother told and placed the bag inside the chest and pushed it carefully back under the bed. When she exited the bedroom, her mother, who suddenly seemed invigorated by the conversation, came inside and sat at the dinner table. For the first time in many months, she cleaned her plate. The unease Lina felt over their strange conversation disappeared, replaced by hope for her mother's recovery.

That night, Hazel embraced her daughter a little tighter before settling into her bed. Lina quickly noticed a new sense of calm regarding her. She sat with her mother, softly singing until the woman drifted off to sleep. Even then, Lina found it difficult to pull herself away to her bed.

Lina rose the next morning to the sun streaming into her room. Birds sang sweetly outside, and Knox's tune was easy to pick out. With a good stretch, she rose and dressed. After lighting the fire, she set the kettle over it for their morning tea.

Lina opened the bedroom door with a smile on her face, but quickly froze. With one look, she knew. Her mother lay still, flat on the bed, an expression of peace on her lifeless face and the velvet bag clutched to her heart.

CHAPTER 2

The last of the handful of mourners said their goodbyes. Lina stood alone at her parents' grave, one side just budding with new grass, the other a dark pile of earth. A gloomy sky hung overhead, clouds ready to burst at any moment. Her swallow, Knox, sang a mournful tune from the trees above as thunder rumbled across the small cemetery.

For the first time in her sixteen years, Lina was alone. Still, her parents being together again was a small source of consolation for the girl. They had always been two halves of a whole, and Hazel was never the same after Felix's passing. Their small cottage belonged to her now, its gardens providing ample food for the warm months. It would be up to her to perform all the harvesting and preserving which winter required.

A fat raindrop fell on her face, followed by several more. By the time she neared home, the skies had opened up in earnest. She ran onto the front porch, sopping wet. A neighbor had left a pie by the door which she collected and brought into the kitchen. After changing her clothes, Lina prepared a small supper for herself. Alone at the table, she dined, the clink of the fork her only company.

Silence surrounded her in its suffocating grip.

For the next few days, she went through the motions, trying to regain some type of normalcy, but they were now all but hollow actions. She had no extended family, and in the past, only the occasional visitor ever stopped by, yet Lina had never felt lonely with only her mother and father's company. Now, loneliness seeped into every crack of her being. Such a new and unfamiliar feeling was this longing for someone... anyone.

Her future was unclear. She knew the day would come when her parents passed away, but she did not imagine it would be this soon. In her mind, Lina envisioned herself married and with a family before losing her parents. Life, however, as it often does, had other plans. If she chose to stay here, she could make a living selling fresh and canned goods, but it would be a solitary existence. Yet, she would have much to learn if she chose to move to the nearest village or even relocate to a larger town. Such a move would put her entirely out of her depth—no clear decision formed in her mind or her heart.

One evening, she slumped into one of the rockers on the porch, the sun low in the sky. Her eyes stared emptily across the yard as Knox flew down and perched on the rail. He cocked his head to regard her. When she didn't move, he bounced back and forth and cocked his head again.

"What do you want?" she asked, surprising herself. It was the first time she had spoken aloud in days. "Some seed, no doubt."

He called out a few notes and leaned forward eagerly. Lina went inside to find a handful of breadcrumbs, which she laid on the rail. He pecked at the seed and ruffled his feathers in satisfaction when finished. The girl laughed, another foreign sound. The burden on her heart eased a bit, even after Knox flew home to roost for the night.

The next day, she woke early and set about cleaning the house which she had been neglecting. Once all was in order in the main room, Lina went to her parents' bedroom. She pulled open the curtains, dusted the furniture, and aired out the bedding in the yard. Her mother would never have wanted the room to be closed up like a dusty tomb. Later that afternoon, she brought the freshened quilt back inside. When she tossed it across the bed, her toe hit something hard underneath—the chest. On the morning of her mother's death, she hastily threw the bag inside and meticulously avoided all thoughts of it since.

The promise she made to Hazel loomed over her. Slowly, she knelt to slide the chest out. Its lid opened with a tiny creak, and she groped inside to grab the bag. With it in hand, Lina returned to the main room. She sat at the kitchen table, laying the bag down in front of her. There it sat while she stared down at it. A noise from the bedroom startled her. Knox flew in from the open window. He landed on the table next to the bag, again cocking his head to watch her. When she remained still, the swallow took the golden string in his beak and attempted to fly. The weight of the bag held it down, but he managed to move it slightly across the table in her direction. He stared at her.

"All right," she whispered with a sigh, "I will go to Winnie's tomorrow."

As if pleased, the bird flew to her shoulder, where he leaned down to rub his head against her cheek before flying back out the way he came in.

Lina picked up the pouch, her fingers running over the soft napped fabric, which she had considered luxurious as a child. Though heavy for a swallow, it felt like nothing in her hand. Whatever was inside, it could not be much. She debated whether to open it now or wait. The sheer looks of fear on her parents' faces when she first touched it flew to her mind. When she later questioned her mother about it, Hazel said it was essential and must not be lost. It was never mentioned again until the day before she died, but then, there was no fear, only deep respect.

Curiosity finally got the better of Lina. She tugged the strings open and turned the bag over. Into the palm of her hand fell three barleycorns.

That was it?

Whatever her mind imagined the contents to be, these mundane seeds were undoubtedly a letdown. Why her parents reacted so harshly when she first touched it was beyond her. Disappointed, she put them back in the pouch and went to bed.

As promised, the next morning, she headed for Winnie's with the bag in hand. A warm spring sun made the walk far more enjoyable than her last trip. Birds sang happy tunes, swooping from tree to tree. Squirrels frolicked in the underbrush, their bushy tails popping out every so often. Flowers burst into bloom around every footfall.

The lilt of wind chimes floated through the air long before Lina saw the cabin, her amulet vibrating at the sound. The structure appeared to melt right out of the forest in front of her. A few steps from the porch, she halted in surprise. Winnie stood on the porch with Knox on the railing next to her as though they waited expectantly for her arrival.

"There, there, child, do not be alarmed. Come." The witch gestured her forward and said, "It is time for you to learn the meaning of those barleycorns."

CHAPTER 3

While Lina mounted the steps, the swallow chirped excitedly. Winnie put a guiding hand on her shoulder and led her inside. They settled down at a small dining table piled high with papers and books. The old woman cleared a large space and laid a plate of cookies down. Knox landed on the back of the girl's chair. Silently, Lina laid the bag on the wooden surface between them. Outside, the chimes and birds tried to outdo each other's clamor.

"Did Hazel ever speak of this?" the witch inquired, a nod at the bag while she pushed the plate of cookies closer. Lina took one to be polite.

"No. Once, when I was younger, I picked it up. Both my parents yelled at me to put it down; it was almost as if they were frightened of it. They told me to leave it be."

"And did you?" Winnie pressed.

"Yes, until the day before my mother died. She asked for it and made me promise to bring it to you," the girl replied, uncomfortable under Winnie's curious gaze.

"Did you look inside already?"

"Yes, last night." Lina felt as guilty as the first time she had touched it and incurred her parents' anger. She took a small bite of cookie out of nervousness.

"Not what you expected?" the witch surmised.

"No. To be honest, I thought it would be something of value."

"I see," was the enigmatic reply.

Silence again. Even the birds and the chimes quieted in anticipation of what would be said next. But the witch seemed in no hurry to talk. She drummed her fingers on the table, her brow furrowed in thought.

"Are you ever going to tell me what it all means?" Lina blurted out, exasperated by the witch's nonchalance.

"Yes," Winnie said. "I'm merely trying to decide where to start."

"How about at the beginning," Lina urged.

"Yes, but whose beginning? Yours? Mine? Times? Which would be the most useful, I wonder?" She deliberated a bit longer. "What did your parents tell you about your adoption?"

"That you helped a young woman deliver me, but she passed in childbirth. You knew my parents always longed for a baby and asked if they would take me," she exclaimed, annoyed that she was the one answering the questions. "Why? Is that not what happened?"

"In a way, it was."

Lina sighed in disgust. They were talking in circles, in riddles whose meaning she did not grasp. Sorry she came, the girl reached for the bag, but Winnie snatched it up.

"Patience, child. It is a long story and will take time for you to digest. Don't rush me." Something in Winnie's tone intrigued the girl.

"Very well," Lina agreed begrudgingly and took another bite of cookie before crossing her arms in irritation.

"I knew your mother well. She and I grew up together," Winnie finally said.

Lina looked at her dubiously. The witch was much older than her mother could have been. Knox flew over to Winnie's shoulder as though he wished to add to the story himself.

"She didn't die giving birth to you," Winnie stated softly. "She died shortly after. She sent me away with you. She died to protect you."

"From what?" the girl exclaimed, surprised by the direction of the story.

"Evil, of course. What else could it be?" The witch shrugged as though the answer was obvious.

"Why didn't she just protect me herself?" It seemed a fair question to Lina, who held the witch's gaze.

"Because I alone could get you out of reach, and your survival was of the utmost importance. *Is* of the utmost importance," Winnie quickly corrected herself.

"To who?" Lina asked in exasperation.

"The Fairy World."

Lina thought perhaps she misunderstood. "The what?"

"The Fairy World, child," Winnie repeated as though that cleared everything up.

Lina regarded her for a long moment. The old woman nodded solemnly. Now, she was doubly sorry she came. Whatever these barleycorns signified, she was not going to learn here. She held out her hand in hopes of retrieving the pouch so she could leave.

"I know you doubt me," the witch acknowledged.

"Doubt seems too inferior a word," Lina declared.

"Please, just hear me out. For Hazel's sake. She would want that."

The reference to her mother lessened her irritation. Hazel asked her to come here. She could at least hear what Winnie had to say. Knox now flew to Lina's shoulder. He walked to her ear and nibbled on the lobe as though imploring her to listen. "Very well."

"I could spend a whole day explaining this and still not finish, but I will start with the basics. You are the daughter of Queen Ivy and King Theros, who were monarchs of the Volant Fairies. Their kind, the Hirundo, ruled over the entire Fairy World, maintaining freedom and balance. But an evil queen named Dahlia toppled their reign and brought chaos and darkness to the land. There is a prophecy linked to a child who will one day restore the kingdom and bring peace to the land. That child is you."

Hazel always loved to tell Lina a good story at bedtime. She created quite a world full of fairies and other mythical creatures, as well as their beloved swallow. They had been a favorite part of the girl's childhood, a comforting place of escape, but in the end, only a fantasy. In the real world, Lina's parents were gone, and she was alone. Alone and wanting *real* answers.

"I'm a bit old to believe in fairy tales, Winnie. If you don't know what the barleycorns mean, it's fine. Please tell me so I can seek answers elsewhere."

"Clearly, words will not convince you. So I shall show you. I will need a day to prepare for the journey. We will leave in the morning. Do you promise to come back?"

"Yes," the girl replied reluctantly, unsure what else to say under the circumstances and anxious to leave. "How long will we be gone?"

"Quite a while." The witch escorted her to the door. "Go home, set your affairs in order, and return at dawn. I will keep these safe until then." The pouch disappeared into the folds of her robe. Now, Lina had no choice but to return tomorrow. "And most importantly, make sure to wear your amulet."

All the way home, Lina pondered the conversation, analyzing it from all sides, but only found herself more confused. She fingered the amulet around her neck, contemplating what could possibly make it so significant. Knox followed closely above, settling into his nest when they arrived at the cottage.

Back in her small abode, she prepared a light dinner. Her mind still debated what to do and what she believed. Even though Winnie's story was preposterous, she would not find out anything more by staying here. Wherever the witch was taking her, perhaps she could extract some answers from others. By the time Lina finished her meal, she had resolved this was the best course of action.

There was not much for her to pack except a few clothes, a comb, and some bread. She looked around the house, but there was nothing else to bring except for the rowan chest. It was not cumbersome, and its value sentimental enough she did not want to part with it. Once out from under the bed, Lina opened it to look over the remaining contents, which no longer seemed relevant to anyone. A sealed envelope with the word *Lina* written in her mother's handwriting sat inside. Though she had not been in the box often, she was sure this had never been there before.

Lina wondered how her mother held the velvet bag the morning she found her. When she left her on that final night, it was still in the box under the bed, yet somehow Hazel had retrieved it and left this in its place. She had not noticed it when she hastily threw the bag in nor when she blindly pulled it out.

Carefully, Lina pulled out the paper and unfolded it into her lap. The words before her caused a gasp to escape her lips.

Lina,

Believe everything Winnie tells you. 'Tis all true. You were a wonderful daughter to us.

Now reclaim your life as the fairy you were meant to be. I will always love you.

Mother

CHAPTER 4

At dawn, Winnie awaited Lina on the porch, Knox by her side, chirping along with the chimes and bells. She regarded the small bag of belongings the girl shouldered and the rowan box she clasped to her side but said nothing. Once inside, she offered Lina a sweet roll which the girl readily took.

"We will need to walk deep into the forest. It is a good distance and not always an easy path, but I know the way," she informed her.

As far as Lina knew, Winnie never left her cabin. In fact, she did not attend either of her parents' funerals. At the time of Felix's death, Hazel mentioned the healer never went out. Now, all hunched over and hardly agile, she wanted to delve deeper into the woods.

"Are you ready?" she inquired as Lina licked the last bit of crumbs off her fingers. Knox hopped around on the floor, enjoying the rest.

"I suppose," the girl answered hesitantly, wondering if she had made a mistake coming here despite her mother's note.

The witch shuffled to the closet and selected a long cape covered in tiny bells. An airy tune fluttered across the room as she wrapped it around her shoulders. Next, she grabbed a small rucksack. With each movement, the soft bell song cascaded around her.

More bells? Lina thought.

On the way out, the old woman grabbed a walking stick. She offered a second one to Lina, and they set off with Knox swooping above. All morning they hiked through the woods, the undergrowth so thick in spots, it was treacherous. The endless ringing of the tiny bells blended in with the singing birds and the rustling leaves. Around mid-day, they stopped in a small clearing. Winnie drew out some bread and cheese from the rucksack for their lunch.

"You have done well so far, Lina," she said while they sat against a sturdy tree trunk. "Do you have any questions?"

"How much farther?" Her brow dripped with sweat from the exertion, but the old witch seemed hardly winded by the journey.

"Not much longer," the woman replied, handing her another hunk of bread. "I understand this must be confusing for you."

Knox flew down to her side, and she gave him some small pieces of bread. After eating them, he hopped up to her shoulder. They sat in silence for some time, the girl deep in thought, absently fingering the amulet around her neck. Winnie's gaze settled on the stone, a reverent look in her eye.

"I found a note my mother left," Lina finally admitted. "It said I was to believe whatever you told me. So I will try."

"Good girl. When we get there, you must be cautious and listen to my every instruction," Winnie announced with seriousness. "No matter how strange it may seem," she added with a knowing leer.

"All right," the girl agreed, though this was as mysterious a thing to say as everything else had been so far. She could only hope it would all make sense soon, or they would end up lost in the depths of the forest with no hope of finding help.

Winnie gathered the uneaten food to place back in her sack, the little bells adorning her cape jingling in time with her movements.

"You like bells a lot," Lina blurted out, the tone almost accusatory. "I mean, you have so many at your home and now, the cape."

"Yes, they are beneficial." Winnie smiled over at her.

"For what?"

"Keeping evil away." The witch rose, signaling the end of the break.

"Evil? What kind of evil?" Lina glanced about her, suddenly aware of their complete isolation in the woods.

"Patience. In time you will know all."

The old woman took up her stick and walked off, leaving Lina no choice but to follow, her question unanswered. She would add it to her ever-growing list.

They hiked again for a long while until they came to a large hill. Lina's feet dragged more and more with each step, and she thought of protesting against the entire journey. Winnie halted at the top while the girl, less than half her age, struggled to keep up. When Lina finally reached the top, the witch pointed down the other side. There stood a circular grove of rowan trees, more enormous than any she had ever seen in her life. The land was empty around them, as though this spot was specifically marked before the forest picked up and continued some ways farther.

"Here we are at last." Winnie hurried down the far side of the hill with Lina on her heels.

The outer trees were the tallest, standing as if they were sentries to whatever lay inside. Once they slipped past them, the land outside disappeared from view. Dapples of sunlight filtered to the floor through the leaves above, dancing in irregular waves on the ground. The air itself tingled with an otherworldly vibration. For the first time, Lina believed there might be something to old Winnie's story when her amulet grew warm against her skin.

They reached a small clearing barely wide enough to fit them both. High above, Lina could see specks of blue sky peeking in between the highest leaves. The swallow fluttered around them with excited chirps while Winnie produced the velvet bag from her cape and dumped the barleycorns into her hand.

"Knox will be happy when you get there," the witch mused. "Are you ready to go back?"

"Back where?" Lina asked, her stomach sinking.

"The Fairy World, my dear."

"As ready as I'll ever be, I suppose," the girl mumbled, second-guessing all the decisions which had brought her here. Her heart pounded against her ribs, and her mouth went dry. She clutched the rowan box to her chest.

"Very well. Stand here and be very still."

The old woman pulled Lina close with one arm. With the other, she tossed the barleycorns overhead where they remained suspended in the air for a moment before bursting into golden dust. Winnie used her free hand to motion in a circle above them. She chanted words in a language the girl did not understand. Ever so slowly, the golden dust spread out and encircled them. It surrounded their heads and wafted lower, around their chest, waist, and knees. When it touched the ground to enclose them completely, Lina heard a click. Before she could think, she felt a sensation of heat burst from her center outward, followed by the sheer terror of plummeting down a long tunnel.

Just when she thought her body would be torn inevitably apart, the heat drew back into her, and she fell or landed, she was not sure which, onto the ground. Dizzy and bewildered, it took a few moments to re-orient herself. Once the spinning sensation dissipated, she looked around.

In a dark place, full of what look to be massive tree roots, she stood. No longer did she wear the simple clothes of a poor peasant girl, but a soft, pink dress with delicate slippers on her feet. Next to her, the rowan box sat on the ground, askew but unchanged. Beyond that was the sack she brought from home, now large as her house. But the biggest shock was the woman in front of her. Tall, with long brown hair and a lovely face, stood a woman in a cape of bells, now too short for her frame, which she removed to expose a pair of gossamer wings. In Winnie's unmistakable voice, the fairy said, "Welcome back, Lina."

CHAPTER 5

Dahlia woke with a start. Blackness lay heavy around her, and lightning flashed, illuminating the shadowy outlines of the room. Perhaps it was only the noise of thunder that woke her from her slumber. But no, after a few breaths, the feeling grew stronger. Often she had wondered if she would sense the actual moment.

She rose, slipping a dark robe around her. It pooled along the floor like inky black water in her wake. The low hum of fabric on stone followed her to the balcony, where she watched the early morning storm rage. Dark clouds blocked out the dawn's first light, punctuated now and again by bright lightning bolts.

Her empire spread before her beyond the reach of her vision in every direction. Sixteen years had come and gone in her unchallenged rule, each day enfolding more lands into her iron grip. Some called her merciless, even heartless. She cared not. That was all life ever taught her.

Even here in the violent storm, she closed her eyes and remembered the gleaming castle, the glorious kingdom her parents had reigned over all those years ago. Back then, a large part of her believed in the world's goodness, and that hope always won out in the end. Her eyes snapped open. *Not anymore.*

Fragments of memory lingered on the edge of her mind of Ivy and herself. Inseparable they had been, together since the womb. They were only parted for three minutes when her sister, Ivy, entered the world first. Three minutes, a small fraction of time, but enough to decide the fate of an entire kingdom. In their early youth, they had not comprehended the enormity of these three minutes. With the innocence of childhood, she and her sister planned to rule together one day. How simple the world seems to an innocent mind.

Their parents had allowed them to think this, never discouraging the fantasy. Every waking moment they passed together, rarely apart for more than a moment. The princesses were beloved throughout the kingdom, one as fair as ivory and the other with hair as fiery as flames. They spent their days pretending to rule as co-queens, never planning to be parted from one another. Dahlia had felt as though they shared one heart.

But as time wore on, the subtle favoring of Ivy grew stronger. Her sister began having lessons from which Dahlia was excluded. One day out of nowhere, Ivy was joined in her studies by Edwina, a pupil of Priya's, the queen's enchantress. No explanation was given, but Edwina never spoke to Dahlia and eyed her suspiciously whenever they were together. She envied the bond which developed between this fairy and Ivy, worried she was no longer her sister's most trusted confidante. One day, when she felt significantly hurt and out of sorts, she wandered into the gardens. High up in a tower window, blue lights flashed. It was Priya's tower. Without much thought, she headed up. Perhaps the enchantress missed her pupil as much as Dahlia missed her sister.

A soft breeze helped carry Dahlia up to the balcony, where she alighted and folded her wings. Gently, she tapped on the door.

"Who's there?" Priya snarled, the harshness in her voice making the girl sorry she came.

"It's just me, Dahlia."

The door cracked. Priya's face peered out, framed by long black hair streaked with white.

"I didn't mean to disturb you. Ivy is busy, and I am alone. I thought maybe you would like some company…"

The enchantress's eyes narrowed, a wave of calculation playing over her face for a second before a decision formed. "Yes. Come in, child."

Dahlia left the warm sun of the balcony for the chill darkness of the chamber. When her eyes adjusted, she stood mesmerized. She noticed a bed, a table, chairs, and other such ordinary furnishings, yet scattered about them and atop were fascinating objects—crystals, vials of vibrant colored liquids, feathers of all shapes and sizes, and the skull of what looked to be a mouse or chipmunk. A small bowl on the table caught her attention. Blue flames flickered over it, somehow suspended in mid-air.

"How did you do that?" she asked.

"I'd like to tell you; however, many of the crafts I practice are not looked upon favorably by all."

Dahlia knew that *all* meant her parents, who were adamant about the evils of dark magic. With a disappointed sigh, she replied, "I wish you could."

"Well," Priya said with a conspiratorial smile, "I suppose it could be *our* little secret."

And so, her lessons with Priya began. Dahlia was thrilled with the complicated magic and, to be honest, by the secrecy. It was nice to feel trusted and essential again by someone. For months, they trained while Ivy had her separate instruction. So focused on grooming their heir, her parents did not notice where Dahlia was during these times.

It was the first time Dahlia had ever kept anything from her sister. When they were together, they still acted as if nothing changed, planning how they would rule together one day. A few times, she almost confided in Ivy, but for reasons she could not quite explain, something kept her from mentioning it. The timing never felt right. Besides, her sister never mentioned what went on in her lessons with Edwina, which Dahlia found hurtful.

One hot afternoon, they lolled in their favorite spot inside the garden maze under the leaves of a large daisy. Ivy picked up a petal off the ground and wrapped it around her head like a crown. Pollen motes flew in the air around her. She offered a petal to Dahlia, who refused.

"Take one. When we rule together, we will have matching crowns."

The thought that her sister still planned to rule with her heartened Dahlia. Perhaps she was wrong to envy Edwina so.

Suddenly, a bee came buzzing down to circle Ivy, its bulky body hiding her in shadow. Bees, who were fond of harassing fairies, were kept out of the kingdom, yet somehow the giant insect had gotten past all the guards.

"You smell like pollen, girl. Let me have some." He sneered and tried to land on her.

"Leave us," Ivy commanded, and the girls ran away, but the insect flew after them. When it caught up, it wrapped its legs about Ivy.

"Stop! Get off me!" she cried, struggling to free herself.

Terror-stricken, Dahlia watched the stinger protrude from the bee, who prepared to strike. She could hear their guards running to them, but the girls were deep in the maze. The bee would sting and wound her sister, possibly mortally, before they could reach her. Without thought, Dahlia pointed a hand at the insect and whispered a spell. The creature released its prey just as it burst into flames. It fell to the ground, where it disintegrated into a large pile of ash.

Relieved, Dahlia raced to her sister. But Ivy recoiled. "How did you do that? That is dark magic."

"It was going to sting you. You could have died. Priya showed me some spells. I had to save you."

"Black magic is evil, Dahlia. Priya should not be teaching you these things. I must speak to our parents."

Ivy flew off, leaving her sister hurt and confused. The king and queen were equally disturbed by the news. Both Priya and Dahlia were reprimanded. The enchantress apologized profusely, assuring them the lessons would end. And they did, but not for long.

A loud clap of thunder brought the dark queen back to the present, where she stood amidst the raging storm. With a sigh, she left the balcony and walked down a long circular staircase to her throne room, the feeling of unease that woke her growing in her mind. All about her, dark obsidian glowed in the light of torches. A guard snapped to attention at the sight of her. "What can I do for you, My Queen?"

"Fetch me Kafir and Purus."

"At once, My Queen."

While his hurried footsteps faded into the darkness, she stepped onto the dais where her throne sat. She ran a hand along the smooth, black stone and took a seat. Her hands fell onto the carved armrests, two menacing vipers with their fangs bared. Only a moment passed before she heard the whisper of scale on stone. Two enormous snakes slithered into the room, the guard giving them a wide berth. In unison, they stopped before her, dipped their heads, and uttered, "My Queen."

"A moment I have long awaited is upon us. Go with all haste to Oakgarde Forest. My niece has returned to our world. Find her and bring her to me."

"Yes, My Queen," their hissed voices echoed throughout the chamber.

CHAPTER 6

"Winnie?" Lina gasped.

"Yes, it's me, though in this world I am known as Edwina," answered the beautiful fairy in front of her.

With so much to process, the girl hardly knew what to say. Winnie—or Edwina—was not the same hunchbacked old woman. Nor was anything else the same. From her clothes to the rowan box, to her giant bag, to the strange area they stood, questions hurtled through Lina's mind.

"It is overwhelming, I'm sure," the fairy said while the girl's eyes darted from one place to the next. "Let me answer a few things straight off," she said with a reassuring smile.

"Your bag is from the mortal world. It does not belong here and so remains its original size. Rowan wood is sacred to the fairies; therefore, it transformed with you and me, who also have a place in this world. And your outfit, I produced with a simple spell."

"And you? You are completely different," Lina commented, finding her voice.

"In the mortal world, I adopted a disguise to protect me from both fairies and humans. Here, I take my true form." She led the girl over to a tree root whose ridges formed a natural bench for them to sit on. "The bells, you see, they ward off fairies with evil intentions."

"Why did you need protection from fairies?" Lina eased down onto the seat, the dress softer against her skin than anything she had ever worn. A quick hand to her neck found the amulet there, safe and sound. The air was heavy with a cloying, earthy scent.

"Because I hid you. If they found me, they would have found you."

"Who would have found me? Who were you hiding me from?" Lina inquired in exasperation.

"I was the enchantress of your parents' Hirundo Kingdom found in Roshall Grove. As one of the only ones who had the knowledge to travel between worlds, the task fell to me to protect you until you were grown."

Lina's eyes scanned the chamber and landed on what looked to be a skeleton, the shaft of an arrow stuck between two rib bones. Goosebumps rose on her skin. "Protect me from what?"

Edwina followed her gaze and frowned. "That, my dear, is a long story. Let us find somewhere safe to stay, and then I will answer all your questions."

"Can't we just go to my kingdom?" Lina asked, exasperated by the lack of information. If Edwina had so many powers, why were they in this dank place among the tree roots?

"Roshall Grove is far from here, and this is one of the few portals to the mortal world. We will need to journey to your kingdom, but first, we must prepare." She rose to leave.

It was all so much to take in. The logical side of Lina never believed Winnie was genuinely taking her to the Fairy World. She considered the idea merely the ravings of an old woman. However, since Lina heard the story of her past, her gut felt it was true as much as she tried to dismiss it. Now that she was here, a feeling of dread crept in. What if the prophecy was about her after all?

Edwina set off at a brisk pace, leaving Lina only a moment to grab the rowan box and follow. They walked through the threshold of a broken door, moss now growing on the splintered projections of wood. After a long trek down a dark tunnel, they emerged into the daylight, where the girl gulped the fresh air into her lungs. Towering trees soared overhead out of sight. Grass as tall as Lina herself grew along the sides of a clearly defined path, giant flowers hanging over the top like massive umbrellas. Lina marveled at it all, even the clearly defined clumps of dirt underfoot.

Edwina halted up ahead and whistled. To the girl's astonishment, two swallows swooped down to land. Though they were large as horses, one had the unmistakable red heart Lina had known her whole life.

"Knox!" she cried and ran over, throwing her arms around him, his feathers soft and warm against her face. The relief at finding him here brought her a margin of relief and comfort.

"Hello, Lina," Knox said in greeting. The girl blinked in wonder. The bird had chirped, but instead of unintelligible sounds, his words had been crystal clear.

"I can understand you! I'm so glad you are here. Why are you so big?"

"Swallows and other kinds of animals can go between the worlds," Edwina quickly explained. "They remain the same size in both places, so they appear smaller in the human world and larger in the Fairy World. You and I would have been tiny in the mortal world, Lina, had it not been for the spell I used to make us both seem the size of people. In this world, animals and fairies can understand one another as well."

How this could be possible, Lina could not guess. Then again, three days ago, she would not have thought any of this was possible. The birds and the enchantress waited for the girl while Lina tried sorting it all out in her head. In the end, she was happy to have the swallow she had known for so long here with her, and decided all the details did not matter.

"This is my friend, Finley," Knox told them, and the two fairies greeted him warmly.

"We need to go to one of the safe houses to plan our trip," the enchantress said.

"I know just where to take you," Finley confirmed.

"Here, Lina, get on," Knox instructed, bending to accommodate her.

She mounted and sat amid his plush feathers. He assured her she could hold on to them tightly without causing him pain. With a rush of his wings, he took to the sky, the panicked girl clinging on for dear life. Finley led the way with Edwina alongside him, her wings shining brightly in the sunlight. Lina watched as the ground sank farther and farther below, her heart lodged in her throat.

After a short distance, they circled up around the trunk of an oak tree. On one of the uppermost branches, they landed. Lina climbed carefully off. Though the branch was wide enough to hold her, she reeled at the sheer drop to the ground, so far below, she could barely discern it. She stood rooted to her spot in fear. Edwina, on the other hand, landed and strode across the limb to Knox with all confidence in the world.

"I am not sure if Dahlia watches for Lina's return or not. Go and see what information you can gather," Edwina ordered.

With a nod, both birds flew off, leaving the two fairies on the high branch, not exactly Lina's idea of a safe haven. The enchantress walked to where the branch met the tree's trunk, and a knothole sat. She pushed on it, and it swung open like a door. She motioned for Lina to join her as she went in. The girl took one small step and stopped, then another, at length; she managed to edge her way carefully to the door.

Inside was a comfortable room. A large table sat in the middle, a bright red tablecloth atop it. A few cabinets lined the right-hand wall, a haphazard pile of bowls and pots stacked like a crooked tower on their counter. On the left, two cozy chairs flanked an unlit fireplace. Against the far wall, two large beds stood in opposite corners, between them a large wardrobe. The whole place was dusty and smelled a bit stuffy from apparent lack of use, but it was far better than the empty and dangerous branch outside.

"There now. You settle in, and I'll make us some dinner."

There was not much to do besides lying her rowan box down on one of the beds. She went and sat mutely at the table, digesting all that had transpired while Edwina lit a small fire to prepare the meal. The enchantress flitted out the door and returned a few moments later with a large nut and some other items Lina did not recognize. With a flurry of movements, she prepared the meal.

"Will you be a dear and go shake that tablecloth out?" she asked, nodding toward the door.

Lina grabbed the cloth as instructed. She took a timid step out the door and gave it a few shakes. A scrabbling noise caught her attention, and she looked down the tree to the squirrel climbing his way up. He disappeared into a knothole. Fascinated, Lina took her first good look around from the treetop. A few birds nest dotted branches on the neighboring trees, all empty as far as she could tell. Her eyes rose up even farther to the high branches of a tall oak. There sat an owl, his large yellow eyes looking straight at her. He gave a nod of his head. She nodded back in wonder before returning inside with the tablecloth.

She spread it over the table, which Edwina quickly set with bowls and spoons. The elder fairy served the meal, and the ladies sat to eat. Whatever the food was, it was tasty, and her appetite appeared at the right moment after the long day. When they finished eating, the enchantress stoked the fire to a cozy blaze and sat in one of the chairs. Lina joined her, and the woman studied the girl for a long time.

"And now, it's time you heard the story of where you came from and the prophecy about you."

CHAPTER 7

Before they could speak another word, a peck at the door interrupted them. Finley had returned with information. Edwina stood at the open door with him for a few moments to receive his report. Lina strained to hear, but the popping wood of the fire drowned out any chance of that.

"It does not appear anyone has noticed our return... yet," Edwina announced with a sigh of relief. "Hopefully, this buys us some time to get you closer to home."

"Which is where again?" Lina asked. She curled up comfortably in the other chair, a cup of tea in hand, still too hot to sip.

"Roshall Grove, home of the Hirundo Kingdom, ruled by the highest of fairies known as the Avian Volants."

Lina only blinked at the sentence, so full of strange words.

"There are three main types of fairies," the enchantress explained, "Volants, Groundlings and

Fluvials. Each one is associated with a particular element—Air, Earth, and Water, to be exact. You are a Volant Fairy or an Air type, as am I. Our order is the Hirundo. We are the highest in the fairy hierarchy and, most importantly, the holders of the Primal Crystal."

"The what?" First, she was expected to wrap her head around all the different types of fairies, and now, another strange reference. This story became more and more confusing at every turn.

"The Primal Crystal held the energy which kept the Fairy World in balance. Our kind's duty is to safeguard this relic, to maintain harmony and peace throughout the land."

"But something happened to it?" Lina guessed.

"A cruel fairy turned to the Fire element, the darkest of all fairy magic. This Ignis Fairy tried to bend the Primal Crystal to her will, but it broke apart before she could use it for her wicked purposes. However, your mother, a powerful fairy, was there. She retrieved a small piece of the stone, thereby preventing the evil fairy from making it whole again. I placed a strong spell on the shard until her successor was ready to set things right. *You* are that successor, Lina."

"Me? Set things right?" she questioned in quick succession. Lina's face portrayed her confusion.

"Yes, you are the heiress to your mother's throne. She was Queen of the Hirundo, the protector of the stone. Power to protect the Primal Crystal passes from queen to queen, usually from mother to daughter. And that stone is the piece I speak of." She gestured to the girl's necklace. "With it, you restore the Primal Crystal and bring peace to the kingdom."

Lina's hand flew to her amulet around her neck; never had she imagined it held such power and value. Her head pounded with all the information; it was too much to process. Only days ago, she was a simple peasant girl. Now the fate of an entire kingdom rested on her shoulders. She sat quietly, a log cracked and split in the fireplace sending down a tiny shower of sparks.

"But how can I do this? I know nothing of this world!" she finally said.

"I foresaw a prophecy of the kingdom in ashes, destroyed by evil only to be restored when a child, the true successor, received her wings. When I explained the prophecy to Ivy's parents, who were queen and king at the time, we came to realize that child was you," Edwina spoke sharply.

"And how exactly am I to receive my wings? Do you just give them to me?" Lina asked, anxious for a straightforward answer in this complex story.

"No, dear." Edwina chuckled, "You only receive your wings with the kiss of true love."

Lina stared at her mutely. She knew even less of romance and love than she did of the Fairy World. If the fate of this realm depended on that, Lina had severe misgivings about restoring the kingdom and happily ever after.

"I think that is enough for you to take in right now," the enchantress concluded.
Not inclined to talk anymore, Edwina rose from her chair and tidied the kitchen. All the while, the girl remained seated, her empty eyes trained on the fire. She missed her tiny home, so comfortable and safe, and she missed the two people who had raised her. The only kind of love she ever experienced was from them. She had never wanted anything more. This thought brought her the unfamiliar feeling of resentment. If only they had not kept this a secret from her, she would have had some time to prepare. To have it thrust upon her like this was unfair.

"Go to bed, dear," the older fairy said at length, "and rest up for the journey tomorrow."

Dutifully, Lina slid between the covers of one of the beds. Soon, the enchantress extinguished the fire and settled in the other bed. Lina's body was exhausted from the day's journey, but sleep eluded her in the dark, quiet room. Questions careened across her mind until she could no longer keep them all inside. She needed answers, and she needed them *now*.

"This cruel fairy," Lina whispered in the shadow-filled room, "she will try to stop us, won't she?"

"Yes," was the terse reply.

"And she rules the Fairy World now?"

"She does. Nevertheless, without the Primal Crystal whole, it is not *true* power."

Irritation rose in Lina; her cheeks flushed with anger. Edwina's account left out much of the story, yet she was reluctant to give up more details. How could she ask all this from her and not tell Lina the entire tale? Well, she would keep asking questions until she felt satisfied.

"What is her name? And how shall I take the kingdom back?" she asked, her tone leaving no room for silence or incomplete answers.

"Her name is Dahlia, and once you restore the Crystal, she will be rendered powerless. All we need to worry about right now is getting you back to Roshall Grove in one piece."

"And finding true love?" Lina questioned doubtfully.

"That will not be the hard part, dear. A fairy named Cornelius was selected as your match before birth. He will take care of the kiss."

So true love, was that easy? Lina could not argue since this was unfamiliar territory to her. If the enchantress were this confident on the subject, Lina would take her word for it. At least it sounded easier than defeating an evil queen.

"Surely, all inhabitants of the Fairy World want the balance restored here. There must be many allies out there to help us," Lina ventured.

"Yes, and no."

Lina sighed audibly in frustration at yet another unclear response.

"You see, dear," Edwina continued, "the imbalance hurts the land and all who live in it, but there are always those who look to use hardships to their advantage, to profit off of others' struggles. Likewise, some of the Groundling sects see this as an opportunity to claim more power in the hierarchy for themselves. So while some will look to aid us, others will *not*. Your identity must remain a secret as long as possible."

Happy to have some actual details, Lina started to picture what they faced. Of course, this led to several additional thoughts.

"How long will it take us to get to Roshall Grove?"

"It depends on how secretly we travel," Edwina replied. "My presence alone may endanger you. In the mortal world, there were certain protections I could use. Dahlia will see through them all here."

Evilness and cruelty were but foreign thoughts to the girl. Both had rarely touched her life. She realized now how small her universe had been, how sheltered her parents kept her. Edwina's story sounded like one of Hazel's fairy tales to her. But it was not. It was very real.

"This Dahlia, was she always evil?"

Edwina was silent for a moment before answering. "I don't know if she was evil before birth or if life itself turned her to the dark side. All I know was when she revealed her true self, it was too late for us to stop her."

"You knew her, then? She was not a stranger to you?" Lina was surprised by this information.

"Yes, I knew her. And that made her betrayal all the worse when it occurred. You see, Dahlia is your mother's sister."

"My mother's sister?" the girl reeled from the blow. "The woman who wants me dead is my aunt?"

Lina said no more, but a deep sadness filled her. As far as she knew, Dahlia was her only living relative, her only connection to her past. Yet, already they were sworn enemies.

CHAPTER 8

The next morning, they set out and left the comfort of the tiny tree house. Knox assisted Lina to the forest floor, where he deposited her next to Edwina. The swallow updated the enchantress on his findings. "So far, there seems to be no awareness of your arrival back. However, one of the Ephemera Fairies I met spoke of roads in and out of Roshall Grove being watched by Dahlia's spies."

"It's good news Dahlia has not detected our presence," she assured him, "yet I am concerned with these watches you speak of. Go and see how far west you can fly before you encounter one."

Knox nodded, and Lina gave him a quick hug before he flew off. Watching him disappear across the sky made her heart feel heavy. She would miss his familiar face in this strange land.

"Here is a bag with some food." Edwina handed her a sturdy sack. "You can put your rowan box in there."

After storing the box away, the pair departed on foot. It was pleasantly warm, a soft breeze wafting with a woodsy scent all around them. They followed a clear-cut path through the vegetation. Large leaves canopied overhead, and Lina cried out when an enormous drop of water fell on her head. The girl dodged another headed her way. It landed with a great splash nearby.

"Be careful of the morning dew," Edwina warned a bit too late.

The enchantress led confidently onward while Lina marveled at her surroundings—grass stems rising like tree trunks, an acorn the size of a boulder, a spider's web as lofty as a building soaring between two branches. The actual trees towered so high Lina could not discern the tops of them. The flowers amazed her the most, so vibrant and fragrant. Every part of their petals, the round pistils and centers looked as though the most talented artist had taken a brush to them. Tiny details her mortal eye could never discern to appreciate.

All morning they walked, the scenery changing little. Only once did they see another fairy. She was a slight being, dressed all in brown, perched on a large rock combing her long hair. She stopped mid-stroke to regard them. Instinctively, Lina kept her head down.

"Let me do the talking," Edwina whispered.

"Good day." The fairy eyed them suspiciously as they neared. "What brings you to the forest floor?"

"Good day. This little one has lost her way. I am helping her home," the enchantress answered casually.

"Oh my," the fairy exclaimed, suddenly full of concern. "Do you need anything? Food or water?"

"No, thank you, dear, we are fine," Edwina assured.

But despite her assurances, the fairy picked up a small bag and offered them two little cakes. Edwina nodded at Lina to accept one while she took the other. The fairy's skin was brown like an autumn leaf, complete with vein-like lines. Her hair, though soft enough to brush, resembled twigs with small clumps sticking out at random. She had no wings, but her arms and legs were long and graceful. Happy they accepted her cakes; she wished them well on their journey. When they were safely out of earshot, Lina asked what type of fairy she was.

"A lower Groundling type called Arboreas. They are associated with the trees, some small insects, chipmunks, squirrels, and the like. Though easily frightened, they are very kind and extremely nurturing.

Knowing you were lost struck a chord in her. Don't worry; you will not find a more trustworthy sect of fairy."

It reassured Lina to know there were some hospitable fairies in this world. She would need all the help she could get to defeat her aunt. Perhaps someday, this fairy would be her ally. First, Edwina must transport her to Roshall Grove.

They stopped only once at midday to eat. The weather remained warm and dry, the terrain easy to navigate, but Lina's legs felt more like lead with every step. When the sun dipped in the sky, Edwina stopped in a clearing. She whistled loudly to the sky. Down swooped a sparrow, who let Lina board her back. Again, a bird lifted her to a tree branch where the enchantress entered a knothole, much like the one from yesterday.

"Shelters like these are scattered across the kingdom for traveling Volants to use," she explained at the girl's confounded countenance.

When they sat for dinner, all of Lina's muscles protested against the day's vigorous activity. From the small of her back right down to her toes, she ached. Irritably, she picked at her food. "Why don't we just fly to Roshall Grove? It would be a lot faster."

"Faster, yes, but far more dangerous," Edwina warned with a knowing look. "Dahlia will expect this and watch the skies. There are fewer options for hiding in the air than on the ground. Remember, she knows the spell I used on your amulet. She knows you will come sooner or later now that you have grown up. Her power depends on you, never restoring that, Crystal. She wants to take your shard to accomplish this herself. Do not doubt that she has a large network of spies, both fairy and animal, on constant alert."

Lina trusted the enchantress knew what was best and let the matter drop, despite her aching feet. Later, she fell into a deep slumber where she dreamed of a beautiful fairy with long golden hair like her own and with the most magnificent pair of wings she could ever imagine. When morning dawned, she was unsure if she had seen her transformed self or her late mother, Queen Ivy. In the wake of the dream, emptiness lingered for a long while.

Off again, they trod along a more difficult path. An overnight shower riddled the way with puddles and muddy tracts. Some of the areas were so waterlogged, they had no choice but to walk through them. Edwina used an enchantment to keep them dry and clean, for which Lina was grateful. Though a chipmunk crossed their path at one point, they met no fairies all morning.

When a strong rustling sound emanated from the high grass on their right, the enchantress froze. It started out soft, but the volume increased to a flowing swoosh. The girl had no idea what it could be but sensed it was not good.

"Quickly, behind that mushroom." The enchantress shoved her into the cover of a fat stalk.

Lina peered from behind it and waited. The sound grew louder until, to her horror, two large black snakes slithered out of the grass. They encircled her companion, towering above her with fangs bared, but Edwina did not cower.

"Hello, what brings a Volant down so low?" one hissed, the sibilant sound echoing across the path.

"Nothing of your concern. Now be gone," Edwina replied with a dismissive wave of her hand.

"No need to be rude. We are all friends here, right?" the other chimed in, looking far from amicable. "We were worried you may be unwell since you are not flying."

They wriggled around in an intricate pattern, making it hard to keep eyes on both of them at once. Lina was mesmerized by them—supple black bodies, green diamonds on their heads, and the bright orange tongues cast a sort of spell which held her rooted to the spot.

"I am fine and would like to continue my journey alone if you don't mind." Rather than fear, Lina could discern a hint of annoyance in Edwina's voice.

Again, they swirled around the enchantress in a graceful whirl of movements. So entranced was Lina with the snakes, she did not hear the stealthy steps behind her. A cold, slimy hand clamped over her mouth, while other sets of hands snatched her up and instantly carried her off into the forest.

CHAPTER 9

"These are the new arrivals, My Queen," said General Sepitus.

Dahlia stood with him on a platform overlooking the training fields where dozens of soldiers were going through their paces. The general had served her from her initial attack until now. A Vespertilio fairy, his bat-like fangs and skeletal wings made for a formidable presence. He ruled her troops with an iron fist even she admired. Over the years, Sepitus had earned her respect.

"And the forges are always busy crafting armor and weapons." He nodded at wisps of black smoke against the grey sky over the armory.

"Excellent work, general. You have done well. We will meet soon to discuss battle strategy."

He saluted her crisply and returned down the stairs to his troops, chest puffed out with pride at her words of approval. More troops arrived every day, some from settlements overtaken by her army, some freely, excited to join her cause. Almost exclusively, they were

Groundlings. Volants proved more difficult to enlist, with many joining the Resistors. General Sepitus had a knack for getting the most out of every fairy, regardless of type.

She watched for a few more minutes, smiling as more seasoned fighters schooled the recruits. The numbers were definitely in her favor. This thought comforted her way back to her tower. Up the circular steps she walked, she preferred the rigor of the stairs to the effortlessness of flying. Her maid jumped to her feet when she entered her chambers.

"Be gone," she hissed, and the fairy scrambled away.

Long years now, this space had been her refuge, first as Priya's chamber, now as her own. She thought back to when she killed the bee to save Ivy, and it seemed as though her training with the enchantress was over. Heartbroken, not only because her family was disappointed in her, but also because she lost the one thing that gave her life meaning, and she wandered the palace forlornly. Then, news of her killing the insect spread about the palace, and people looked at her with anger and fear. She took to staying in her room, only coming out after dark.

One such night when sleep would not find her, she went for a walk in the gardens. Lightning flashed in brief snatches, the rain not caught up to it yet. Dahlia looked up longingly at Priya's tower, an amber glow in the windows. Her parents forbade the enchantress to teach her, but perhaps she could still speak to her. Buoyed by the thought, she flew to the balcony and tapped on the door.

Priya cracked the door. "Dahlia! Does anyone know you are here?" she whispered, whipping her head left and right to make sure they were alone.

"No," she replied, instinctively shielding her face as lightning flashed again.

"Come in." She pulled her quickly inside. "I was hoping you would come to visit me."

Dahlia looked longingly around the chamber, which had become special to her, at the piles of books with lessons she had learned and ones she still hoped to learn from. "I miss our sessions so much. If only that stupid bee had never come around. It wasn't my fault the creature got to my sister."

"Of course, it wasn't. Who would have thought such a dangerous insect could find its way into the kingdom?" With a wry smile, she directed the girl to sit, and they eased down across the table from each other.

"Sadly, your parents and I have some fundamental disagreements when it comes to magic. They see the Air, Water and Earth elements of conjuring as good and the Fire element of conjuring as evil, but I feel magic is neither. It is the fairy who chooses to use them for good or evil. Like the bee, you killed—not out of malice but to protect your dear sister."

"Exactly!" She leaned across the table closer to Priya. "If only my parents could see that."

"I don't think we could ever convince them to see things as we do. However, if you want to continue our training in secret, I am willing to teach you."

"Yes!" Dahlia cried, rising to fling herself into Priya's arms. "I have missed it so much. I have missed you."

In the secrecy of night, Dahlia continued to learn the dark side of magic. Her parents suspected nothing, only happy she kept to herself all day and caused no more trouble. The only one who may have suspected was Ivy, who in the rare times they were together, glanced at her knowingly, but never said a thing. She was too busy with her lessons with Edwina, after all. Every day from her window high above, Dahlia watched them walking with each other. A pang of hurt pierced her heart each time, thinking the person she had treasured the most in this world had replaced her with another. And Edwina did little to help the situation. On the infrequent occasions, they were together, she watched Dahlia with a most untrusting gaze, and there was little pretense of friendship between the two young fairies.

"I wish it weren't just you and I who felt this way about magic," she said to Priya one night as they worked alone in the chamber mixing potions.

"There are others. Many, in fact." The enchantress put down the vials she held and came to stand by Dahlia.

"Here in the kingdom?" The girl put down her flask and gave her full attention to the conversation.

"No. In the far western forest of Elderbreach, an entire colony thinks as we do. I will take you there someday."

Dahlia had heard of this forest, a place with many mysterious tales attached to it, an area that filled most with suspicion and unease, with whispers of dark magic. Not her, though, now that she listened to Priya. She imagined how reassuring it would be to meet like-minded fairies, ones who did not cast wary looks at her every time she set foot outside her room. Her heart instantly felt lighter. Perhaps one day, she would show her family how the use of fire magic could at times be beneficial.

"Maybe we could make my parents see, make them understand magic as we think it should be used," Dahlia said, a voice full of hope.

"That will not happen," Priya declared.

"But maybe if…"

"No. Nothing will change this." She came and took the girl by the shoulders. "There is more to this. I shouldn't tell you, but any increase in your powers threatens them."

"How?" she asked, a frown knitting her brow.

"They fear you are more dominant in magic than Ivy. That is why your lessons stopped. They can't risk you outshining her. She is the heir, after all…"

"Only because she was born three minutes sooner." Dahlia squared her shoulders in defiance. "It's not fair."

"I agree. You have as much claim to the throne as your sister. But the law is the law. What are we to do if they are dead set on Ivy succeeding your mother?" Priya gave her a long, serious glare before she returned to her task.

That light feeling in Dahlia's heart from a moment ago suddenly hardened in the grip of anger. She would be a wise and powerful ruler if only given a chance. But if her parents wanted to restrain her powers, how could she ever prove to them she could be a leader? Why should she be repressed only to make her sister look stronger? As she went back to mixing her potion, hatred filled her to her very core.

Now, all this time later, Dahlia stood alone in that very chamber. For many years in the beginning, she harbored the wish that her family would see her side of things and all would be well, but not anymore. On the back wall, a winding staircase took her to the top of the tower, where she entered a windowless circular room. With a whisper of words, blue flames sprang to life in the fireplace. She sat and pulled her scrying ball across the table until it sat in front of her. "Show me my snakes."

The ball clouded over with a deep blue, which rippled and waved before an image formed of Oakguarde Forest. Kafir and Purus reared up menacingly over someone. Dahlia took in a sharp breath. Edwina. Hatred surged in her at the sight of the enchantress, the many years doing nothing to assuage this visceral reaction.

Edwina and the snakes exchanged words until suddenly, she flew off with the reptiles in hot pursuit. When Kafir was almost upon her, the ground gave way before him, where the fairy turned it into quicksand. Purus immediately anchored himself to a nearby branch and pulled his cohort, Kafir, to safety. By the time they collected their wits, Edwina was gone. There had been no sign of the girl.

Dahlia waved her hand, and the ball went dark. In silence, she brooded, her fingers steepled at her chin. The Queen cursed the snakes for their stupidity, but there was nothing to be done. The important thing was to capture Lina before she made it to the Resistors. Fortunately, the girl was far from them; much time remained before she arrived there.

She descended to her lower chamber and went onto the balcony. The sun dipped low on the horizon, only the top of its orange orb visible. The first night stars twinkled in the skies above the ragged black clouds floating past. At her shrill whistle, a raven appeared in the sky, swooping down onto the railing. Though his ebony form dwarfed her, he bowed reverently.

"Cotswold, gather some others and scour the land between here and Oakguarde Forest. Bring me any word you hear about Lina. And when you find Kafir and Purus, remind them I have little patience for failed missions."

With a nod of his head, the bird flew off. She watched him until the black speck of his outspread wings disappeared into the darkening sky.

CHAPTER 10

Lina's struggles were useless; too many hands held her captive. The one clamped firmly on her mouth prevented any scream for help to escape. Leaves and stems bounced off of her as they ran across the forest. Eventually, the ground changed, and she heard their footsteps sloshing through water. Cold mud splattered all over her. Finally, they dropped her down in a murky puddle, too startled to even make a sound. A fairy woman stood over her, three smaller young men at her side. Her skin was smooth with a soft green cast. Green and brown strands of hair tumbled over her shoulders. The boys were of similar coloring with short cropped hair.

"Yes, she will be just perfect for Bacchus," the woman proclaimed.

"Who are you?" Lina demanded, finding her voice, "Take me back this instant."

"Ooh and feisty too. Bacchus will like that," one of the boys declared.

She stood and tried to walk away, but they grabbed her again. Their skin was smooth with a cool, almost wet quality, but their grip was unyielding.

"Now girl, don't worry," the woman assured, "I have been looking for a nice fairy to be my son's bride, and I think you will do splendidly."

"I don't want to be anyone's bride. Now please release me. I have important things to do."

"Important, eh?" the fairy mimicked with a strange cackling laugh. "Take her to the house, boys."

Lina struggled at first but realized it was futile. They brought her to a tiny house made of brown sticks, the roof green with moss, on the banks of a lake. Behemoth frogs sat just inside the lip of water that lapped onto the shore. The boys opened the front door and unceremoniously shoved her inside before taking up a post outside to prevent escape. A few moments later, the woman entered.

Lina stood in the cottage's cozy main room, nicely decorated with fresh flower petals and tiny doilies on every surface. A hutch stood on the wall displaying hand-painted plates. Not at all what one would expect from the outside or such indecorous fairies. Soon, the woman had a kettle singing over the fire. She poured them each some tea in finely sculpted cups, whose delicacy belied the clumsy green hands that set them down.

"Bacchus will be along shortly. He will be so happy I have found a match for him." She motioned for Lina to sit at the kitchen table.

Lina only nodded, all the while plotting how to escape. Perhaps if she went along with the woman's ravings, the fairy would lower her guard. The girl needed a better idea of what she was dealing with before she tried anything, so Lina took a seat.

"Oh heavens, me, where are my manners? I am Juniper," she introduced, laying some unappetizing looking food on the table.

"You're worried about manners after you kidnapped me?" Lina snapped.

The fairy bristled. "There is no need to be rude. I told you my name, now what is yours?"

The girl did not answer. Edwina warned her about keeping her identity a secret. She would have to come up with a plausible story. She thought of eating some food to stall for time, but it looked inedible. The silence between them lengthened.

"Come now, dear, if you are to be my daughter-in-law, I will need to know your name," the woman pressed.

"Hazel. My name is Hazel. I am traveling with my aunt, who must be worried and looking for me."

"That Volant Fairy was your aunt? Then where are your wings, girl? Surely you would have them by now, unless…"

Lina froze. Had Juniper already guessed her secret? But the woman's face softened.

"Not to worry, dear. It's all right if you're a Poxy." She patted the girl's hand.

Lina only blinked.

"There is nothing to be ashamed of. Sometimes Volants simply do not grow wings. Though your kind shuns you, we welcome you here. Not like with the Arboreas and the Rodentia, but you know how some Groundlings like to put on airs. You will not find that here among us, Herptiles."

The girl tried hard to process all this new data thrown at her. Clearly, though, these Herptile fairies were not as kind as the Arboreas she met. She did not trust this woman one bit. If nothing else, a Poxy sounded like a reasonable alibi for now. It kept suspicion from her real story.

The front door banged open. A rotund young fairy stomped in, a scowl on his face. "Mother, Weldon said you were trying to play matchmaker again." His gaze fell on Lina; the distaste he saw was palatable. "Please tell me not *that* pale, scraggly mess."

"Now, now, Bacchus, I know she is dirty. We stole her and had to run through the muddy woods. Just let me clean her up a bit," his mother urged.

"That will not help. She looks sickly. She is not good Groundling stock. She is likely some Volant castoff. And can you blame them? She's horrifying."

Lina listened to the exchange. While happy the fairy, Bacchus, did not want her, she felt the heat rise in her cheeks at his insults. They obviously had different ideas about what constituted horrifying—and manners.

He flung himself into a chair at the table, where his overweight frame hung off the sides. Large warts covered every exposed section of his skin, and long whiskers grew oddly from his lips, curling across his face to meet his unkempt hair. His entire demeanor suggested he got exactly what he wanted from his mother at all times.

Juniper bustled to the cabinets, her hands a flurry of activity. She returned with a heaping plate of what looked like grubs. Lina's stomach turned, watching Bacchus stuff his face full.

"I'll not have her. I'm sorry you went to the trouble," Bacchus uttered, grub goo dripping down his chin. He flung the plate across the room, where it landed in the sink with a loud clatter. "I'll be back later. See that she is gone."

Once the door slammed behind him, Juniper turned to Lina. "Not to worry, he will come around. Let's get you cleaned up."

Juniper washed the girl in a warm bath, taking extra care with her long, golden hair, which she fashioned into a long braid tied with a green ribbon. Once finished with this process, she handed the girl an outfit quite similar to her own—a green tunic made of a fabric pattern of overlapping leaves with a pair of dark brown stockings. The garments looked large on the hanger, but once put on, shrunk to fit Lina perfectly, evidently some Fairy World magic. The woman handed her a pair of soft, green boots, which likewise contracted around her foot.

"There now, pretty as a princess. And here is your lovely necklace back."

"Thank you for your kindness, Juniper. However, since Bacchus doesn't seem too interested in marrying me, I should be going to find my aunt," Lina said, trying to keep her voice casual while putting on the amulet and tucking it under the tunic.

"Nonsense, girl. He will come around. He's just stubborn. Trust me; you two will be happy together," the woman said, picking up a wet towel from the floor. "Besides, your aunt was too busy with those awful snakes. What are the odds she even survived?"

The thought hit Lina hard. Without Edwina, she would be lost. Her stomach sank while she thought about what to do. Escape was her only option. Before she could ponder further, there was a loud rap on the door. When Juniper opened it a crack, a large male fairy pushed his way in.

"Bacchus tells me you have stolen another girl?" he huffed, his large belly covered by a velvet vest, whose buttons were taxed to the extreme. A watch fob hung from a clip on his jacket, its other end disappearing into a pocket. Unlike Bacchus and the other boys, he was well-dressed and carefully groomed. He obviously felt himself of some importance, as did Juniper, who shrank back in his presence.

"Well now, *stolen* is such a harsh word," the mother answered in a deferential tone. "Truly, she will be a fine match."

The man's eyes fell on Lina and instantly narrowed. "She is no Groundling."

"No, she is a Poxy. I told her that was no matter here," the woman replied, nervously twisting the bath towel.

"You know the law, Juniper. All Volants must be assessed by me the moment they enter the village." His green eyes were still fixed on the girl.

"Oh, but, Leander, what is to assess? She is a harmless fairly bereft of a true home, not anyone Queen Dahlia would be looking for."

Lina's heart skipped a beat, but she forced her expression to remain neutral. Dahlia took no chances. Her aunt had issued a mandate to look for her, even after all these years. A real sense of danger filled her, and the amulet vibrated softly against her chest. Escape was now imperative.

"Nonetheless, I will take her with me until we are sure. Come, girl." He grabbed Lina's arm and pulled her toward the open door.

"Now, now, she can just wait here with me. There is no need to take her," the woman said, clamping on to Lina's other arm.

"I must follow the law, Juniper," he replied, a false apology in his tone.

"Since when are you a stickler for Queen Dahlia's laws? I can see what's going on here—you want her for yourself!" Juniper exclaimed.

"Are you accusing me of dishonesty, Juniper?" He released his grip on Lina to take a menacing step toward the woman. "I am offended to have my character called into question in such a way."

"Says the man who has fifteen wives. The whole village knows you are always on the lookout for more." She also let go of the girl's arm to meet Leander face to face.

Forgotten in their anger, Lina picked up her bag and inched over to the open doorway. In a flash, she took off running, the shocked cries of the two fairies behind her. She headed for a break in the foliage, her feet sinking in the wet ground with every step. It would be dusk soon, and the light would fail her. Only steps away from the gap, two large hands seize her and wrestle her back. Bacchus wrenched her around to his approaching mother and Leander, a smug look of triumph on his face.

"You see? She tries to flee. Isolate her immediately!" Leander exclaimed.

Bacchus dragged her to the water's edge, where he shoved her into a small boat, which two small fairy boys manned. They rowed way out into the lake where a lone lily pad sat. With a shove from one, she fell onto it and watched them grow smaller, rowing back to shore. All around her, the water of the lake darkened quickly in the fading remnants of the day. It lapped on to her feet as though to remind her how trapped she now was.

A pink flower bloomed in the center of the lily pad, its petals radiating out like a rosy sun. She walked to it and sat against its folds. The sweet scent of it wafted across the air. Though beautiful, it was still a prison from which there was no escape.

CHAPTER 11

Darkness settled over the lake. The first twinkling stars appeared in the sky, and a nearly full moon rose above the tree line. With each passing minute, fear grew in Lina. It was only a matter of time until the Herptiles returned and discovered her true identity. She paced the edges of the lily pad, desperate for escape. All around her lay the shadowy water. If only she could swim, but that was a skill she never learned. She tried mightily to row the pad with her hands, but its stem stuck fast to the lake floor. Defeated, she sank to her knees and dissolved into tears.

"What makes you so sad, pretty girl?" the voice as melodic as running water startled Lina so much, she jumped up with her arms out as if to fend off danger.

"You need not fear me. Here I will show you."

A tiny fairy pulled herself out of the lake onto the lily pad. The moonlight shimmered off her smooth skin in iridescent waves. Her long hair resembled seaweed but glistened when it fell down her back. She stood up straight and rose to only about half of Lina's height, delicate enough to be carried away by a strong breeze.

"There," she said, spreading her hands that were webbed like a duck's feet, "do I look dangerous?"

"No," Lina admitted, her guard dropping ever so slightly. "What is your name, and where did you come from?"

"I am Lula, a Fluvial fairy who lives in a kingdom at the bottom of this lake."

"And you can breathe underwater?" Lina asked, so fascinated she forgot her troubles for a moment.

"Of course. I was out for a swim and heard you crying. Why are you so sad, pretty girl?" The concern on her face was genuine.

"The Herptile fairies who live on the shore are holding me captive."

"That's not very nice. Indeed, Herptiles are mean and spiteful fairies. We try to keep our distance, or they bring us trouble. Why are they keeping you captive?"

"One of them wants me to marry her son, so she kidnapped me," Lina explained, but decided to keep all the other information a secret.

"That is horrible. They are going to imprison you out here until you agree?"

"Honestly, I don't know what they will do, but I am afraid."

"Well, that won't do. That won't do at all. Let me help you," Lula declared, an earnest expression on her face.

Gratefulness welled in Lina's heart at the diminutive fairy's offer, yet she did not see how it could be possible. "I can't swim or breathe underwater."

"You won't need to," Lula assured her. "Just give me a moment."

She slid back into the lake, her tiny form disappearing in the murky water. For several long minutes, Lina waited, part of her wondering if she imagined the whole encounter until Lula's head reemerged from the lake. She climbed back onto the lily pad.

"All taken care of," she beamed. The pad swayed ever so slightly. Panicked, Lina dropped to her knees. Lula's laugh rang over the water like a song. "Fear not, pretty girl, I told the fish to eat through the stalk. In a few moments, the leaf will be free."

Sure enough, after some diligent nibbling by the fish, the pad broke away from its stem and spun free into the lake's current.

"I don't want to go back to shore," Lina cried, "The Herptiles will catch me again."

"Not to worry. I will steer you to the far banks where the lake merges with a stream which will take you far away from here."

Lula positioned herself in the water near the back of the leaf and guided it across the lake with a swiftness that belied her size. The moonlight glittered on the surface, smooth as glass in front of them, a cool breeze gusting Lina's hair back from her face.

"It was so kind of you to help me. How can I ever repay you?"

"There is no need to repay me. Fairies help other fairies. That is the code of our world, though some have forgotten." She gestured her head to the Herptile village. "Years ago, this whole land was beautiful and harmonious. Now, this realm slowly fades into darkness. You must have heard stories of how the Volants, Groundlings, and Fluvial fairies lived and worked together for the greater good. I wish one day to see such a world restored. For now, my kind looks to go deeper and deeper into the waters before the shadow overcomes all above us. I am trying to say that I believe in the old ways and strive to live by them. You do not owe me anything except repaying a kindness to others."

Lina smiled at Lula, who diligently paddled the leaf further from the Herptile shore. Hope blossomed in her heart that escape was near. When they were almost to the other side, a commotion of yells and curses rang out behind them, and Lina stiffened.

"Looks like they figured out you were gone," Lula said with mischief in her tone. "But, not to worry, they will never be able to catch you. I'll push you into the stream's path. Hold on tight."

The sound of rushing water grew louder up ahead, the current becoming choppy. Lina grasped the flower in the center of the leaf while she cascaded down a small decline. Lula maintained her grip with ease and steered the lily pad into the center of the waterway, where it quickly picked up speed.

"This is where I leave you, pretty girl. Good luck to you."

"Thank you, Lula. I promise to repay your kindness and do my best to make the world what it once was."

With a wave and another melodious laugh, the fairy disappeared back into the depths. A twinge of sadness came to Lina's heart. Dahlia's reign had affected every creature in this world so much a whole group of fairies was withdrawing entirely. How could one girl conquer such evil?

Fast but smooth, the stream's current carried the leaf away, nearly unnoticeable in the darkness. Soon, Lina, worn out by the day's events, drifted to sleep against the flower's soft petals. The moon set, the stillness of night enfolding the world for a time. Gradually, the eastern sky turned from black, to steel grey, to the pink hues of dawn.

The girl startled awake to find the shores rushing past on both sides. After a brief moment's confusion, relief flooded her. She had escaped Leander and his village. Indeed, he would not have hesitated to hand her over to Dahlia. But her comfort at this thought was short-lived. Doubt and frustration marched back in to remind her she had no idea where she was or how to get where she needed to go. Her stomach grumbled moodily as well. Yes, she was free from the conniving Herptiles but still a prisoner on this lily pad. She rustled through her sodden sack and found a quick bite to eat.

She sat down, hands under her chin, and tried to conceive some sort of plan. Her sheltered life in the woods with her adoptive parents had left her ill-equipped to deal with such difficult situations. There, she had only worried about a failing crop or a sick animal, and her parents always led the way in solving any dilemma. Now, the fate of an entire kingdom was in her hands, and she was lost.

"Are you Lina?" a gentle flutter of a voice asked. The girl looked up to find a white butterfly perched on the pink flower. She was too astonished to answer, and the insect cocked its head. "Can you not understand me?"

"No... I do... you just startled me. I've never spoken to a butterfly before. How do you know my name?" Lina could not take her eyes off the magnificent insect, its alabaster wings slowly opening and closing while it regarded her.

"Edwina has many creatures out searching for you. She is most worried that some harm has befallen you." The butterfly flew down to her side.

"You know Edwina?" the girl gaped at the unexpected but happy news.

"Of course, dear. Everyone knows her. She is the most powerful enchantress in the land," her soft voice filtered from her cylindrical mouth.

"Can you take me to her?" Lina cried, her heart dancing with joy.

"That is why I am here. I can direct you if you have some sort of paddle unless you have something to tie to me."

Lina's hand flew to her hair. "I have this ribbon. Are you sure it won't be too hard for you to pull me?"

"It should be fine. The wind will assist me. It's getting stronger now, ahead of some afternoon storms, I suspect."

Lina looked up at the unbroken blue canvas of the sky. If storms were coming, they were still far off. She undid the long ribbon Juniper tied on. How ironic it would now further aid her escape. The butterfly graciously allowed it to be tied around its waist. Lina secured the other end around the base of the flower.

"This will do nicely," the butterfly exclaimed. "I will get you to where Edwina waits in Cedar Knoll."

With a burst, it took off into the sky, dragging the leaf in its wake. Lina's loosened hair flapped behind her like the tail of a kite. They moved toward a bend in the stream and exited to a smaller waterway overhung with thick bulrushes. Dragonflies, mosquitoes, and jewel beetles, all gigantic to Lina, darted around the air. Fish nibbled at the surface algae. A turtle, three times the girl's size, sunned himself on a log. He watched them with suspicious eyes but did not move. It was a peaceful place to behold. Lina felt encouraged she would soon be reunited with Edwina.

An unexpected shadow fell over the leaf, covering the sunlight. Lina looked up to see a contingent of large fairies flying above them. One darted down on thick wings and snatched her off the lily pad. The next thing she knew, she was flying away while the lily pad continued down the stream, the butterfly unaware she was even gone.

CHAPTER 12

"Wait!" she screamed in the fairy's tight grip.

Down below, receding farther into the distance, the lily pad grew smaller. She watched helplessly and hoped the butterfly would be able to untie itself; otherwise, it would likely mean its death. The fairy flew up into the boughs of a river birch and landed on a long branch. A rudimentary hut formed by leaves wrapped around a twig, much like a tepee, stood nearby.

"Why did you take me?" She rounded on him, anger coming far quicker than it had with her last abduction.

"Your long hair looked so beautiful, blowing in the wind. I simply wanted to talk to you," he replied, as though his reasoning made his actions acceptable.

He had a smooth, tanned body with large oval-shaped wings, mostly clear but dappled with black. A loincloth was all he wore. His captivating eyes took up most of his face. They were large round discs with a grid-like pattern of lenses, which reminded Lina of the center of a daisy. His head was as smooth as his skin, without even one strand of hair. Perhaps that contributed to his fascination with her locks.

"Why did you not just talk to me then? Why did you have to take me? Is that what fairies do in this land? Just take whoever they want?" she yelled.

He flinched, and she felt a twinge of sympathy. Of course, this poor fairy did not know about her recent ordeal.

"I am very sorry. I just wanted to show you to everyone so they could enjoy your beauty as well. Please don't be angry. Let me get you a nice treat to eat."

Although enraged, her stomach grumbled at the thought of food. The fairy disappeared into the leaves above, returning a few moments later with a tray of honey cakes and berry juice. He eagerly watched while she nibbled on one.

"Thank you," Lina said, her irritation subsided when she deemed him no threat. "I was starving."

"We have plenty of food. You will like us, so stay and visit here. You will enjoy our company."

"I wish I could, but I cannot. I lost my traveling companion and must reunite with her in Cedar Knoll," she explained with a grimace.

The head of another fairy popped through the leaves above. "Hi-ho, Kai. Rumor is you have a guest."

"Yes, come down and meet her, Calder. She is so lovely."

A fairy, seemingly identical to the first one, flitted onto the branch. While he scrutinized her, Lina looked between the two for a discernible difference: Kai's nose was slightly rounder, perhaps, but that was a stretch. Other than that, she saw no deviation even the giant eyes were indistinguishable. Maybe they were twins.

"What kind of fairy are you? Clearly not a Volant." He nodded at her lack of wings.

"I'm a Poxy. My name is Hazel." She stuck to the same story, hoping it would work. "I was traveling with my aunt before I was stolen away by some Herptiles." They both scrunched up their noses at the mention of Herptiles. That sect was not well thought of in this world. "I managed to escape from them, and then your friend here seized me up."

"Now, Kai, you know it isn't polite just to take someone. We've talked about this," Calder admonished.

"But she is so beautiful with that long golden hair, don't you think?" He pulled Calder towards Lina for closer inspection.

"For a Poxy, I suppose. However, they are the most useless of fairies, no magic at all. Her hair looks like straw, and her skin is so pasty. Not my type at all." Like the Herptiles, they spoke about her as if she were not there to hear it.

Offended, Lina was about to tell him what she thought about their looks when a third fairy emerged from the foliage. Everything about this one looked like the others except clothing covered the top half of its body, indicating she was female. Either they were triplets, or this type of fairy all looked exactly alike.

"Who's this?" the female asked, her giant eyes fixed on the girl.

Kai repeated the story, and the fairy shook her head. She walked over to Lina and extended a hand. "Hi, Hazel, I am Ezlyn. I am sorry for Kai. We have told him before not to capture random fairies. He is particularly fond of Arborea. A Poxy is definitely a first."

Softened by the apology, Lina replied, "Well, I was quite hungry, and Kai did give me some delicious cakes."

"See—delicious cakes." Kai pointed at the tray with a proud flourish.

"What is all the commotion down here?" a new voice questioned.

Yet another fairy arrived on the bough. Lina marveled at the clone-like appearance of them all. It must be a challenge to tell each other apart, though they seemed to have no problem. This latest addition, Westley, was brought up to speed on the situation.

"Well, I agree with Calder, she is rather plain, but if you find her pretty, Kai, who am I to judge?" he deemed, as tactless as the rest.

Doubt crossed Kai's face. Without the approval of his friends, his certainty on the matter faded. "Well, I just thought she was—"

"Different?" Lina supplied, hoping to fill the awkward silence when he could not find a proper word.

An audible gasp followed this declaration. Though Lina wondered at their eerie similarity, it seemed a source of pride among them. *Different* was not attractive here. Kai looked crestfallen at the realization of her appeal to him.

"Well, now that I've gotten a good look at her, she is rather pasty," he volunteered.

"And no wings either. How would she navigate around here? Calder added. "You may as well take her back where you found her."

Kai did not debate with them, only nodded sadly. Satisfied they had convinced their friend of the girl's unworthiness, they left en masse. Ezlyn called back over her shoulder, "It's going to storm at any moment. Perhaps let her stay the night."

The butterfly had predicted accurately. Indeed, even on the most covered branch, the signs of a storm were clear. A darkness fell over them, and strong gusts of wind whipped up the undersides of the leaves. Finding her way in a downpour would prove troublesome.

"Would you like to stay?" Kai asked, the first drops of rain splashing down around them.

"If you don't mind, I think that would be best."

With a renewed smile, he led her over to the hut, and they sat inside its tapered roof. It held up surprisingly well against the squall that surged around them. For a while, they sat in silence, lightning flashing and thunder rumbling. The tempest eventually dwindled to steady rainfall, quieter now. If nothing else, Lina felt safe here.

"I'm sorry I took you." Kai's voice broke the stillness. "My fellow Ephemeras' were correct; it was wrong of me. Tomorrow I will take you to Cedar Knoll myself."

"Ephemera? Is that what your type of fairy is called?"

"Yes, we are the Ephemera order of the Volants. You would have been Hirundo, am I right?"

"Yes," she said, surprise in her tone.

"I've only seen a couple in my life, and you share their traits. Now, the good ones are mostly in hiding. I should think you would want to go in the opposite direction of Roshall Grove to escape the queen."

"I am merely following the wishes of my aunt, who I must meet in Cedar Knoll. Do most Hirundo hide from Dahlia?" She wanted information but knew she must tread carefully.

"Did you learn nothing before they exiled you?" His giant eyes seemed to grow even bigger.

"Not much," she admitted, which was not too far from the truth.

"Queen Dahlia rules with an iron fist. Her desire for power is merciless. She blights the land and hoards all resources in an ever-widening grip of control over the kingdom. Her servants, snakes, and spiders, scour the kingdom, trying to ensnare new orders of fairies under her command. Those who rebel are annihilated. Our entire order is now confined to this tree and the two other such colonies nearby. Our leader attempts to conceal us here to avoid attracting her evil eye."

"Why do all the good fairies not join together to overthrow her?" A question she wondered about since she arrived in the Fairy World.

"In order to break her spell, the Primal Crystal must be restored. She is too learned in dark magic for anyone to defy her." Kai painted a grim picture of what the good fairies were up against.

"If the spell was broken, would you fight against her then?"

Kai was quiet for a moment, staring out at the rain. "That is a very big *if*. I am afraid there is little hope of anyone breaking the spell. Legend says Queen Ivy's daughter was transported to another world to save her life. Who knows if she will ever return. And if she does, Dahlia waits to destroy her. The queen's spies are everywhere and see everything."

The hair on the back of Lina's neck bristled. Her aunt knew she would one day return. The safety she felt a moment ago dropped away. Would Kai possibly add up the pieces to discover her identity? But he continued to speak, unaware of her worry.

"They say the daughter will return in a flash of lightning—a mighty warrior princess, who will battle the evil queen to her death," he declared, a brief flicker of optimism in his eyes.

So the kingdom waited for a conquering heroine to return. Her only hope, the kingdom's only hope, was to find Edwina and get to Roshall Grove. Even then, what threat could a girl as powerless as herself be to a mighty sorceress?

"Well, enough of my babbling. It's late. Let me get you some bedding."

He briefly left and returned with some soft grass which he fashioned into a mattress. Across it, he laid two large petals to act as blankets. Grateful for the kindness, Lina settled down in the makeshift bed.

"Have some rest. Sweet dreams, Hazel," Kai whispered with a smile and strode out of the hut.
Lina heard the murmur of his wings as he took off, leaving her to fall into an uneasy sleep.

CHAPTER 13

Lina roused early the next morning, with Kai nowhere to be found. She crept out of the leaf hut and sat on the branch. The air was fresh from yesterday's rain, and sunlight dappled through the leaves. At least she would have fair weather to start the day.

Kai flew down to the branch. He handed her some honey cakes. "For your journey to find your aunt."

"Thank you, that was very thoughtful," she said, placing the food in her bag.

His cheeks reddened ever so slightly. "I hope you enjoy them. And if you are ever back this way, promise, you will drop in and say hello."

"I certainly will." She enjoyed her time with the Ephemera far more than the Herptiles.

"Are you ready to go? It's not far."

Once she nodded, he picked her up and flew off. Away from the tree, he glided low along the water to avoid detection from above. On the bank of a stream, he sat her on a cattail that bowed slightly with her weight.

"Good luck to you, Hazel," he said, never landing, "I am happy to have met you."

"Thank you," she called to his fleeting form.

Lina slid down the fat stalk to the ground. Around her, cedar trees loomed high into the sky, more stately than the willow trees which hung slovenly over the bank. Lush foliage grew on the riverside. Clusters of flowers dotted the landscape of reedy grass and mossy stones. Birds flitted among the trees, happy songs ringing out. Insects buzzed from flower to flower, a calming hum created by their wings. But, Lina saw no sign of Edwina or any fairy for that matter.

A sense of aloneness engulfed her, panic about to rear its head. Her adoptive parents had always been there for her. Never had she spent even one night alone before their deaths. Even after being separated from the enchantress, she was aided by Lula and Kai. Every decision in the fairy world to this point had been made by others. Now it was up to her.

For some time, she debated what to do. The higher ground should provide some clues on how to proceed. The rise would not have been steep to her mortal feet, but it was a small mountain to a fairy. Up she trudged, all the while looking for some indication of Edwina. Halfway up, tired and hungry, she sat on a rock to rest. She ate a honey cake, touched by Kai's thoughtfulness. Now the poor Ephemera hid in the trees to avoid Dahlia. She owed it to them and all the other oppressed fairies to do what she could to conquer her aunt, Queen Dahlia.

A rabbit hopped into view, its brown fur dark against the green grass. It nibbled at some and hopped closer. This rabbit was larger than a horse would have been in the mortal world. A soft gasp escaped her lips. Instantly, the rabbit turned his eyes to the stone where she sat. After watching her a moment, he looked all around.

"Hello," the rabbit announced in a tone of caution.

"Hello," she whispered back, nervously fingering her amulet.

"What brings you here?" he questioned and hopped closer.

Kai's words about Dahlia's spies being everywhere flashed through her mind. Unsure how much to share, she replied, "I'm waiting to meet someone."

The rabbit's eyes narrowed, his nose twitching furiously. Again, he looked all around before he hopped right next to Lina. "Do you hope to meet Edwina?"

Lina's eyes widened. "Yes. Do you know her?"

"Yes," he said, still on guard for any movement nearby.

"Where is she? Can you take me to her?" She could barely contain her excitement at the thought of reuniting with the enchantress.

"She was here but had to leave. Come, I will show you."

The creature broke off with great speed, and Lina struggled to keep up. Down the hill, he bounded. Around a corner, she lost sight of him but soon found him up ahead by a scorched pile of earth. While panting to regain her breath, Lina arrived at his side and studied the burnt ground at her feet.

"She was here for a few days asking for help to find a girl. You, I assume." Lina nodded. "Then, two snakes came. It seemed as though she knew them, but not in a friendly way, and they exchanged words. When they attempted to capture her, she cast a spell and disappeared."

Not the same spell she had used to bring Lina to the Fairy World. That spell left a golden circle of dust on the ground, whereas the land was pitted and charred here. It must have been the same two snakes who caused them to be separated. Kai mentioned Queen Dahlia had some in her service. They had already found Edwina twice in the short time since they arrived in this world. Lina's heart pounded against her chest.

"What happened to the snakes?" They spoke to one another in a soft voice.

"They were burned, not badly, I think, but scared them enough to leave with all haste." He continued to look around vigilantly.

"Do you think they will return?" Lina shuddered at the thought.

"I cannot say, but so far, they have not."

"What about Edwina? Will she return?" Lina inquired with exasperation.

"I don't know the answer to that either, I'm afraid," he uttered with a shrug.

Lina stared at the circle of black marring the otherwise bright green grass. For the moment, her hopes of finding the enchantress were dashed. The rabbit regarded her, an unreadable expression on his face. His whiskers bounced with his twitching nose, while he debated the situation. A soft breeze wafted the scent of the blackened earth across the glade.

"I am Zander. If you are the one Edwina searched for, then I trust you. You are welcome to come to my burrow while you sort everything out. There is a place right outside you can stay if you prefer to be above ground."

"I would truly appreciate that." Lina had no idea what her next move should be, and though she sensed the rabbit was her ally, she would stick to her "Hazel" story if asked about her identity.

She followed him to his burrow not far away, a hole in the ground hidden by a downed tree. When she peered in, she saw only blackness and had no desire to go inside. Zander poked his waggling nose at a tiny knothole in the fallen trunk. Inside was a small area covered in moss, some cracks on the side let in the light, but the wood overhead protected it from the elements. Lina stepped onto the soft green floor—it would provide excellent shelter until she decided her next move.

"You are welcome to stay as long as you need. I will find you something to eat. There are no more fairies left around here, but I can ask some of the animals if they have any word on Edwina's return."

"Thank you." The sentiment was not adequate to describe Lina's relief.

A small head poked out of the burrow. The new rabbit, brown like Zander, took in the scene with saucer-like eyes.

"This is my sister, Zara," he introduced. Zara slowly emerged from the hole and went to sit by her sibling.

"This girl is the one Edwina was searching for," he explained to his sister. "She will wait here for a while to see if the enchantress returns."

"I hope it is Edwina who returns and not the snakes," Zara cried. "What if they come looking for her instead?"

Lina noted the sheer terror in the rabbit's voice. The snakes could return, and she was putting these animals in great danger. "Maybe I should go. I don't want to cause any trouble for you."

"Nonsense," Zander declared. "Trouble has been brewing for a long time. We know who you are. We know who Edwina sought. We will help keep you safe until she returns. Isn't that right, Zara?" Zander urged.

"Yes," his sister conceded. "If you are who Edwina says you are, we need to find her and get you home. We will help you any way we can, Lina."

For the first time since the Herptiles stole her away, the girl felt a burden lifted from her shoulders. These rabbits wished to aid and protect her on her journey. Plus, she would not have to pretend to be someone she was not with them, and that in itself was helpful enough.

CHAPTER 14

Dahlia wrapped her cloak tightly around her shoulders against the creeping chill. Winter would be here in earnest soon. For now, it settled for sheathing everything in a layer of frost each morning. She scraped her long nails on the terrace railing before rubbing the ice crystals against her fingertips. The garden grounds spread out below her. Long had it been since any flower bloomed there. Once, it was a place of splendor, beautiful topiaries, exquisite smells, even a hedge maze. If Dahlia closed her eyes, she could almost feel the summer sun warm her skin while she ran along its paths with Ivy on those long-ago days of camaraderie and secrets shared that only happened between sisters.

They had been opposites from the start, Ivy was fairness and light, Dahlia fiery and brooding, yet the bond between them was undeniable. Two halves of a whole, their mother used to say. While Ivy tried to rein in Dahlia's cynicism, Dahlia grounded Ivy's imagination in reality. The two were inseparable until the incident with the bee caused an unraveling of their bond. The last time they were ever alone in the gardens was a glorious summer afternoon, so perfect, one believed it would never end. The sisters raced along the path to the hedge maze, where they stumbled and giggled, confident they knew the way. Their guards waited dutifully at the entrance. Finding their favorite secluded spot, they settled on the grass.

"Can you believe it?" Ivy said. "Theros and I are to wed?"

The girls had just come from a meeting where their parents laid out the plan for Ivy's future and, with it, the future ruler of the kingdom. Dahlia had not been mentioned at all. Ivy, giddy with delight when it was over, grabbed her sister's hand and ran straight to the maze.

"At least he is handsome," Dahlia suggested with a smile, not wanting to ruin her connection with Ivy after so long. Nevertheless, after the conversation with her parents, Dahlia felt stung—stung as if by the giant bee who threatened her sister all those months ago.

"True. But me... a wife?" They snickered at the once girlish fantasy now solidly before them. "Not that I need to worry anytime soon."

Fairies could live for untold years. Ivy would only be required to marry when their mother died, which to their young minds, not yet hardened by the tragic turns of life, seemed an impossibility. For their entire childhood, their parents had reigned in peace.

"At least you know what your future holds. They do not care enough about me to even have a plan." Dalia tried unsuccessfully to keep the bitterness out of her voice.

"Dear sister, do not fret," Ivy exclaimed, taking her hands. "We've always talked about this. You will be my most trusted advisor, my right hand. Do you think I would listen to Theros over you? Or even Edwina, for that matter? You and I will rule together in all but name, just as we always planned. I promise."

At these words, some of the hurt melted away in Dahlia's heart. She enjoyed the rest of the afternoon with Ivy and hoped the fracture between them was on its way to being mended. But later, Priya scoffed at Ivy's promise to Dahlia.

"Your parents are too afraid of your power to let you anywhere near Ivy for any length of time, and I doubt you could convince Ivy of the benefits of our lessons—not to mention Theros. You watch; she will fall under his spell. Love does that. It clouds the mind, makes people forget their promises." At Dahlia's crestfallen face, the enchantress added in an unconvincing tone, "But not to worry. I am sure your parents will rule for many years to come. Perhaps there is still time enough to have Ivy accept your powers for what they are," Priya smirked for effect.

    The girl nodded, even as an inkling of doubt filled her. Priya was right, her parents had already created a rift between the siblings, and Theros would not want her usurping his place at Ivy's side. Her sister *would* break the promise, of that she was sure. The certainty of this thought wound around her heart, strangling it with malice.

    "I cannot believe my parents did not make a single plan for my future. I stood there like a spectator, not a princess. It's so unfair," Dahlia complained, arms crossed over her chest.

    Priya crossed the room and put her arms around the angry girl. "I agree. It is unfair, and we are not the only ones to think so."

    "What do you mean?" she asked, her voice filled with surprise.

    "My friends in Elderbreach think your parents should give you more consideration. They were surprised your training was left to me with no interest from the queen and king."

Dahlia knew her parents were not aware of her lessons with Priya, but this meant they did not care whether she received any training at all. She was still a member of the royal family, and they omitted her from learning her heritage and the knowledge a leader would need. At least, Priya's friends thought she was worthy of these teachings.

"The more I hear of your friends, the more I appreciate their input," she asserted.

"Yes. My friends are very wise fairies, even if your parents have no use for them *either*," the enchantress remarked, further driving home the point.

Now, more than ever, Dahlia felt justified in her secret lessons. Priya was a wise teacher and had her best interest at heart. Together they could figure out a way to make her parents see she deserved more.

The flapping of wings brought Dahlia back to the frosty garden terrace of the present. A dark figure descended from the sky, a speck of black swirling and ever-lowering until it alit on the railing.

"I bring news from Cotswold, My Queen," the raven said with a bow of his head into the cloud of coldness brought on by his words.

"Go on, Rhys."

"It seems, shortly after her arrival in Oakgarde, Lina was abducted by a Herptile woman who had some nonsensical scheme of marrying off her son. The girl claimed to be a Poxy, and the woman did not realize who she was. Our agent, Leander, however, had sense enough to question her identity. They imprisoned her on a lily pad in the middle of the lake until one of us could arrive."

"And…" the queen asked when the pause lasted too long.

"Unfortunately, Lina was able to escape with the help of a Fluvial who loosened the lily pad and took her to the river."

Dahlia cursed under her breath. The water fairies usually kept to their own, not bothering with the affairs of those above ground. They thought themselves untouchable in their watery kingdom. Once she conquered all the land, Dahlia would make sure they regretted bestowing help on the girl.

"One of my flock mates spotted Lina floating down the river with the assistance of a butterfly. He thought to swoop down and grab her, but an Ephemera beat him to it," the raven continued, head down as he delivered this unfortunate news.

"An Ephemera?" Dahlia was incredulous. The three Ephemera Queens had taken steps to protect their kind from her reign. They hid in their tree kingdoms meticulously, avoiding both Dahlia and the Resistors. She had only left them alone thus far, because knowing they would be an easy defeat, she chose to concentrate her resources elsewhere.

"Yes. They had Lina briefly, but one brought her to Cedar Knoll. He could not catch her at that time because Edwina had some creatures and fairies keeping watch and was able to fight him off. The enchantress herself was nowhere to be seen."

"Very well," the queen replied after a moment's thought. "Return to that area and tell Cotswold to patrol between there and Roshall Grove. Hopefully, one of you will prove competent enough to capture her," she seethed.

"Yes, My Queen." He dipped his head and took off into the grey morning sky.

The girl was more elusive than expected; even Edwina had lost her. No matter, though. She was still far from the Resistors. There was more than enough time to seize her.

And if that failed, Dahlia's army was too great, her magic too powerful to be defeated. The thought brought a smile to the Dark Queen's face. She returned inside, her cape scraping across the frosty ground with each retreating step.

CHAPTER 15

The rabbits agreed to keep Lina's identity secret if possible. No one wanted to endanger any of the forest inhabitants. So, Hazel the Poxy's story was promulgated around the woods when they spoke of their guest. Two weeks passed with no sign of Edwina or the snakes. Zander and Zara, along with their brother Zavier, were kind companions to Lina. The boys liked to bring her food, and Zara helped gather grass to weave a bed for her dwelling's moss floor.

Lina quickly fell into a routine, arising each morning to toss off her leaf blanket and explore the area for some sign of Edwina. There were plenty of nuts to eat and the occasional berry. However, each day, autumn's grip tightened, chilling the dawn a bit more before whisking daylight away earlier and earlier. Besides the rabbits, she saw chipmunks, squirrels, and a deer so massive, she barely topped its hooves. She tried to avoid contact with any of them; best not to have her presence noted. As Zander had said, she never once saw another fairy of any kind.

One afternoon, with him by her side, she came across the overgrown remnants of a cluster of fairy houses built on the side of a knoll. Grass now choked the windows of the wind-eroded walls, the doors but faded thoughts of their once glorious colors.

"Where have they all gone?" she asked.

"Some went far South to escape Dahlia's reign, and others joined an underground movement where a group of Resistors plots to overthrow the evil queen. An eternal spring season once blessed this land, but the Primal Crystal shattered, and it broke the spell. Many fairies did not have the wherewithal to survive the harsh winters. Plus, the snakes and the spiders, once banished to certain areas, now roam freely across the land. This forest used to be a far lovelier place."

"So there truly are no fairies left anywhere near here?" she asked, saddened by his story. A natural breeze lifted the hair from her shoulders. Colored leaves wafted down from the treetops, slowly dancing to the ground. Spring was *not* eternal here anymore.

"No more Volants at all. Of the Groundlings, all Arborea are gone, only a few Rodentia remain near the cornfields out west, but they stay under the earth, out of sight. The snakes are a huge threat to them."

Lina imagined a warm and verdant forest full of animals and fairies, the small village bustling with activity. Melancholy filled her heart as she stared at the abandoned cottages. She saw little of the Herptile town and even less of the Ephemeras' home, but these tiny buildings spoke to her, reminding her of places she'd visited in the mortal world. This forest village represented community and the peaceful co-existence of many kinds. They deserved to have that life back.

On their way back to the burrow, the crunch of leaves thundered out, and a shadow fell across their path. Lina looked up at a enormous stag, who leaned his head down to them. Frightened, she took a few steps back, but Zander said, "Hello, Cyrus."

"Hello, Zander," he returned the greeting and turned to the girl, "and you must be Lina."

It was hard to say what amazed Lina more, his baritone voice or that he knew her name. Either way, she felt a connection to the majestic animal and decided to trust him.

"Yes," she acknowledged.

"I heard you rabbits were hosting a Poxy, but something told me to keep an extra eye out. I am sorry for eavesdropping, but I promised Edwina I would guard you if you came." He settled down onto the forest floor in front of them.

"Have you seen her? Do you know where I can find her?" Lina asked quickly.

"Not since she last fought off the snakes," he replied with a shake of his magnificent antlers. "She told me then that she would be back as soon as she could, but I've heard word that both snakes and ravens follow her every move."

"I am not the only guardian you have. She met a few fairies, who were traveling west to join the Resistors and tasked them with keeping you safe until she returned."

"There are fairies here? Can you take me to them?" she exclaimed.

Before he could answer, three fairies flew down from the branches above. Lina gasped at the sight of them—they looked very much like her, with pale skin but with navy hair instead of blonde. Their wings were a pale iridescent blue. The trio, two girls and one boy, looked back at her with the same fascination.

"Is it really you, Lina?" one of them asked, turquoise eyes wide with wonder.

"Of course it is. She looks just like Queen Ivy and her mother before her," the second fairy declared and turned to her. "Your Highness."

They bowed as one, Lina awkwardly staring back.

"Forgive me; I am not used to people bowing to me," Lina explained, "and you are the first fairies I have seen who look like me. All the others have been so different."

"I am Cassia, and this is Sorrell and Tamsin. We are Cyano Volants," the last one said, stepping in front of the other two and continuing "a very close relative to the Hirundo."

"And you know of Edwina and the Resistors?" The very thought filled her with hope.

"Yes. We were headed to join the Resistors when we met Edwina. Once she returns, we will continue on that path." A proud glint filled each of their eyes.

"Do you know when she will return?" Lina asked eagerly.

"As Cyrus told you, the agents of the evil queen pursue her. She has to shake them before it is safe for her to return here."

"But there have been other dangers as well," Tamsin piped in before a withering look from Cassia quieted her.

"What other dangers?" Lina cried.

"A few days ago, a flock of ravens swirled overhead," Cassia explained. "One swooped down to the forest to look around. We were able to impair him enough that he flew away, but now he knows fairies are here, and he may return or send something worse."

"How did you impair him?" Lina asked, imagining how large a raven would be.

"Like this," said Sorrell. He held out his hands, and with a quiet spell, shock waves flew across to a nearby flower. Its stem quickly burned under the attack.

While Cyrus and Zander watched as though it were the most ordinary thing, Lina was amazed. "How did you do that?"

"Volants have many abilities the lesser fairies do not," Sorrell ventured and aimed at another target.

"Enough," Cassia ordered, slapping his hands down. He immediately stopped and backed up to stand by Tamsin. "We saw some swallows high above, but the ravens chased them off."

Perhaps Knox searched for her as well as Edwina. The thought brought her comfort, but neither one evaded Dahlia's spies. Journeying to Roshall Grove alone was daunting, but she did not want to put any animals or fairies in danger. "Do you think I should wait here for her? Or is it too dangerous? Should I try to find Roshall Grove on my own?" Cassia did not answer, her brow furrowed in thought. A gust of wind tore more leaves from their boughs, and Zander huddled close to the stag's side. Neither had said a word since the fairies arrived. Whatever their opinions were, they kept it to themselves.

"Here is what I think we should do," the Cyano fairy said, "let's wait here for a little while longer. Hopefully, either Edwina will show up or someone who has news of her. Autumn is upon us. Any journey we make in the cold will be treacherous and require much forethought and scouting. However, if the situation becomes more dangerous, we will talk about moving and protecting the forest inhabitants. Does that sound reasonable to you?"

"Yes, it does," Lina answered. "For now, we will wait."

CHAPTER 16

And so, wait, they did. The weather turned cold, the last leaves detaching from their limbs and blowing to the ground. Each day saw the sunrise a bit later and set a bit earlier. The rabbits did their best to keep their guest comfortable in her small nook. Chipmunks, who had taken to visiting Lina, brought her a piece of deerskin from a carcass in the forest. She used part of it to fashion herself a cloak and stuffed another piece full of rabbit hair to create a warm blanket. The remaining fur Lina earmarked for a pair of boots.

After their encounter with Cyrus and the fairies, Lina's true identity was quietly whispered among the animals in the woods. The creatures all took it upon themselves to help and protect the girl as best they could. Their constant patrol of the forest put Lina's mind at ease, knowing any sign of danger would be quickly reported to the Cyano fairies.

"Do you think the Resistors are strong enough to defeat Dahlia?" Lina asked Cassia on a brisk afternoon.

They sat together inside her log home, a tiny fire conjured by the fairy keeping them warm.

"I often wonder that myself," she replied with a sigh. "They are small in number compared to what the queen can summon, but your return gives us hope of the Primal Crystal being restored, and hope is something we haven't had for a long time."

"I would need a lot of help to wrest the crystal from her. If fairies who fled and the ones in hiding come to help, perhaps we could challenge her," Lina mused aloud, her back resting against the soft green moss.

"The most important thing is to get you to Roshall Grove. Sorrell maps our route as we speak. When he returns in a day or two, we would be wise to set out. It will not be easy going, but it is better than waiting here and doing nothing," Cassia said, pacing the length of the partial tree trunk.

Lina watched the flames dance in a gust of wind. A storm was brewing, a harbinger of what awaited them on the trek to her home. Though she preferred to stay in the safety of the forest, she knew Cassia was right.

"I guess I better get to work on those boots." She nodded at the extra fur, but her voice gave away her doubt.

Cassia smiled. "Don't worry, Lina. You will be with me, Sorrell and Tamsin. We will get you there in one piece."

"I know. It's just I can't help wondering why Edwina brought me here without teaching me more first. She never even discussed a backup plan if we were to become separated. It is only because of the kindness of strangers that I was able to survive. But I know there are those with evil intentions who are looking for me, and I feel unprepared to deal with them. Please promise to give me some instruction on what I should do if I become separated from the three of you." This thought plagued her mind.

"You make a good point, Lina. I will discuss this matter with Tamsin tonight. We will make plans for you in the event you are left alone. When Sorrell returns, the four of us will address all your concerns," the Cyano assured her, stopping to take her hands.

"Thank you, Cassia. I feel much better about the journey now."

The fairy bade her good night and flew out of a slit in the log, a flutter of blue hair and wings. Lina picked up the fur and got to work. Zara had given her a piece of cork-like bark for the soles and some sturdy dried grass for the laces. It took her the rest of the afternoon, but in the end, she was proud of the product her efforts produced. At least there was one thing she accomplished besides worrying about the future. Her thoughts flew to Edwina—the enchantress underestimated the ease of her task. Lina fought down the anger she felt. She missed her home, her parents, the way things used to be. Exhausted, she huddled under her blanket though it did little to warm the coldness in her heart.

The next morning, Sorrell returned. Cassia told her to be ready to leave the day after next. The rabbits sat with her while she packed some food in her small bag next to her rowan box. Snow lightly fell outside, a stray flake finding its way into her small chamber every so often. She told them the fairies would plan for any eventuality on the trip back and proudly showed them her boots.

"They are beautiful," Zander complimented. "Please be sure to send word to us the moment you have arrived safely. We will be so worried."

"I promise I will."

"We will be sorry to see you go," Zavier voiced the thoughts of his siblings. "We've gotten used to having you around."

"I will miss you all and will never be able to thank you for your kindness," Lina spoke with feeling. She watched a fat tear fall from Zara's eyes. "But, let's not be so sad. I still have a couple more nights. Let's plan a nice dinner to celebrate."

"Yes!" exclaimed Zara. "A going away party."

The brothers nodded in happy agreement. After a brief discussion about food and decorations, they hopped off to prepare. Lina was glad to lift their spirits, and it would be nice to have a proper goodbye.

That afternoon, while snow fell around her, she walked one of the regular routes. She searched for any sign of Edwina, a long shot, but done more out of habit than anything. She pulled her cloak tightly around her shoulders. In the mortal world, this storm would have been a mere flurry to her, but here, the large flakes fell heavy on her petite body. When it became too complicated to walk any further, she turned back toward the rabbit's den.

A sound caught her attention, rustling in the brush up ahead. Something was coming. Lina cast a glance around her. The only place to hide was behind a small snow-covered rock, it would not cover her completely, but she had no other choice. She raced over and cowered behind it. Two chipmunks burst out of the brush and looked around frantically.

"What's wrong?" she asked, standing to face them.

"Snakes!" one cried.

Lina's blood turned as cold as the snow. "Where are they?" she urged.

"Back by the warren. Zara saw them coming and sent us to warn you not to come back," one said while the other shuddered by his side.

All Lina could think about was the safety of the rabbits. Without thought, she took off running while the chipmunks watched, their mouths agape. She prayed her friends were all right and cursed herself for putting them in such danger. Hopefully, the Cyano fairies had protected them.

She reached a slight slope, and the burrow came into sight. Lina hid inside the curtain of a fallen branch. Peeking out, she could see the log was displaced, pieces of down and straw strewn about. A crashing noise rang out, followed by more debris falling from the hole. She heard nothing more but darted for cover. Lina crept closer to the burrow and stopped behind a large tree root. Rustling sounds emanated from the warren. To Lina's horror, a snake's head emerged. He slithered out fully, twining into a coil. Another head, with a green diamond-shape, followed. Dahlia's snakes had found her at last.

CHAPTER 17

"She was here, Purus," one snake hissed while the other slipped out of the hole and coiled up next to his cohort. "If we wait, she may return unless the escaped rabbits can warn her."

The snakes had come upon the rabbits without warning. Now, their home lay in ruins, destroyed by these merciless serpents. To her horror, Lina noticed a spot of blood on one snake's fangs. Her heart sank at the thought of them not escaping in time.

Suddenly, breaking from her depressing musings, one of the snakes swung around in her direction—its green diamond-shaped head aglow against his inky black scales. A trembling Lina ducked lower behind the tree root.

"No, Kafir, if they found her, they will not be back. They know luck was on their side this time. I picked up her scent going south. I say we follow it," the second snake replied.

"Very well, we can check back here later," Kafir agreed.

They slithered off—as one—in the direction she had traveled earlier that morning. Lina stood frozen for a moment. The thought of putting her friends in such danger caused her breath to hitch. Knowing she must make haste, Lina was still too distraught to move. *I must find them. They are on the run because of me;* Lina mentally scolded herself. Thinking they must have gone searching for the fairies, Lina took off toward the glade they frequented. Cassia would know what to do. Every few moments she stopped to listen for the slithering of the snakes, but she heard nothing.

The glade came into sight, a fresh patch of fresh snow, marred by dark blue stains. She stumbled ahead, looking at the sky above for some sign of the Cyanos, when her foot struck something. Before even looking down, her heart knew what it was—Tamsin lay lifeless at her feet. Not far away, Sorrell and Cassia had met the same fate. Their navy blood seeped out of their bodies, tarnishing the pure white ground. Instead of sorrow or fear, a great anger rose in Lina. She had brought about the deaths of three innocent friends. Friends who not only offered their aid, but bestowed kindness upon her as well.

Even knowing the immense danger, they hadn't hesitated to help Lina.

Wracked with guilt, she crept back to the burrow and retrieved her bag. Through glossy, wet eyes, Lina noticed the snakes had ransacked the warren, but they had not found her room. Thankfully, all her belongings, including the food, were still inside the toppled log. Armed with the knowledge her enemies' went south, Lina headed west towards Roshall Grove, though she did not know how far away it was. Luckily, Zander taught her how to hide her tracks, a skill which was handy now that she was being followed. She kept out of sight as much as possible, but the trees thinned out as the land rose, leaving little cover. Soon, Lina was farther from the burrow than she ever had been. Her legs ached on the ever-upward climb, but she pushed on.

When night fell, she stopped and took refuge in the hollow of a downed log, a space not nearly as homey as her previous lodging. Her deerskin cloak provided inadequate coverage for the freezing temperatures of the day, but night-time was far worse. Lina wrapped herself in whatever foliage she could find, but it did not do much to warm her. Sleep was elusive, her ears always alert for the sound of rustling of snakes.

In the morning, she ate some of her provisions, but there was not much. She had only packed a few day's worth of meals because Cassia told her there would be safe houses along the way. Even if Lina found one, she could never reach the treetops by herself, and it would be risky to call for help with the ravens around. During her hike, she kept an eye out for any food to replenish her supply, but nothing survived in this harsh winter weather.

For two more days, she hiked up and down one hill after another. The forest, though thinning, continued on without end. An anemic sun tried to shine through low clouds in the dull sky. Frigid gusts of wind punctured the air, and Lina's cheeks ached, every step laborious. The first night she slept in an abandoned den of some small creature and the second, a hollowed-out tree stump. Both nights were freezing, but she dared not light a fire. Her fingers and toes were constantly numb, and she barely slept. More treacherous than the journey were her thoughts, filled with doubt-ridden sentiments of a weak girl, like herself, ever being able to defeat Queen Dahlia. She considered giving up, but somehow her resolve returned each morning.

On the third day, she rose tired and travel-stained, wondering how far she still had to trek. After finishing the last of her food, Lina set out. By mid-morning, she could see the end of the tree line. When she exited the forest, there was yet another hill to climb. Lina felt exposed in the uncovered terrain and glanced up at the sky for any sign of the ravens. At the top, the land leveled out, and in the distance, the long, flat expanse of a cornfield spread before her as far as the eye could see. She put one tired foot in front of the other, knowing the field would provide her with a place to hide and perhaps even a kernel or two of corn.

It took a good while, but she finally reached the field's edge. Lina crept among the dead stalks, the sky ever-darkening above her. Cold, tired, and hungry, she took refuge in the dark brown folds of a fallen husk to debate what to do. Nighttime would be upon her soon. She flexed her fingers and toes, trying to banish the numbness. Her mind told her she needed to search for food before the daylight vanished entirely, but her exhausted body could not find the strength to move.

For a while, she sat wishing for warmth and a full belly. At this point, she was not even sure she was heading in the direction of Roshall Grove or if she had the stamina to keep going. She had encountered no one on her journey to either help or hinder it. Her determination to find the Resistors weakened each day. She was not sure how much longer she could go on, especially without food. Silently, she prayed for someone to show her what to do.

A banging noise startled her, and she crouched low in her hiding place. Nearby, a trapdoor opened, and a small fairy materialized onto the bleak landscape. Lina caught a glimpse of brown skin with long grey hair sticking out of a fur cap. In sturdy boots, the fairy walked right past where Lina hid. She rolled out a walnut stuffed between the leaves of another downed stalk.

"Almost the last of them," she muttered to herself. "Blast this darn snow. Earlier and worse every year."

With a shake of her head, the fairy pushed the wobbly nut back toward the door. Lina knew this may be her only chance for help and weighed her options. Not all fairies could be trusted, but spending another night freezing to death was not what she needed right now. Her choice made, she stepped from her hiding spot as the woman passed and said, "Excuse me..."

The fairy whipped around with surprising agility, her eyes targeting the girl. "Who are you? What do you want?"

"I'm just a poor lost Poxy who needs some food," Lina answered, stepping out of the shelter of the husk.

"You need more than that, I'd say," the fairy replied after giving Lina a once over. "Come with me. You'll freeze out here in the cold."

At the trapdoor, she gave the walnut a mighty shove. They watched it fall over the edge. She signaled the girl to go next. As Lina scrambled down a ladder, the fairy followed, sealing the exit tightly behind them. Whatever fate awaited Lina down here, there was no going back now.

CHAPTER 18

They descended five rungs to a corridor, bright with the light of sconces interspersed along the wall. The walnut rolled in unsteady loops ahead of them. Not far along the tunnel stood a bright red door. The fairy opened it and motioned Lina inside, "You go in and get warm while I put this acorn in storage."

Inside was a comfortably sized room with a pleasant fire crackling on the far wall. A large square table with mismatched chairs anchored a space cluttered with curios, bookcases, and shelves, each overflowing with a host of items of various size, shape, and use. Although it was not nearly as neat as her old house, the sense of hominess reminded Lina very much of the cottage she grew up in, familiar and lived-in.

Her new companion returned and nudged the girl on her shoulder. "Go stand by the fire and warm up, dear."

Lina did not need to be told twice. She happily warmed herself in front of the flames, flanked by two overstuffed chairs whose fabric was well worn. Several wicker baskets filled with fabric pieces and sewing paraphernalia sat nearby. Water dripped off of her cloak and boots, pooling into small puddles at her feet. Slowly, the life filtered back into her fingers and toes.

"My name is Cora. Let me take you coat and boots, dear." The fairy hung her coat on a peg and put her boots underneath as though order mattered in that particular area of her dwelling. Lina offered hers, and they were placed beside the owners.

"Give me a moment, and I will start us some dinner. But first, come with me," Cora ordered.

She led Lina into a small bedroom where she rummaged inside the drawer of a dresser. With a whip of her hand, she gave Lina a long woolen dress. "This should do. It was my daughter's. Now, get out of those wet clothes."

"Thank you, Cora. My name is Hazel," she replied.

The fairy placed some stockings on the bed and left her alone to change. Lina stepped into the garment, thankful for both its warmth and dryness. After tucking her amulet safely under its neckline, she left her bag on the bed and rejoined Cora, who was in the main room knee-deep in meal preparation.

A flurry of activity filled the small counter space, the fairy's movements, so swift, Lina's eyes had trouble keeping up. The fairy hummed a lively tune while a delicious aroma spread from a pot she stirred.

"Do you need any help?" the girl felt compelled to ask.

"You could set the table. Dinnerware is in there." She gestured to a large hutch on the sidewall.

The shelves were littered with papers, notebooks, paintings, and an old silver tea set. Lina found cups, plates, and utensils in the drawers, all with different patterns, which she dutifully laid out on the dining table. Cora set the steaming pot of stew in the middle and dished out two heaping servings.

"So you are a Poxy?" Cora asked once they were settled.

"Yes," she acknowledged warily.

"How long have you been on your own?" True concern laced the fairy's question.

"For a few months." Lina knew she better stick as close to the truth as possible, so she didn't confuse her story if she spoke to anyone here in the future.

"What kind of Volant were you?"

"Hirundo." The question made her heart skip, but she knew she had to answer truthfully.

"Yes, I expected as much; you have their fair coloring. I'm sorry you were exiled, especially in these uncertain times. Do you have any plans? Any place to go?"

"Not really." The truthfulness of this answer stung Lina more than a lie would have. She looked at her bowl and stemmed the tears which formed in the corners of her eyes.

"And were you headed east to flee from the reign of Dahlia?" The woman stopped eating and looked at her pointedly.

"Yes," Lina agreed, better if Cora thought she was headed away from Roshall Grove to keep her identity safer. "But, I am afraid at this point, I am lost."

Cora nodded and returned to her meal. Silence fell over the room, only the sounds of their spoons against the bowl to be heard. When she had scraped up the last drop of stew, the fairy set down her spoon. She looked at the girl for a long time. Lina sat quietly, afraid to say anything.

"Well, Hazel, there are many bad fairies around who are agents of the evil queen. However, I don't think you are one of them. So, I have a proposal for you. Winter is upon us and travel would be perilous. How would you like to stay here with me until Spring? You could help me with my everyday tasks and keep me company. It's been pretty quiet here since my daughter left."

Lina weighed her options. She had no idea how to get where she needed to go and no one to help her. Surviving the harsh winter on her own would be next to impossible. Here she would remain warm and, more importantly, hidden until she could figure out her next move. Perhaps she would even learn information that could help her to go forward. This was the best possible solution for the time being.

"That is very kind of you, Cora. I accept."

"Wonderful!" The fairy's face lit up. She rose to take the empty stew bowls to the sink and returned with two large slices of honey cake.

"Where did your daughter go?" Lina asked, taking a large forkful.

Cora's smile faded, the gleam in her eyes now extinguished. "She left to join an underground movement to overthrow Queen Dahlia. Along with many of the young fairies who used to live here. Once, these tunnels bustled with Rodentia, the proud city of Maizeridge. But, the harsh winters make it difficult to survive here. Those who did not join the rebellion went to seek a more favorable habitat."

"Where exactly is the rebellion?"

"Far from here, near the outskirts of Roshall Grove. Most Volants there now dwell underground, if you can believe it, gathering all resources to defeat the evil queen. I'm surprised you didn't know where they were... since you came from that direction." She placed her fork down on her empty plate.

"I was shunned for many years. My old aunt tried to take care of me, but when she passed, I was left alone. There are many histories and knowledge about our kingdom that I never learned." Lina surprised herself with the false story, but Cora nodded along. "Does your daughter give you news of the Resistors? Are they great in number?"

"I've not heard from my Delphine in a long while. When she arrived, all those months ago, she sent one letter back. Full of excitement, she sounded, ready to take on the world. I wish she had just stayed here with me." She drifted into melancholy silence before rising to grab a book from the hutch. Flipping through the pages, she stopped on one and turned the volume toward Lina. "Here is what the palace at Roshall Grove used to look like, the crowning jewel of the Fairy World, but no more. My daughter hopes to one day see it restored."

The beautiful white castle in the picture shined majestically in the sun, an edifice whose virtue transcended the power it represented. Lina imagined how magnificent her family's legacy had been. She thought about the rebellion—the more fairies who joined the Resistors, the better her own chances of defeating Dahlia. There would be strength in numbers, she hoped. There must be other towns abandoned like this one where some went to join the fight. Perhaps it was a hopeless cause, but could the fairies who fled get far enough away to evade Dahlia's grip, or would her reign eventually spread to the end of the Fairy World? Sooner or later, her evil realm would extend to all.

"Enough sad talk for now," Cora stated, shaking the gloom away. "I am here, healthy, and now I have you for company. There is Mr. Tyson as well. You will meet him soon enough. He is the Mayor of Maizeridge. Now finish up that cake."

Cora sat with Lina by the fire amiably after dinner. To Lina's relief, the woman loved to chat about sewing, painting, and other such light topics. She did not ask the girl many questions about her past. When it was time for bed, Cora gestured to the room where she had gotten the dress. "You are welcome to sleep in Delphine's old room. Make yourself at home. Let me know if you need anything."

"Thank you so much," Lina said, rising from her seat. "Your kindness to me is a blessing."

The older fairy reddened at the compliment and retired to her room. Lina's new room was a comfortable space furnished with a canopy bed complete with an overstuffed mattress and an inordinate number of pillows. A cozy armchair, a night table covered in a ruffle-edge tablecloth, and the dresser finished off the chamber. The overabundance of cheerfully patterned fabrics almost counteracted the absence of any windows.

When she pulled the thick covers over herself that night, Lina was grateful to be out of the cold. Delphine was brave indeed to leave such comfort for the hard life of a Resistor. Lina vowed to find that same courage for the sake of her rabbit friends, the Cyanos, and all who lived in her aunt's evil shadow.

CHAPTER 19

Lina and Cora got along well. They spent most of the first few days together except for a few errands which took the older fairy into the city. Cora had a never-ending list of tasks to accomplish each day. She made preserves to see them through the winter, which Lina stacked with many other jars inside a tightly filled pantry. They gathered a few more walnuts hidden amongst the cornstalks. Once in the storeroom, they broke them apart and separated the nuts from the shell. A mountain of sewing overflowed a basket by the fireplace, and Cora took great pains to help Lina learn to mend various garments and household items.

On some cluttered shelves, Lina found a few books that chronicled the history of the Fairy World. The stories went back many generations and continued until the reign of Queen Amaranth and King Tarron and their two daughters, Ivy and Dahlia. Lina was disappointed the account stopped when the girls were only babies with no hint of her aunt's rise to power. However, the book contained one crucial item—a map. Finally, she had directions to Roshall Grove.

One evening after dinner, Lina sat poring over the map, determined to memorize it so she would not have to rely on anyone or anything for directions home. Cora wiped the last of the dishes dry and sat across from the girl. "I have exciting news. The mayor of Maizeridge will grace us with a visit tonight. He wants to meet you."

Lina instantly felt her stomach knot. For the week or so she had been here, she had met no one and preferred to keep it that way. A loud rap sounded on the door. Cora jumped from the dining table where they sat and hurried over to it. Tensing, even more, Lina prayed the mayor was not an agent of Dahlia's like Leander in the Herptile village.

"Hello, Mr. Tyson. Do come in." Cora swung the door wide.

A dark fairy strode into the room, his large frame looming inside the small space. He towered over his host, who cowered in his shadow. Where Cora's features were dainty and refined, his were coarse and ungainly. A commanding presence, his tweed suit was trimmed with fur, and a large crystal ring flashed on his finger. On an ornately carved walking stick complete with a golden knobbed top, he walked toward the table, his eyes falling forcefully on Lina. They narrowed in scrutiny.

"Mr. Tyson. Please meet Hazel, the Poxy girl I spoke of. She will be spending the winter with me."

"It's nice to meet you." Lina welcomed while warning bells went off in her head.

"A Poxy, you say? She is so fair and unspoiled for one," he said to Cora. "Such a shame. She had so much potential."

Lina bristled. Again, fairies spoke about her as if she were not there to listen. "My hearing is just fine," she grumbled.

"Apologies, young miss, I meant no offense," he stated. "You are more than welcome here with us. Let us sit by the fire and get to know one another better, shall we?"

Mr. Tyson settled into one of the large armchairs and waved for Lina to sit in the other. Cora pulled one of the dining chairs over to join them at the fireside. He made quite a display of propping the walking stick against one side of his seat and crossed his arms over the paunch of his belly.

"It was truly quite a bit of good fortune for you to come upon our Cora, now wasn't it? It would have been a long winter wandering alone." he spoke pleasantly with an underlying tone of prying interest.

"Yes, sir. She has been most kind, and I am grateful," Lina replied. Her face a mask of neutrality. She would not satisfy him with an abundance of information. The fairy woman, flustered by the praise, shook her head to downplay the moment.

"My family built this city from the ground up, as it were." He chuckled at his own jest. "It was once among the most bustling cities in the kingdom."

Lina nodded. Cora beamed proudly at the gentleman. "Mr. Tyson's family is one of the wealthiest anywhere."

"Yes." He sighed. "But, as they say, with great wealth comes great responsibility."

Again, the girl nodded, though she was unsure what he meant by the comment. He did not need any encouragement to continue.

"Hundreds of fairies resided here in the golden days. My family took great care to know each of them, right down to the smallest babe. The welfare of our citizens was always on our minds and of utmost importance. Our mansion was always open to any who needed us."

For the next hour, Lina politely listened to the man detail his benevolence and generosity throughout his outstanding lifetime. Apparently, his idea of getting to know each other was to list his credentials and heroic actions. Lina had never met such a self-important creature before and did not know what to make of him. While she was tired of the boasting, she was happy to have the subject remain on *him* instead of a barrage of questions aimed at her. Cora, who must have known his story already, hung on every word. Even the fire crackled quietly in deference.

"Now, of course, all has changed. There are too few of us left. Still, I take pride in the maintenance of every corner of this place, the shops, buildings and parks, he assured, turning the ring around his finger in a habitual motion.

"That must be a lot of work to keep up with by yourself," Lina commented.

"Yes, it takes a toll." He waved his hand in a dramatic flourish. "But well worth it. My few stalwarts, like Cora here, help me when I need it. I dream of the day when these tunnels are filled again, when the city is restored to its former glory."

"Do you think that will ever happen?" Lina questioned.

"I hope so. Needless to say, I will be a great asset to the Resistors' effort when the time comes." He nodded in a pompous way, again crossing his arms over his belly.

"In what way?" Lina asked with raised brows, her curiosity piqued. It was the first time he hinted about which side he was on in the divided kingdom.

He made a grand show of removing a pocket watch from his vest. "Oh heavens, look at the time. I must be going. Tomorrow, Hazel, I will give you the grand tour of the city. Two o'clock, shall we say?"

"Oh, that would be lovely. Thank you, Mr. Tyson," Cora answered for Lina. She showed the guest out, then tidied up the room while Lina dragged the dining chair back into place.

"Tomorrow will be quite a treat for you. Now off to bed, so you are ready for it, my dear."

"Yes, it should be interesting. Good night," Lina said and yawned.

She retired to her room and lit the small bedside lamp with a match. Shadows of the flame licked around the walls. While Cora clearly worshipped Mr. Tyson, he left Lina with a sense of disquiet. Though she did not think he sided with her aunt, the evil queen, his actual motives to side with the Resistors were unclear. Perhaps she could get a better hold on his character during their outing tomorrow. But for now, uneasiness filled her mind, and Lina was acutely aware he had not answered her *last* question.

CHAPTER 20

Promptly at two the next afternoon, Mr. Tyson rapped on the door with the golden tip of his cane. Cora, ready since the early morning hours, rushed Lina out to join him in the hallway. They each carried a shawl since the tunnels were cold in the harsh winter months. Their guide wore a soft brown fur coat, which only left his ankles, and gold-tipped boots exposed. The mayor was no stranger to luxuries.

Lina had only been in the tunnel section between Cora's house and the trapdoor in her short time here. Now, Mr. Tyson set off in the opposite direction. The path was lined with the same bright sconces and dotted doors just like Cora's, although decorated differently according to the dweller's style. This added a nice touch to the otherwise bland corridor, though Lina guessed many of the homes were empty now.

They reached an intersection where a broader road crossed their path and turned onto the larger thoroughfare—here, wood-beamed ceilings rose higher overhead. The beams were carved with intricate patterns, lending a majestic presence to the avenue. Shops of all shapes and sizes came into sight, spaced apart at first, but then colliding into the busy jumble of a city street. Vibrant awnings and distinctive signs vied for one's attention, suggesting the lively bustle of metropolitan life. Mr. Tyson pointed several out to remark on their popularity and the quality of their goods. Yet, the area was empty of any fairies, and most businesses shuttered, but for a few which showed indication of activity. They ducked into one such shop with a large wooden needle and thread sign swinging over the door.

A chestnut-colored fairy sat at a counter—her long hair hung down around her bent head while her petite hands stitched a decorative flower on the lapel of a shirt.

"Hello there, Teagan," Mr. Tyson boomed.

"Good afternoon," she replied, a gasp when she looked up and saw Lina. Her friendly face broke into a smile.

"This is our new friend, Hazel. She will winter with Cora. And this is Teagan, our seamstress extraordinaire." The fairy, embarrassed by the compliment, looked back down at her work. "Teagan is one stalwart who remains here waiting for the end of Queen Dahlia's reign."

"I would see the city restored to its former glory," she said, her response automatic in delivery.

"Yes, we all hope for that," Tyson said, happy with her appropriate response. "Now if you will excuse us, I am giving Hazel the grand tour."

"It was lovely to meet you. Stop in any time," the seamstress said with a warm smile when they exited her shop.

The three made a few similar stops to visit the handful of others who still lived in the forsaken city. Each fairy repeated the same sentiment as the seamstress almost verbatim. Over all, the excursion showed Lina how desolate Maizeridge was, a shadow of its former self. She suspected this same story played out in many locations now that Dahlia ruled. She tried to imagine the shops burgeoning with customers; the restaurants packed with diners; the benches filled with onlookers. It must have been quite a sight. Nothing Lina ever witnessed in her sheltered upbringing.

More tunnels followed. The ones closer to the city center were wide with elaborate doors of carved wood and wrought iron. As they moved further away, the roads became narrower with more modest entries. On the outskirts of the town, they climbed to the top of a high slope. Over its edge a round, flat grassland sat like the inside of a bowl, its roof opened in the center to the sky. The snow-covered area scattered with benches and bare foliage. A regal gazebo stood in the center like the pupil of a large eye.

"This is Tyson Park, the grandest park in all of Maizeridge. In better times, it was a place for celebrations, concerts, and plays. My family prided itself on the cultural enrichment of all its citizens," he proclaimed, chest puffed with self-importance.

"It must have been wonderful." Lina bestowed the expected reply.

Wind blew down from the opening above, and the fairies closed their shawls around them. Lina noticed several tunnels leading out of the sloped sides of the park, other avenues in and out of the city center. A fat brown field mouse poked her head from one hole in the wall on the far side. She scurried over to them. Three smaller heads filled the space but stayed put.

"Good day, Mr. Tyson." The mouse bowed her head.

"Good day, Madame Mouse. How are you and your fellow mice doing?"

"As well as expected. Most of us have enough nuts stored to get us through the winter," she said, the trio of youngsters watching excitedly from their vantage point, whispering and nudging each other.

"Very good to hear. I'd like you to meet Cora's new friend, Hazel." He stepped aside, so the girl faced the mouse.

"Lovely to meet you," Madame said warmly.

"And you as well," the girl replied. "Are those your children?"

"Yes. Ellis, Finn, and Ari." She beamed in their direction. The youngsters halted their conversation and stared at the new fairy, all three faces aglow with excitement.

"We are giving Hazel the grand tour," Cora interjected. "She will stay with me for the winter. It's nice to have both her help and her company."

"How wonderful. If you are ever looking for some exercise, my pinkies would love to run around with you for a bit," the mother suggested, her offspring bobbing their heads in agreement.

"Thank you. I will keep that in mind," Lina said, expecting she would enjoy time with the young mice more than the pretentious Mr. Tyson.

After bidding the Madame farewell, the mayor said, "Let us return to Cora's through the upper tunnels. They are colder but it will take us half the time."

The two fairies followed him across the field to an opening in the wall. Lina marveled at how anyone could keep the maze of tunnels straight. This passageway was just below the ground outside, every few feet a hole exposed the world above. Snow lay in circles on the ground under each one. Other tunnels broke off on the sides with similar openings in their ceilings. Mr. Tyson glanced down at each one as they passed. Something caught his attention in one and he stopped so abruptly, the ladies nearly walked into him. Lina gasped at what she saw.

Underneath an opening lay a swallow, eyes shut, wings folded around itself. Mr. Tyson took a few steps to halt in front of it. He tapped it with his walking stick, but it did not move. Neither did Lina. The bird's red heart of feathers was all too familiar to her—Knox. A strong intuition rose in her to remain silent about her knowledge of his identity. She sensed the safety of them both depended on it.

"Alas, the poor fellow," Mr. Tyson declared. "Oh well, there is nothing to be done."

"He's dead?" Lina whispered, her heart sinking to the floor.

"Seems to be. It happens sometimes," Tyson replied, unmoved. "Come, let us keep going. "

He joined them in the central tunnel, and they continued home. So saddened was Lina; she did not remember the walk back to Cora's. The death of Knox broke a part of her will to continue on her quest. Next thing she knew, Cora laid a plate of dinner in front of her. Food was the furthest thing from her mind, but she forced some down.

"Quite a tour today, wasn't it? Mr. Tyson knows more about Maizeridge than anybody," Cora commented, sensing the girl's mood but not understanding it. Their excursion with the mayor himself exhilarated Cora. Lina nodded quietly. The fire crackled in the silence that followed.

"Is everything all right, dear?" The fairy's brow wrinkled in worry.

"I suppose I am just tired from all the walking. If you don't mind, I think I'll just go to bed." The girl stood and went to her room, her feet as heavy as her heart.

"Of course, let me know if you need anything, dear," she called as the girl reached the door.

"Thank you," Lina muttered on a choked sob. Although she found Cora's concern true, she still felt the urge to keep her secret. Knox must have been looking for her. How many more deaths would she be responsible for?

Only once in bed, the tears came freely for her dear swallow friend, for her lost life, for the empty city, and for the threat of her aunt. It was all too much to bear. Her major trouble of finding Edwina and defeating Dahlia diminished for the moment, her heart so broken for Knox. The thought of him dying cold and alone haunted her. She vowed to go back, find him somehow in that labyrinth of passages, and properly honor his passing. It was the least she could do for him, and she ached at how inadequate it felt.

CHAPTER 21

Torchlight flickered off the throne room's obsidian walls, any glow cast nearly swallowed up by the dark stone. Deep in thought, Dahlia tapped her forefinger on the armrest. Footsteps echoed in the hall outside, growing loud enough to rise above her drumming. General Sepitus entered. At the sight of her, his face grew pale. He approached the seat and knelt. "My Queen."

Dahlia motioned him to his feet. It had been months since she felt the stirring of Lina's arrival, yet the girl still roamed the land. Annoyance was turning to fury at her servants' inability to capture one mere fairy. Winter had set in with its full wrath. She had expected to have taken care of her niece by now. The icy weather only complicated the matter.

"I bring news. Kafir and Purus have returned," he stated, hands nervously fidgeting at his side. When Dahlia said nothing, he continued, "Cotswold was able to locate and direct them back to Cedar Knoll. They tracked Lina to a rabbit warren, but she was nowhere to be found when they arrived. However, they picked up her scent but lost her trail in the woods when the snow became too heavy. Cotswold sent word that he discovered some tracks in the snow which led to a cornfield, but no further. She was definitely headed in the direction of Roshall Grove."

Rage simmered in the queen, but she mastered herself. She shut her eyes and pondered the situation. If the girl were on the move, she would be spotted eventually. There were many miles for her to cover until she reached her destination. Dahlia leveled her eyes with the General. "Tell Cotswold to continue his surveillance between that field and Roshall Grove. Send Kafir and Purus back out with him to capture the girl once and for all. Carry my orders out immediately! My patience is at an end."

"Yes, My Queen," the General croaked through the invisible grip he felt around his throat. "We will not let you down."

"See that you don't." With a nod, she broke the spell. Sepitus staggered out of the room, fear in his eyes while he rubbed his neck.

The girl was lucky and must have inherited her mother's good fortune. Dahlia rose and exited the back of the throne room. At a narrow door in the hallway outside, she stopped, pressed her hand against the dark ebony, and whispered an incantation. The door swung inward. On the far wall stood a table, a dark cloth over its contents, though shimmers of light still shone out in small patches when a draft caught the fabric in its path.

The Primal Stone.

Dahlia and Ivy used to sit captivated by it in their youth when it sat atop their mother's throne. Its brightness dimmed when it broke, but not by much. This stone was Amaranth's birthright, passed on to the eldest daughter of the royal line throughout generations. With it, her mother held sway over the entire Fairy World, a reign of peace, until one fateful day.

It started like any ordinary day until the rap on her door. Dahlia looked up from her desk, a book of spells open before her. More books were piled up to the side, awaiting her attention. The mid-morning sun shone through her open window, the gauzy curtains floating out in the breeze. Myrtle, her maid, stood at the open door, a messenger at her side.

"My Princess, I am here to escort you to the throne room," the boy announced.

"Certainly," she said, closing her book and rising.

With a quick bow, he led her from her chamber down a series of hallways toward the throne room. Fairies bustled about, some whizzed by swiftly overhead. The palace was always a hive of activity that her mother oversaw to perfection. Several fairies cast wary looks at the fiery-haired princess and took a wide berth around her. Dahlia kept her eyes cast on the pristine marble floor.

Her skin prickled with apprehension. Her parents had not summoned her in ages. Had her training with Priya been exposed? When they reached their destination, she forced her expression to one of indifference. Better not to show guilt before it was necessary. The doors swung open before her, and she entered. Her parents sat on their thrones, and Ivy stood before them.

"Come in, dear," her father beckoned. His tone was kind, but Dahlia saw the deep lines of worry on his brow.

She advanced to them and bowed low. When she rose, her sister smiled warmly at her. Dahlia returned it but could not muster the same affection Ivy displayed. They had barely seen each other in weeks. It ate at her heart to be so easily disposable to her twin. Her mother regarded them from her throne, the Primal Stone casting rainbow prisms around the room.

"You look lovely, Dahlia," her mother complimented, a tinge of nostalgia in her tone. The comment made the girl bristle, but she managed a polite nod to the queen.

"Now that you are both here, we have something to tell you," King Tarron began. "Word has reached us of unrest in the west, a rebellion by a sect of Groundlings. We will send troops to quell it before it develops into anything larger."

"Why on earth would people rebel against you?" Ivy cried, horrified at the thought. She wrung her hands in despair.

"Groundlings are a fickle lot," Queen Amaranth answered. "Every so often, a group of insurgents causes trouble, hoping to grab a larger share of power than they have."

"Where exactly is this rebellion?" Dahlia asked, surprised to hear of any sort of uprising.

Her mother eyed her intently before answering, "It is just outside of Elderbreach."

Dahlia suppressed a gasp. Perhaps Priya could help by alerting her contacts there. They could bolster the kingdom's efforts to defeat the rebels. She decided against saying anything before speaking to the enchantress, but the thought gave her hope that her parents may finally see some value in her, Priya, and the *magic* they believed in.

"Do not be alarmed," the king reassured them, stroking his fair beard. "It is but a small rebellion. However, your mother decided that she would like us seen by the fairies on both sides, so we will be the ones to lead our troops."

"No!" Ivy exclaimed. "Please don't go. Don't leave us."

Amaranth rose from her throne and descended the steps to her daughters. With outstretched arms, she motioned them to her. Embracing each around the shoulders, she ventured, "A queen must look after her people. I have not been to the western regions for too long. My subjects need to see me, to remember who serves and protects them. It will make the kingdoms stronger. Remember this when you are queen."

She spoke these last words directly to Ivy. Any hope Dahlia had crashed down around her. They would never consider her for a queen or any other position of power. The king and queen bade them goodbye, sure of the fate and endurance of their kingdom.

Now, in the darkened hallway, Dahlia could only stare at the shrouded, broken crystal with a sense of redemption. Things had not worked out in her parents' favor after all. She sealed the door with another incantation, then walked out onto a balcony to survey *her* kingdom.

CHAPTER 22

Lina woke from a restless sleep to the sound of Cora at work in the kitchen. The familiar clink of the kettle on the fire did little to comfort her, but she would not succumb to self-pity. That is not what Knox would want. Her plan, set in the wee hours of the night, was her main focus. It could take her days to find the tunnel where the swallow lay, but she had some ideas about finding it faster.

Cora's worried eyes greeted Lina when she came to the table. Before she could even take her seat, the older fairy set down a large, steamy bowl of porridge. "Feeling better this morning?"

"Yes, much better, thank you," she replied. She still had no intention of mentioning Knox.

"I'm glad to hear it. That was quite a tour Mr. Tyson gave us yesterday. No wonder it wore you out," Cora said, her eyes following every spoonful of breakfast to the girl's mouth. "And no wonder, you were already so worn down when I found you."

"I enjoyed the tour very much. Maizeridge must have been something to see back when it was full of life. I wish I could have seen it. Do you have any books about it?"

"As a matter of fact, I do," the fairy announced with pride. She went over to a small table with books piled haphazardly around. On the bottom shelf, she dug through various volumes before crying in triumph. "Aha. Here it is."

She laid a thin volume called *Maizeridge: A City in Pictures* on the table. Lina scraped the last of the porridge from the bowl and set it aside to give her full attention to the book. Cora came to sit by her side. Each page contained a large color picture of one building or another with descriptive text at the bottom. Lina recognized one shot of the city square, its streets, shops and benches bursting with life. Another photo showed Tyson Park with a live band in the gazebo and brightly colored paper lanterns dotting the sky.

"That was the Lantern Festival," Cora told her. "We held it every summer. There was a contest for the best lantern, music, and food. It was one of my favorite days of the year," she gushed with a dreamy smile.

"I can see why," the girl replied, turning to a page with a picture of a younger Mr. Tyson cutting the ribbon on a new store. "Maizeridge looked like a wonderful place to live."

"Oh, it was." The older fairy sighed.

"I'm still surprised at the sheer size of it. I grew up in a much smaller place. It must have been hard to find your way around. Does this book have a map?" she asked innocently and held her breath, waiting for the reply.

"No, I don't believe so." Cora took the book and thumbed through the rest of the pages. "I've lived here all my life and never really thought about needing a map."

Lina tried to hide her disappointment. Her first plan did not work, so she would have to try another, and she had an idea who might help. She rose and brought her bowl to the kitchen, where she washed the few dishes in the sink. Cora settled down to mend some shirts.

"Join me, won't you, dear?" she asked when Lina finished the dishes.

"I will soon, but I think I would like to take a walk. The city is so interesting, and I think it will help me regain my former strength." She took off the apron she donned for the dishes and hung it on a peg.

"That sounds like a fine idea. Perhaps that will bring some color to those pale cheeks of yours. Take your time, but be careful. It's easy to get lost in the tunnels if you don't pay close attention," Cora warned, her face scrunched as she threaded a needle.

"I will," Lina promised, relieved she did not arouse the fairy's suspicion.

She remembered the way to the city center. The tunnels leading there were deserted, with no signs of life to be found. When she stepped onto the main thoroughfare, the dirt under her feet was packed hard. There was a time when these roads bustled with fairies. The photos attested to that. Now, under the reign of Dahlia, an eerie sense of emptiness filled the hollow place.

Once in the main square, she retraced her steps to Tyson Park and climbed up the slope on its side. A bright blue sky above belied the chill in the air—a gust of wind burst past every few moments. Stepping out on the large expanse, she dubiously eyed the numerous holes to exit on the far side. One was where Lina met Madame Mouse, but which one, she could not guess. She cursed herself for not paying better attention yesterday. At best, she could narrow it down to four of them. Confused, she sat down on the steps of the gazebo and wrapped her cloak tight against the cold.

"Hazel? Is that you?" So deep in thought, Lina did not respond to her alias. "Hazel?"

She looked up to see the mother mouse emerge from one of the holes, her three pinkies in a dutiful line behind her. At the sight of Lina, they started whispering furiously to each other. The family approached her across the grass, the winter sun in the exposed sky overhead brightened the ground below them.

"Hello, Madame," she replied, grateful to have found them so easily.

"Back out for another look around?" the mouse asked.

"Yes, I was feeling anxious and wanted some exercise. Perhaps your children would be able to join me?"

The three eager youngsters waited for their mother's answer with bated breath. So did Lina. It was critical that the little ones join her. Without them, the time it would take to find Knox would double.

"That would be nice," Madame Mouse finally agreed. "But, only for a little while, boys, there's work to be done."

"Yes, mother," they answered in unison.

"And behave yourselves," she warned before exiting through another hole.

"You are lucky to have found us. We know every inch of this city," the smallest one declared while they jostled for a spot in front of her.

"Don't brag, Finn. It's not polite. I'm Ari, and this is Ellis." He pushed his brother out of the way and gestured to himself and the other mouse. "Where do you come from? Where is your family?"

"From a place far from here. I have no family." *Except for my evil aunt*, she thought ruefully.

"No family?" Finn exclaimed. "That is so sad."

"It is," she conceded. "But I am lucky to have met nice fairies like Cora on my journey."

"Yes, she is kind to us, pinkies," Ellis added.

"Why do they call you pinkies?" Lina asked, a gust of wind nearly blowing her question away.

"We are born with no hair, just tiny pink squirmy little things," Ari explained, only to be shoved out of the way by Finn.

"So what do you want to do?" he asked, chomping at the bit to get started.

"Well, Mr. Tyson had us exploring some outer tunnels on the way back to Cora's yesterday."

"Oh yes, Mr. Tyson. *Good day,*" Ellis drawled in a spot-on impression of the mayor that left his brothers doubled over in laughter. Even the girl had to giggle.

"I would like to go there if you know the way." Lina's plan depended on their familiarity with the tunnels, and she was rewarded.

"Of course, we know every inch, though our mother doesn't like us going there alone," Ari said. "She's afraid a bird might swoop from the sky and get us. But we would love to show you."

Quick as a flash, they were off with Lina scrambling in their wake and entered one tunnel without hesitation. The mice scattered off into all the secondary tunnels but always ran back together and returned to the girl, who walked behind carefully inspecting each tributary. The youngsters excitedly brought her the occasional leaf, stone, or seed, eager to share their discoveries. This quickly evolved into attempts to outdo one another, and the additional exploring time gave her the chance to get a bit ahead of them as she had hoped. Anxiously, she checked each passageway that seemingly went on without end.

At last, she glanced down one tunnel, and her heart stopped. She had found Knox.

She backtracked to the mice who had scampered from different openings. Soon they ran to her side, each with an object meant to impress.

"Look at what I found," Ari exclaimed, producing an almost whole walnut. His brothers shook their heads, knowing this finding signaled their defeat.

"It's incredible," Lina praised. "You should take it home to your mother at once. She will be very proud."

"Oh, but we are having so much fun, can't we keep going?" Finn protested.

"Your mother said to only be out a little while. If I keep you too long, she won't let us do this again. We don't want that, do we?"

"No." Three heads fell in disappointment at the truth of the statement.

"I promise I will come and play with you again this week. You have my word."

"Can you find your way back to Cora's?" Ellis asked.

"Yes, I will be just fine from here. Go on. I'll see you soon."

Reluctantly, they left, struggling with the nearly round walnut, which did not quite roll in a straight line. Lina watched until the pinkies were out of sight. When she was sure they were gone, she crept back down the tunnel, heart in her throat. Her whole focus had been on finding Knox. Now that she had, her strength faltered.

A shaft of sunlight filtered through the hole above the bird, bathing him in an ethereal glow. Tears came to her eyes when she walked to him on shaky legs. He looked so peaceful it made her heart break *again*. Knox had watched over her in the mortal world, been an essential part of her childhood. He continued to watch over and protect her here in the Fairy World only to die cold and alone away from everything he knew. Overcome with emotion, she threw her arms around him, her tears falling on his soft feathers. He was still warm, a fact Lina attributed to the sun shining directly on him. Then she heard it—a faint thumping. She held her breath to listen. Weak, yet unmistakable, was the sound of a beating heart. Knox lived, but only barely.

CHAPTER 23

She gently shook him to see if he would wake. His eyes merely fluttered, but a moment later, he opened them, and Lina saw a spark of recognition. As they fell shut, she cooed, "There, there. Be still. All will be well. I am here to take care of you."

In the main tunnel, she collected some large leaves and gathered up the seeds the young mice collected. She arranged the leaves over Knox as a makeshift blanket and piled the seeds nearby. Finally, she took an acorn top and filled it with snow to melt it into water. Knox sensed her movements and stirred again. She knelt by his head, gently stroking it.

"Lina?" he whispered, eyes flickering open.

"Yes, I'm here."

"Edwina has been looking everywhere for you," he managed to say.

"We have plenty of time for you to tell your story. First, let's concentrate on making you better. Are you wounded at all?"

"No, I'm just weakened from the cold. I thought this tunnel might shelter me, but I couldn't manage to go any farther." With a raspy sigh, he closed his eyes.

Happy she did not have to deal with any injuries, which would have certainly been difficult, she asked, "Are you hungry or thirsty? I brought food and water."

Knox nodded, and she lifted the acorn next to his beak so he could sip. Next, she fed him some of the seeds. He filled up quickly and laid his head back down.

"I think we should try to move you to a more sheltered spot. Do you think you are up to giving that a try?" Lina was worried it might snow again and was not sure he would survive that.

She helped him move away from the hole to a hidden nook a little way down the tunnel, more protected from the elements. Here she covered him with the leaves again while she briefly filled him in on where he was and how she was rescued from the cold by Cora. He had little strength to ask questions but focused on her words.

"I should go," she said when the sunlight rose higher over the opening. "Cora will be wondering where I am, and I can't arouse suspicion. I don't want anyone here to discover you. Especially Mr. Tyson. "

"I think you are right; we don't know who to trust these days," he agreed. "What I need now is rest and a safe place to recuperate, which I now have thanks to you."

"It was the least I could do for you, my precious Knox. I will be back tomorrow as soon as I can get away. Sleep well."

With a final hug, she left. Lina marked the outer tunnel on the way home to Cora's with stones so there would be no guessing the next day.

The fairy was happy to see her, remarking on Lina's improved color and mood. "The walk and fresh air have done you good, I believe." She then suggested the girl make it a daily habit, to which Lina readily agreed.

Lina helped Cora in the morning, then went to Knox every afternoon, doing whatever she could to aid his recovery. Cora, happy the daily walks brightened the girl's mood, never questioned Lina. Mostly, Knox needed rest, and she was content to sit with him and replenish his food and water. A few times, she was able to sneak him some broth, and after a few days, he gained enough strength to stay awake for longer periods. Then, leaving out nothing, she told him about all the adventures that brought her to Maizeridge.

"So while Edwina was fighting the snakes, I hid behind a mushroom. The next thing I knew, some Herptile fairies abducted me," Lina explained one morning, sitting against Knox's silky feathers.

"Herptiles are dreadful," the swallow commented. He pecked up another seed and swallowed it.

"I think the mother, Juniper, could have been nice if it weren't for…"

A noise in the main tunnel caused them to freeze. Lina put her finger to her lips, and Knox nodded his acknowledgement as she crept toward the sound. Reaching the tunnels' junction, she stopped, and ever so slightly, peeked out her head. At first, she saw nothing until a movement caught her eye. Someone quickly pulled a mouse, by its tail, behind a large rock. A little smile formed on Lina's face, and she relaxed. She approached the rock and confronted those hiding.

"Oh, Lina, hi. We didn't know you were here," Finn ventured, his brothers huddled around him.

"Really? Because I think you have been eavesdropping on me?" she admonished.

"Tell her, Finn. We *were* eavesdropping, and we're sorry," Ellis admitted.

"He made me!" Finn yelled, nudging his nose at his brother.

"Did not!" He pushed his brother back.

"Enough! We all wanted to," Ari declared. "Please don't be mad, Lina."

After a few moments of careful thought, she replied, "I'm not mad. Come with me. I want you to meet someone."

They followed Lina to the swallow, their eyes growing round as saucers at the sight of him. Knox studied them too, just as curiously. Lina knew letting the young mice in on her secret was a risk, but including them may be an incentive to keep their mouths shut.

"This is my dearest friend, Knox. I am helping him recover from an illness. Knox, this is Ari, Ellis, and Finn."

"Hello. Nice to meet you," Knox greeted with a nod of his head.

"Wow, I've never met a swallow before," Finn exclaimed in delight.

"It's nice to meet you too." Ari bowed low, and after a shove, his brothers followed suit.

"Hazel, how do you know him? And what made him sick?" Finn asked, and the bird gave Lina a questioning look.

"Don't be rude! That is none of our business," Ellis scolded, creeping closer to the bird.

"It's quite all right. I got caught in a storm and took refuge in the tunnel..." Knox began.

Afraid he may give away her true identity, Lina interrupted, "I was lucky enough to find him, and when I discovered it was Knox, I knew I had to help him get better."

"We can help you take care of him," Ari offered, his brother's heads bobbing in agreement. "Bring him food and water."

"Well..." she hesitantly said. "Maybe I could let you, but only on one condition."

"Anything!" the boys cried in unison.

"I don't want Mr. Tyson to find out about Knox because I do *not* trust him. That means you can't tell *anyone* about him. Not Cora. Not *even* your mother. It has to be our secret, like a classified mission. Whoever tells can no longer come here or be my friend again. Do you think you guys are up to the challenge?"

"Yes! Yes! We can do it! Please give us a chance," they pleaded. "You have our word!"

"Very well, then," Lina consented, satisfied they were more interested in Knox than telling her secret.

"No one will hear of him from our lips," Ellis guaranteed. "Especially Mr. Tyson. No one trusts him."

As for the mayor, he came every evening to visit Cora and bored Lina to tears with stories of the grandeur of bygone days. While stifling yawns, Lina was pleased he was too involved with himself to question her comings and goings more carefully. Her moments with Knox were the treasure of her days. Though Cora's sweet temperament made easy company, Lina only truly felt seen and understood by her swallow.

Ari and his brothers came every day and proved to be great helpers. They scoured the tunnels, bringing food and checking on Knox whenever they had a chance. Madame Mouse knew her children spent time with Lina each afternoon, but they kept the swallow a secret. One day they came with a large blanket they managed to procure from their mother. Proud of their cunning, Finn said, "We told her it was for our picnics with you."

After a week, Lina and Knox agreed they should tell the young ones her real identity, which left them in greater awe of the pair. Even in the frivolity of their youth, they understood more than ever why she must pretend to be Hazel. They knew about the evil of Dahlia and her penchant for placing spies everywhere. While they all waited for Knox to regain his full strength, the three happily sat and listened to Lina fill him in on the incidents she went through since being separated from Edwina. The Herptiles stories, the Fluvial, and the Ephemera were like something out of a bedtime tale for the pinkies.

As he recovered, Knox was able to speak more of his adventures. The enchantress had flocks of birds scouring the land for any sight of Lina. A stag gave him a tip that she headed in the direction of the cornfield. Without a break for days, the swallow rushed to the cornfield but got caught in a snow squall and took refuge in the tunnel. "As soon as I am able, I will go and find Edwina," he stated.

Lina, who worried every day someone would discover their secret, hoped it would be soon enough.

CHAPTER 24

The days passed with nobody the wiser—the pinkies had admirably kept Knox a secret. Madame Mouse was happy for her children to spend time with Lina, freeing up time for her each day.

One day, the three pinkies tumbled into the tunnel all abuzz. "I think we should tell her," Ellis whispered, a near impossibility with excited children.

"Why does it matter?" Finn murmured, placing some seeds in Knox's bowl.

"Tell me what?" Lina asked with concern mounting in her chest. "Does someone know about Knox?"

"No," Ari assured. "We just found something strange while we were looking for food."

"What?" Knox questioned, while he pecked at his seeds.

"A room stuffed full of armor and weapons. Come on, Lina, we'll show you."

She followed them through the dizzying maze of corridors until they turned down one notably darker and colder than the others. At the end was an immense chamber filled to the brim with fairy armor and weapons. Someone had stacked shiny breastplates, shields, and helmets in orderly rows on one side; the other held enough spears, swords, and maces for an army. Though the room seemed long forgotten, its contents were all new.

Before Lina could comment on finding such a strange stockpile in this forsaken area, they heard voices directly above them. Ari signaled them over to a hole in the wall behind the large breastplates. They all crawled inside just as a trapdoor above opened.

"Put them down there with the others," they heard Mr. Tyson's voice order.

The sound of several fairy steps, in succession, on the ladder echoed throughout. There was a good deal of banging and clanking while new merchandise was delivered into the chamber. Ever so slowly, Lina crept from the hole and peeked around a breastplate. Mr. Tyson stood with a group of Rodentia, who climbed back up the ladder. The mayor grabbed the last fairy by the arm before he could ascend.

"Good job, Silas. Are you sure this is the bulk of it?" he demanded.

"Yes, Mr. Tyson, sir. We have been able to pilfer most of it. At this rate, we will have the Resistors weapons house cleaned out after a few more trips."

"Very good. When I ransom these back to the Resistors, I will reward you and your crew handsomely."

"Thank you, sir." With a deferential bow, he sprinted up the ladder.

Mr. Tyson gave the room a once over, and when satisfied, he followed and the trapdoor shut with a bang.

"What was that all about?" Ellis poked out his head to ask.

"Let's just get back to Knox," Lina answered.

The swallow was as disturbed as Lina when she explained their findings. "It seems Mr. Tyson is stealing supplies from the Resistors so when the time for battle arrives, he can sell it back to them at great profit to himself."

"Yes, that is what I thought," Lina agreed. "But why would he do that?"

"To put it simply... *greed*," Knox informed her. "Sadly, it's an all too common trait among fairies. Many only think of themselves and their needs at any given moment.

Look at Juniper or Kai—they each took you for personal reasons with no regard for you or your wishes."

The mice nodded in agreement; such had their experiences also been with fairies. "Not you, though, Lina," Ari assured. "That is why we like you so much."

"Thank you," she said, saddened at the thought someone would want to exploit the Resistors, who already had such a fight in front of them.

Later, after the pinkies had left, Lina asked, "Do you think we will be able to defeat Dahlia? It seems as though many forces are working against us."

"Hopefully, you are the *key* to restoring peace to the kingdom. Your return should cultivate a renewed sense of loyalty amongst the fairies on our side. They know the prophecy and will want to be on the right side when all is said and done," Knox explained, while Lina settled under the blanket against his feathers.

"If only Dahlia weren't my aunt. I know I have never met her, and she is cruel. She killed my mother after all, but still, to know we are related…"

"Yes, Dahlia's is a sad story," Knox supplied.

"Sad?" Lina retorted, surprised at the word. "In what way?"

"She was always in her twin sister's shadow," he said, as the sun's rays crept down the tunnel towards them.

"Wait, my mother and Dahlia were *twins*?" Lina cried, somehow this detail made her feel much worse.

"Yes, they were twins. Though very different, Dahlia's coloring so fiery while Ivy was so fair— a figurative sun and moon, if you will. Your mother was the oldest by a few minutes, but those *few* minutes made all the difference. It made your mother the heir—the future queen. As youngsters, they were inseparable, but whereas Ivy maintained her sweetness, any kindness Dahlia possessed as a child faded quickly. She grew brooding and envious."

"You knew them as children?" Lina jumped from beneath the blanket and stared at the bird, her mouth formed the perfect *O*.

"Yes. Swallows used to live for untold years until your aunt broke the Primal Crystal. Since then, a few of us have passed, and more will follow until someone stops her." With a melancholy sigh, he hung his head.

A million questions vied for attention in Lina's mind now that she had the chance to speak to someone with firsthand knowledge. "Why was she so jealous of Ivy? Was my mother unkind to her?"

"Oh no, not at all. Ivy was a caring and gentle soul. She showered her sister with love hoping to win back her affection, even at the end. She turned a blind eye to the danger until it was too late. Thankfully, Edwina was able to save you."

"But I don't understand why Dahlia would kill her sister." This was the hardest for Lina to fathom. She paced the tunnel in front of Knox while he revealed more of the story.

"Dahlia coveted Ivy's power and rank. For years, your mother couldn't conceive to procure an heir. Her barrenness would have made your aunt the heir to the throne. When Dahlia became pregnant first, she was sure her daughter would be next in line after her, assuring her long years of power." The swallow shifted his weight and settled on his other side.

"But my mother did get pregnant... with me."

"Yes, she did. There were rumors, Lina, that Dahlia gave your mother an herb to prevent pregnancy. No one was able to prove it. When your father, Theros, learned this, he wanted her exiled. Your mother begged him not to. She forgave Dahlia and still dreamed of reconciling with her. That was so like your mother, benevolent to the very end," he continued the chronicle. Lina wrung her hands during his recount of events.

"So what happened then?"

"Not only was Ivy's pregnancy announced, but Dahlia gave birth to a stillborn daughter. She blamed Ivy for cursing her baby. Your mother tried to comfort her, but the loss was too tragic and Dahlia's anger too great. For years, she studied dark magic, and finally, she saw her opportunity to use it. She attempted to steal the Primal Crystal to bend it to her will. And well, now you know the rest."

He looked at the tears in the girl's eyes. Her heart broke at the thought of the lifeless newborn, her cousin. It was a heart-rending legacy—one mother with a dead child and one child with a dead mother.

"Ah, you have your mother's compassion. But remember, Dahlia vowed to kill you and Edwina had to hide you away. There is no good left in her, Lina, so do not waste your tears," Knox counseled and motioned her back to his side.

"I wonder what makes someone choose evil over good and hate over love?" she asked, slipping beneath the blanket again.

"A deep hurt, I imagine. A longing to fill a painful hole inside. When love cannot fill it, hate will surely take its place until sadly, there is no room for anything else."

To learn this about her aunt's past made the thought of conquering her even more ill-fated. Dahlia's hatred caused waves of suffering which would remain in Lina's heart forever.

CHAPTER 25

Dahlia roamed the hallways of the castle, stopping at a window. Outside, snow swirled fiercely under a steel grey sky. No one had found the girl. There had been no information about Lina during the bitter cold months. Her last sighting had been near Maizeridge, a perfect spot to wait out the winter season. The girl must be there with whatever fairies remained in the once-thriving city, the smug Mayor Tyson, no doubt, still hanging on to its rule for dear life.

When winter was over, Lina would join the Resistors. Dahlia's initial plan was to kill her before she got to them. Yet, in these cold, solitary months, Dahlia had plenty of time to think. Killing her niece was essential, but the Resistors must see it with their own eyes. Otherwise, it would lack the maximum effect, and Dahlia wanted to destroy any last bit of hope they harbored. It would inflict far more pain on their feeble rebellion to have her join them and think they had a chance to win before crushing them all with one decisive blow.

She left the windowsill, her feet following an aimless dusty path since much of the castle went unvisited for many years. As she passed by her old bedroom, the one she cherished as a child, she had no desire to look inside. That girl no longer existed. Next came Ivy's room. Here, Dahlia paused and turned the door handle. Inside, the shrouded furniture sat dulled in the grey light. It was nothing like the vibrant chamber she spent so much time in with Ivy, until that one fateful day.

Dahlia was summoned to her sister's room by a page, an oddity that had never occurred before. On the walk there, she could not imagine the reason. Upon entering the room, she saw Edwina and Priya at the foot of the bed. Ivy laid face down sobbing; Myrtle, the girls' nanny, stroked her shoulder consolingly. Dahlia's stomach sank. Any event that brought the two enchantresses together could not be good.

"What happened?" she asked.

"I'm sorry to tell you this," Priya replied, "but your parents are dead."

"Dead?" she exclaimed while her sister cried harder. "How?"

"The rebels killed them," Edwina declared, her icy gaze on Priya the entire time.

"Amaranth and Tarron underestimated the size of the enemy forces, sadly, and the rebels overcame them. Nobody in their party survived." Priya moved to stand by Dahlia and patted her back.

Despite all the resentment she held for her parents these last few years; their deaths were still a blow. "How could they have miscalculated the situation so badly?"

"The conflict in the west was so sudden there was not enough time for aid to arrive. They sent word to friends in Elderbreach, but alas, they got to the uprising too late to save them," Priya said.

Edwina glowered at the old enchantress with malice. She looked as though she wanted to say something but remained silent instead. Dahlia went to her sister, her instinct to comfort her twin overcoming all else. Ivy sat up, threw her arms around her sibling, and continued to cry. Dahlia held her close, but no tears filled her eyes, the loss still too much of a shock.

"What will we do?" Ivy choked out. "What will happen to the kingdom?"

"Do not worry, sister," Dahlia soothed. "We will figure it out together."

"Together?" Edwina rebuked. "There is no *together*. Ivy inherits the throne with Theros at her side.

After a proper funeral and period of mourning, the crowning and the transition of power will take place."

Dahlia stared coldly at the fairy, who dared to show her cruelty even on the day she found out her parents had perished. She turned to Priya, who shook her head slightly—now was not the time to fight with Edwina. With the death of their parents, Ivy was now the reigning queen and her subjects must be told. Dahlia gently helped her sister from the bed to prepare to address her kingdom. As they passed the younger enchantress on the way to the dressing table, Dahlia's glare left her enemy's eyes downcast.

Once the twelve days of mourning passed, Ivy, older by only three minutes, officially inherited the stone and the crown. Wedded to Theros that very day, Ivy began her reign with Edwina stepping in to usurp Priya's enchantress role. Those were the beginning of dark and difficult days.

"Ivy is too idealistic, too impractical to rule," Priya had said in the confines of her chamber the evening of the coronation. "How could three minutes matter more than actual qualification?"

Dahlia was glad to have the enchantress voice her frustrations. "If only there had been more time to dispute the issue, to show them evidence where succession was not just determined by birth order.

"It would not have mattered. Nothing would have changed their minds. There is more to the story, you see. There is a reason Edwina suddenly became so favored over me."

Dahlia waited for the rest, wild anticipation rising in her.

"During one of Edwina's training sessions with me, she had a vision that frightened her. She told your parents about it and they were convinced she had foreseen the future, that her vision was a *prophecy*. They abruptly took control of her lessons, purposely isolating Edwina and Ivy from you. Edwina was then allowed to learn secret magic, what some may call forbidden magic, such as traveling between the worlds."

"What was this prophecy?"

"That an evil fairy would take over the kingdom and lead it into darkness and hate. And only Ivy's daughter could save the kingdom through the power of true love." Priya paused for effect before adding, "They believed this evil fairy was you."

Dahlia's heart turned to ice. How could her parents ever think that about her? Did they ever even love her?

What of Ivy, her twin sister? They had shared and planned so much together. Was she part of this conspiracy as well? The love and bond she felt with Ivy vanished at that moment.

Now, Dahlia remembered the sting of their faithlessness as if it were yesterday while she lingered in the doorway of Ivy's old room. Closing the door, she moved her feet unconsciously up a nearby circular staircase, which led to a tower—not frequented, but never forgotten. At the top, a door opened to a once bright room, now filled with cobwebs and neglect. In the chamber's center sat an ornate cradle carved of rowan wood. Dahlia sank next to it, a cloud of dust dancing around in the gloom. Slowly, she reached out a hand to rock it gently from side to side.

Ivy tried to conceive for many years without success. Her sister, who always had all the luck, seemed barren. The entire kingdom spread rumors that Dahlia somehow prevented Ivy from becoming pregnant. Though untrue and hurt by them, she was not surprised. Dahlia was used to the evil gossip at this point. In the midst of this came her greatest joy—discovering she was pregnant with the child of one of her beaus. For once, it looked as though her luck was changing for the better. If the new queen could not produce an heir, Dahlia's daughter would be next in line for the throne. Ivy decorated this magnificent nursery for the babe and proclaimed her happiness at having a niece or nephew to all who would listen. Though relations had been icy, things began to thaw between the sisters with a little one on the way.

Until the unthinkable happened. Dahlia braced herself for the physical impact of the memories—Priya laying the stillborn baby girl in her arms, the news that Ivy was in fact, after all this time, with child, Priya's whispering that *it seemed more than a coincidence*, and the anguished feeling of betrayal that her flesh and blood thought her capable of fulfilling an evil prophecy.

Now, Ivy was dead by her hand, vengeance for the death of Dahlia's daughter. And Lina would be next.

She rose and stormed from the room, dust exploding through the air with the slam of the nursery door.

CHAPTER 26

The winter wore on without incident. When Knox felt stronger, they moved him to a remote tunnel to protect against discovery. Lina dutifully helped Cora with whatever work the old fairy gave her each day. Every evening, Mr. Tyson would visit to speak of the past and his great importance in it. Her afternoons with the swallow were Lina's respites from the monotony of her underground existence. She had never longed for spring so much in her life.

Knox told her further histories about her kingdom, dating back more years than she could count. These stories mesmerized both her and the little mice. Her kingdom had a long and proud heritage, one she hoped she could live up to if given the chance. The world Knox spoke of sounded so different from the one she was in now. There was much damage to be undone.

"So apparently, I am betrothed to a fairy named Cornelius," she said one day, curiosity getting the better of her. "Do you know him?"

"Yes. He is a strong-minded boy, knee-deep in the rebellion. For years, many have given up on your return, but not Cornelius. He trusted Edwina would bring you home one day," Knox assured her.

"Is he kind?" Kindness was as important to her as his loyalty now that she knew more of fairyhood.

"I have no reason to say no. Cornelius is fair and commands respect, but like most of his kind, can be fickle."

"Fickle?"

"It's a nice word for always wanting things your way," Ari volunteered. "Mother calls Finn fickle all the time."

Knox chuckled. "Yes, that is one way to look at it. Opportunistic would be another word. A fairy trait, I suppose."

Lina could not disagree, given her time here thus far. Fairies like Mr. Tyson were blatant about it, but even Cora offered to help Lina quench her loneliness. How would Cornelius react to her showing up? After all these years, would he expect to rule *his way,* or would he defer to her?

"My upbringing was different, I suppose," she mused aloud.

"Yes, Hazel and Felix did an admirable job. You could not have asked for better parents in the mortal world," the swallow readily agreed.

Lina remembered her childhood days as she ambled about the woods around her cottage. Hazel had filled her mind with so many fairy stories, and she always looked to discover them. Never would Lina have predicted being thrust into such a place that bore little resemblance to her fantasies as a little girl. A pang of resentment pervaded her blissful memories, if only they had prepared her for what awaited her. The feeling quickly passed when she remembered the burden of the secret they had carried for so long.

"They were ever so loving. I could not have asked for more," Lina sighed. "I miss them, my house, the comfort, and safety of my old life."

"Unfortunately, our destinies often take us far away from who we once were and who we thought we would become," the swallow said.

"I never worried about being enough in the mortal world, but here, well… so much is expected of me. What if I cannot bring about Dahlia's downfall?" The thought plagued the back of her mind every moment of the day.

"Do not worry. That duty does not lie on you alone. There will be many to help when the time comes—Edwina, the rebels, Cornelius. Your true love awaits your arrival to fulfill the prophecy."

It all sounded so simple when Knox put it like that. She tried to gain some hope from his optimism. Settling against his feathers, she shut her eyes and took refuge in the comfort of his presence.

That evening, while Mr. Tyson droned on to her and Cora around the fire, she thought of the swallow's words. Knox soothed a pain in her she had not realized was there. Since Hazel had passed, her heart bore a gaping hole of loneliness. When she was with him, Knox filled it. With Knox, Lina was free to be herself instead of pretending to be someone else. So entrenched in her thoughts, she did not notice Mr. Tyson eyeing the dirt on her shoes.

The next day, she and Knox went to one of the nearby roof openings to check the weather. Though the air still had a chill, it held the promise of warmer days ahead. Spring crept in enough as if to say, "I am on my way." The bird hopped out of the hole for a moment while Lina paced below.

"I think the weather will hold for the next few days," he announced on his return. "Tomorrow, I will leave to find Edwina and bring her back for you."

Lina was both excited and scared at the prospect. She could not imagine a day here without Knox but knew he needed to go. Her arms flew around him in a fierce hug.

"Don't worry, Lina. You will be home soon. I am still too weak to carry you, but Edwina will set everything right," he promised.

"I will be back tomorrow to see you off."

With another embrace, she departed for Cora's, and Knox hopped back to his refuge. Neither saw the large fairy hidden in the shadows, a malevolent glint in his eyes as he turned and scurried away.

The next day, Lina diligently performed her tasks for Cora, her eye always on the clock. She could not bear the thought of Knox leaving without a good-bye from her. How many days would it take for Edwina to return? She finished drying the dishes and neatly folded the towel, readying to depart.

"Dear, before you head out with the young mice, could you run to the Seamstress Shop for me to pick up my new apron? This one has too many holes to cover my clothes properly."

"Of course," Lina replied. Anxious to be done with the errand, she rushed into town.

The sewing shop was empty save for its lone worker, who proudly handed over a dark green apron with intricate sunflowers embroidered along the border.

"This is so pretty, Teagan. Cora will love it," Lina said after admiring the craftsmanship. It was indeed a lovely garment.

"Thank you, I hope so," the fairy said as Lina departed.

Knox's imminent journey filled her mind on the way back. When she walked down the tunnel to Cora's, she was surprised to see the door open. Lina heard voices filtering out into the hallway.

"Well, where is she?" Mr. Tyson demanded.

"Hazel went to the seamstress for me. What is this all about?" The old fairy's voice shook with the question.

"If I find out you knew about this, Cora, there will be repercussions."

"Knew about what?" she quailed.

Angry he spoke to the kind fairy in such a tone, Lina hurried to the doorway. Mr. Tyson stood just inside, poor Cora cowered in front of him. He spun around at the sound of her footsteps. "Ah, so there you are… Lina."

The blood drained from Lina's face to her toes, replaced by a cold dash of fear. For a second, she stood frozen, but if Mr. Tyson knew her real identity, he might know about Knox. The thought of her friend's safety rallied her. Even as he lunged in her direction, she jumped away and ran as fast as her legs could carry her, the apron dropped on the floor forgotten.

The swallow heard her frantic approach and hopped to the end of his tunnel, where he nearly collided with Lina.

"You must go now. Tyson knows who I am," she cried, shoving him back down the passageway. The mayor's furious shouts rang through the air.

They raced for a roof opening, heavy footsteps behind them. When they reached the hole, Knox said, "You must come with me. It is too dangerous for you to stay here now. I can take you as far as my stamina allows, and we will find you another hiding place."

Without argument, she mounted his back, and he leaped for the sky, sunlight streaming down around them. She thought they would make it, but at the last second, a rough pair of hands seized her and threw her to the ground. Knox pecked at their pursuer, but the large fairy pushed him away.

"Go, Knox. You must go!" Lina cried

With one last look at her, he leaped for the opening, but Mr. Tyson grabbed his tail. The swallow called out in pain before spreading his wings in flight. The fairy stumbled back, looking with disdain at the tail feathers left in his hand. Throwing them down, he spat on them, his eyes settled on Lina.

"And now, to deal with you..."

CHAPTER 27

Lina paced the dark room, situated so far underground even the dank air could only imagine the freshness of sunlight. Mr. Tyson dragged her down many inclines to get here. The room was sparsely furnished; dark earth made up its walls and floors, which held the stale, never changing air. There was but one wall sconce in the chamber, its small circle of light hardly enough to illuminate the space.

Tired of being on her feet, she sat in a worn tufted chair and wrapped a blanket around her. She had been here a day, or that is what Teagan told her when she delivered some breakfast. Her lack of sleep made it feel longer. Exhausted from the ordeal, she finally nodded off.

The creak of the door lock woke her, and she bolted to her feet. Mr. Tyson strolled in, diamond-encrusted fingers clutching his gold-capped walking stick. This was his first visit since he had tossed her inside after Knox's escape. He scowled for a long moment, then circled her like prey.

"That silly Poxy story—Hazel indeed. No wonder you kept your identity a secret. You are quite valuable, you know. The question is how can I use you to my best advantage?" He passed in front of her, and their eyes met.

Other than an angry glare, Lina made no reply.

"Cora, of course, thinks I should release you, let you return to Roshall Grove and save us all. But that seems short-sighted to me. After all, should I not be generously rewarded for finding you?" He stopped behind her, his breath hot in her ear. "And, if the Resistors are willing to pay handsomely for you, perhaps Dahlia will pay more."

He saw her stiffen and again stood before her with a satisfied and smug grin on his face. She would not give him the satisfaction of pleading and kept her eyes trained on the wall behind him.

"So many options to think through. Even if your aunt pays well for you, it does not help me in the end. But think, if I return you to the rebels, then I can rule by your side."

"By my side?" Lina finally found her voice.

"Yes, as my wife. We will make Maizeridge our home, build a glorious palace. Once again, my city will shine, and all will hail my wisdom and benevolence." His eyes aglow with the promise of such power.

"Your plan won't work. The prophecy says only the kiss of *true love* will grow my wings and destroy Dahlia. I am betrothed to the fairy Cornelius for this purpose." The thought of him, always so foreign to her, now brought her comfort.

"I've learned in life that money tends to solve any problem you have. A well-placed bribe here and there will bring you to my side. Do not concern yourself with silly prophecies." He waved a dismissive hand and moved towards the door. "We will marry tomorrow, and your future with me will be set."

"And if I refuse?" she countered, her bravery the only device she could hold against him.

"You are not in a position to refuse," he balked. "You belong to me now. Remember that."

He slammed the door on his way out. In the chilly room, Lina sat forlornly. Tears flowed down her cheeks; never had she felt so alone. She missed Hazel and Felix and her simple farm life. More so, she missed Knox. Her thoughts were with him often this past day. Had he been able to fly without the lost tail feathers? Or was he hurt again? Her heart ached at the thought.

In these past months together, a closer connection developed between them. A kindred spirit, he made her feel valued for being herself. Not that her mortal parents had not, but they saw her as a child, someone to protect. Knox saw her as an equal. His presence alone made the world feel whole. She prayed he was unharmed.

Time dragged on slowly in the dimness of her prison. Teagan brought another meal, an apologetic smile on her face. "Don't worry, Hazel… I mean, Lina, I am making you a beautiful gown for tomorrow. You will be the most beautiful bride the Fairy World ever saw."

Lina turned her head away without speaking. Quietly, the seamstress left. Nothing had gone right in the Fairy World since Lina arrived. The Herptiles, the Ephemera, nor these Rodentia had her best interest at heart. Perhaps staying in the mortal world would have been better. Anger found a foothold in her and wound its way around her being. As if having her evil aunt to defeat was not enough, the fairies of the world seemed intent on thwarting her every move. Did they not realize she was trying to save them?

The night elapsed faster than she hoped, given her fate. Instead of Teagan, Cora delivered her breakfast in the morning. She took one look at the girl's tear-stained face and lost her composure.

"Now, now," she sobbed, "we can't be blubbering. This will all work out for the best."

"Work out for the best?" Lina cried, her anger only increasing in the wee hours. "How can you let him force me to do this?"

"You have to understand, dear, Mr. Tyson is in charge. It is by his good graces that I can stay. Cheer up," she said, her tears now gone. "He is an important man, and you will be an important wife."

Lina made no reply. Help would not come from Cora. Not this time.

"Now eat up. Teagan will be here to dress you. Oh, how I love a good wedding," she exclaimed, the door clicking shut behind her.

The girl looked at the food on the tray but had no stomach for it. Time was almost up, and she had no viable plan of escape. "I guess there is nothing to do but go along with the ruse," she muttered to herself.

"Not true," said a deep voice.

Madame Mouse stuck her head out of a freshly dug hole in the side of the chamber wall. Her three offspring peeked over her shoulder. Lina had never been so relieved to see the pinkies.

"We told mother Mr. Tyson was holding you prisoner," Finn explained. "We saw him take you and try to stop the bird. We told her who you *really* are and that we must save you."

Lina's heart warmed. There had been someone looking out for her best interest after all.

"I dug a tunnel to the surface. It will be a tight fit for you, but we will make it work. Come on," the mother mouse ordered.

Without delay, the girl crawled into the hole. After a few inches, it was pitch black. The mother led the way with Lina's hand on the end of her tail. The youngsters followed behind to make sure she didn't get lost. They crept along the claustrophobic tunnel, some spots so narrow, Lina barely edged by. Finally, a shard of light illuminated the space enough for her to discern the sides of the walls. Gradually, more light poured in as they climbed a steep incline to the surface and scrambled out into the morning sun.

After the darkness of the tunnel, the glow momentarily blinded Lina, When her eyes adjusted, she dusted off large clumps of dirt. A stiff breeze lifted her hair, further dispersing the soil. The young mice cheered with glee at her escape.

"Thank you," she said and hugged Madame Mouse.

"You're most welcome. Where will you go from here?" she inquired with concern.

"I suppose I'll head in the direction of Roshall Grove," Lina replied.

"Be careful," warned her rescuer. "I am sure Queen Dahlia is watching for you."

"She is not the only one," an angry voice boomed.

They turned in horror to find Mr. Tyson looming behind them, his large body framed by the rising sun. Malice emanated from him like heat from a fire. The youngsters shrunk behind Madame Mouse.

"Run, Lina," yelled Ari from behind his mother.

But it was too late, and with one quick move, his rough hand seized her arm. Lina stared into his cold, calculating eyes, the daylight fully exposing the greed that shone through them. Desperately, she wrenched her arm to free herself. But alas, his grip was too tight.

"Please, you must let me go," she begged, clawing at his hand.

"I think not. You are far too valuable." His voice was thick with another victory. In the daylight, his features took on an even more wicked appearance.

Despite her best efforts, he pulled her away, heading for whatever hole he emerged from. The mice ran forward and valiantly tried to yank her back in the other direction. What little combined strength they had was not up to the task. Ari nipped at Tyson's hands, but was swatted away with ease.

A blur passed overhead, momentarily blocking the sun. Knox swooped down and pecked at Tyson, who raised his walking stick and struck the swallow. Lina screamed when the bird crumpled to the ground.

"No one can save you, girl. You belong to me now," the mayor crowed triumphantly.

A blinding burst of light knocked them all off their feet; the mice slung in all different directions.

"Release her at once," a stern voice commanded. Mr. Tyson staggered to his feet, and immediately cowered before the illuminated figure, dropping the girl's arm in the process. Lina looked up and gasped. Edwina had returned.

CHAPTER 28

General Sepitus pointed to a location on the map spread out before him and Dahlia in the library. "To the best of our knowledge, the Resistors remain assembled here in a labyrinth of tunnels forming an underground bunker. We could use several strategies to attack them, none of which I feel they could counter. It is up to you how to proceed."

Dahlia's spies were busy all winter long gathering information about her enemy. Once they discovered the Resistor's location, scouts had determined their approximate number. It was hardly impressive next to the force the dark queen could summon. More continued to arrive for her each day, swelling the ranks so much, they had to camp outside the castle grounds. She turned away from the table to look out the window. Dead trees stood in the fragile sun of early spring. Yet, the change in the season would do them no good; their crooked branches had been empty for years.

"I have given this matter a great deal of thought," she told Sepitus. "I would like to let Lina join the Resistors before we make a move."

"Is that wise, My Queen?" the general blurted before he could think better of it.

She shot him a withering look. "You just said they would not be able to counter our attack. Do you think *one* girl could make such a difference to their campaign?"

"She has the rest of the Primal Stone, My Queen, could that not make us vulnerable?" he replied in a hesitant whisper, eyes on the floor.

Dahlia laughed aloud. "She possesses but a shard of it. Don't tell me you still believe in that fairy tale of a prophecy? You doubt me, after all we have done together, all the power you know I have at my disposal?"

"Of…course…not, My Queen," he stammered, cowering low before her. "It is my job to consider your safety, that is all."

She left the window and walked around the table to stand over his groveling form. Raising his chin with her fingertip, she said, "I want the Resistors to see her defeated, which will destroy whatever shreds of hope they have. You have been a faithful servant, Sepitus, but do not make me explain myself to you *ever* again. My patience has its limits."

"My sincerest apologies. Never again will I question your judgment, My Queen."

"Good." She dropped his chin. "You may go."

With a hurried bow, he scrambled out of the room as though death itself were at his heels. She turned her attention back to the map. For a long time, she stared at the borders of her kingdom. Weak light filtered through the chamber, the days growing longer as winter's hold diminished. Her eyes focused on Maizeridge, and a surety filled her. The girl was there.

Now that the weather turned milder, Lina would likely make a move to join the Resistors just outside Roshall Grove's borders. Dahlia just needed to be patient. Better to wait like a spider in its web for the unsuspecting fly. She had seen firsthand the damage being rash could cause. Memories flooded her mind of Priya in this very room during the days just after her stillborn baby was delivered as though reliving the moment.

"I am sure I will find a precedent somewhere in the fairy law," the old enchantress exclaimed, thumbing through the pages of a book that sat amongst the tomes and scrolls she had gathered.

Dahlia hardly cared. Her baby's death drained her heart of all but sorrow and grief. She was curled in the window seat, knees to chest, trying to survive the waves of agony which broke over her constantly. Nothing could penetrate her misery.

"I read about twins born some ages ago. Instead of simply declaring the oldest the heir, they gave them a series of tests to determine whose power was better suited to rule." The old enchantress remained convinced of her ability to put Dahlia on the throne.

"What does it matter? The kingdom adores Ivy, and now she is with child. She will give them a new heir."

"What does it matter?" Priya cried frantically. "It matters because you are more powerful and more deserving. Ivy is like your mother, too short-sighted to realize the scope of magic available to her."

Both Dahlia's mother and sister eschewed the mention of dark magic, deeming it too dangerous to meddle with. But from what Priya taught her, she could see the usefulness of it for a ruler. With their parents' death, Ivy turned more and more to Edwina, who despised dark magic as much as Ivy herself. Priya's influence decreased by the day. Rumors spread that she was somehow responsible for the deaths of Amaranth and Tarron.

"My sister blames black magic for the death of our parents," Dahlia stated. The uprising where they were killed was led by devotees of the dark arts. "No one will persuade her otherwise."

"And yet, Edwina can use illicit magic to travel between the worlds? And, Ivy, who was barren, suddenly conceives?" the old enchantress scoffed. "That is suspicious at best. Surely, she must have used some of the forbidden spells to get with child."

Dahlia leaned her forehead against the cold window. The thought had crossed her mind about her sister's pregnancy. Ivy seemed willing to use forbidden spells for her benefit but not for her people. A hardness formed in the pit of Dahlia's stomach at the thought of her sister holding a newborn child. Suppose she had used dark magic to create her pregnancy; what would have stopped her from using it to end another. Her hand flew to her empty womb. As Priya had pointed out, was it more than just a coincidence that her baby died?

"What if you can't find a precedent?" Dahlia asked, her newly stirred anger making her focus. If there was a case where someone before challenged the line of succession, she needed to bring it to everyone's attention. Ivy and Edwina had stripped her and Priya of any voice or power in the kingdom. She rose from the window seat with purpose, remembering the weight of her dead infant in her arms. She would avenge her daughter.

The enchantress continued her search through the volumes and scrolls while Dahlia put away discarded books and brought her new ones. Hours passed, Priya's persistence never faltering. A few times, some fairies entered the library but left at the sight of them. Dahlia was used to it by now. Back when they were children, Ivy was beloved by their subjects, but they merely tolerated her. Whispers of Dahlia's red hair being a sign of evil reached her ears at a very young age. She ignored it then, content in the bond between her and her sister. Never could she have imagined being estranged by her twin.

"Aha," Priya cried and triumphantly motioned Dahlia over. "Here is what I was looking for and it's as I said. It establishes that in the case of twins, a series of tests should be administered before choosing one over the other. We will show it to your sister tomorrow."

The girl read the words on the pages in disbelief that they were real. There was a precedent, a pathway for her to the crown. For a brief moment, she thought perhaps a shared rule between Ivy and herself would most benefit the kingdom. That thought withered all too soon. Her sister would never rule in collaboration with her. A fight stood before her and Priya, with Ivy already holding a significant advantage.

"What if Ivy dismisses this information as unimportant? I am sure she will not willingly give up her claim to the crown."

"There are other ways at our disposal. Are you willing to do whatever it takes?" the enchantress asked.

"Yes," Dahlia vowed, and a satisfied smile filled Priya's face.

The library door groaned open, startling Dahlia back into the present. A guard hurried across the room and bowed before her. "Cotswold has arrived with an update, My Queen. He waits for you in the throne room."
She dismissed him with a curt nod. Her eyes fell back onto the map, lingering on the word Maizeridge. This time she would not act in haste. This time there would be no mistakes. *Victory* would be hers.

CHAPTER 29

"I'm terribly s...s...sorry for the mis...misunderstanding," Mr. Tyson stammered.

"There was no misunderstanding, you greedy, selfish being," Edwina declared, anger etched on every inch of her face.

"I only wanted to help her. To keep her safe...," he feebly explained.

While he pled his case to the enchantress, Lina ran to Knox. "Are you all right?"

He hopped to his feet and shook out his feathers with a flourish. "Yes. And you?"

"Yes. I was so worried about you," Lina cried.

"And I, you. I brought Edwina back as soon as I could."

They embraced, Lina relished in the soft touch of his feathers against her face. The knot in her heart released, knowing he was safe and they were together again.

"Please," the mayor pleaded, "I never hurt the girl. Here, ask her." He pulled Lina toward him, but she jerked her arm away.

"Lina, has this man hurt you?" Edwina asked.

"He was going to make me marry him to gain power in the kingdom for himself. The mice tried to help me escape," Lina explained, with a cold stare for the mayor.

The enchantress took in the scene. An abashed Tyson looked at the ground. Cora and Teagan, who had just arrived, stared at her in awe. Madame Mouse gathered her children safely to her side. When Edwina's eyes fell on Lina, the girl saw all the anguish she felt since her disappearance. The fairy had never stopped looking for Lina.

"I thank you, Madame Mouse, and you ladies for keeping Lina safe. As for you..." She stood before the trembling Tyson. "I am disappointed to hear of your choices. However, there is no time for me to deal with them now properly."

"Please, I'll do anything to atone for my behavior," he groveled, such a different demeanor than Lina had seen these past few months. She could not help but smile at his muddied clothes and broken cane.

"The moment draws near where all will be called upon to fight against Queen Dahlia. I trust I can count on you to answer that call," Edwina admonished sternly.

"Yes, of course," he spluttered, and with a deferential bow, he hurried back underground, grabbing the pieces of his damaged cane.

"Now we must go." She whistled to the sky, and a second swallow swooped down. "Edgar will carry you, Lina. Come."

Knox gave her a nod, and she boarded the other bird's back. They lifted off into the sky. As they flew off, Lina turned to wave to Cora, Teagan, and Madame Mouse. The youngsters darted along below yelling, "Good-bye, Lina. We will miss you."

High into the clouds, they rose, the enchantress leading the way. Knox soared by his fellow bird's side, his missing feathers causing him to bob and dip. With some noticeable effort, he kept up the pace. Lina relaxed, the reality of her escape sinking in. She closed her eyes and let the wind whip across her face. She was free. Underground for so long, Lina exalted in the fresh air. From the crisp feel of it in her lungs to the strands of hair it sent floating behind her, she reveled in its vigor.

"We are going to the main hiding place of the Resistors," Edwina called back to the girl.

Lina was daunted by the thought of reuniting with her kin. Many would look to her to bring down Dahlia. Was she up to the task? Would her kind accept her after all these years? She would find out soon enough.

Around midday, Edwina descended into a grove of large pines. Lina dismounted Edgar onto the ground, the trees soaring into the sky beyond sight. While the birds pecked around for a quick snack, the girl gaped at a pinecone next to her. It was twice her size. There was still so much to get used to in this new world. With a pang, she realized her bag with the rowan box was still in the dresser at Cora's. Her only link to her mortal life was gone.

"I am so sorry it took so long for me to find you," the enchantress exclaimed with a hearty embrace. "How did you make it on your own?"

Lina recounted her tale from the moment the Herptiles stole her away." The mother, Juniper, took me because she wanted me to marry her son. He was not interested in the whole prospect, but another fairy named Leander, who seemed to be of some importance in their community, wanted to make sure I wasn't the one Dahlia sought. He had his henchmen stick me in a lake on a lily pad."

Edwina, who listened with great interest, laid out some snacks for them. They sat on a carpet of pine needles in the shade of a large trunk and ate. The swallows flew up to explore the trees, where other birds flitted amongst the boughs. Sunlight filtered in long shafts onto the floor from above.

"A fairy named Lula came out of the water and helped me escape. It's funny though, she never even asked my name." This fact had intrigued Lina from the start.

"She was a Naiad, a type of Fluvial fairy. They are known for their kindness. But, generally, they keep to their underwater kingdoms and avoid involvement in the world above. You were lucky to come across her."

"Yes, I was," Lina agreed between bites of a honey cake. "Then, a butterfly found me on the river and was going to take me to you at Cedar Knoll until an Ephemera named Kai stole me away again. In the end, he and his kin were friendly and let me go, although I never told him exactly who I was. His kind fears Dahlia, though. Three different kingdoms of them are hiding in the trees." Lina took a breathe before continuing.

"Kai took me to Cedar Knoll to meet you, but you were gone. It was there I met Zander, who brought me to his siblings. They let me stay with them while I waited for you. Until one day, the snakes came and scared them away, the same snakes that confronted you. I fled and wound up with Cora in Maizeridge and have been there ever since."

"It sounds as though you have had quite the adventure already. It was never my intention, but I am very proud of how well you handled yourself. You've given me valuable information about who may or may not be our allies in the upcoming battle with Dahlia." Edwina patted her hand affectionately.

"Fairies are such contrasting beings," the girl complained, "Juniper, Leander, Mr. Tyson, even Kai only thought of their motives. Yet, Cora and Lula both helped me for no personal gain."

"Don't fool yourself into thinking mortals can't be the same. There are good ones and bad ones in every kind of creature," Edwina warned.

"Most of the animals I met were so kind, the butterfly, the rabbits, the mice," she insisted and brushed crumbs off her dress. Ants the size of her foot scuttled over to eat them.

"Yes, most animals lack the conniving nature that can creep into a fairy's soul," the enchantress agreed.

"Not those snakes. They were terrifying." Lina bristled at the thought of them.

"Yes, and it has been quite an ordeal trying to stay one step ahead of them. My attempts to end their meddling will only hinder them for a time before they are back. Kafir and Purus are their names, and they are Dahlia's most loyal servants. Not to mention the ravens she has searching for you and goodness knows what else."

The swallows drifted down and landed by the fairies. Knox sat next to Lina. She leaned against him, his presence alone filling her heart with satisfaction. Even a few days of separation from him had been torture.

"Knox is a hero," the enchantress stated. "With a damaged tail and all, he managed to find me. He is a true friend."

"Yes," Lina concurred, gently stroking his wing. He nudged his head against hers.

"You two will be safe in this grove tonight," Edwina said to the swallows. "Let Knox rest and gather his strength. In the morning, head for the outposts of Roshall Grove."

"You mean we are not staying together?" Lina cried in despair.

"I'm afraid not. Our path lies underground," the enchantress explained, and Lina groaned. "I know, dear, underground again, but once we get to the stronghold, I promise you will see the sky again." Edwina stood and held out a hand to the girl. Lina saw the familiar glow of fairy dust.

"Thank you for the ride," Lina said to Edgar, and he bowed his head.

"I am sorry we must part again," she said to Knox and threw her arms around his neck.

"Me too. But I will see you soon," he promised.

Weary-hearted, Lina walked to Edwina. With a flick of her hand, gold dust flew up over them, wafting down in a large circle around them. Lina felt the warmth followed by the sensation of falling. The next thing she knew, they stood in a dark tunnel, the pine trees' roots rippling out in all directions. There was no musty dankness in the air, just an earthy smell. The enchantress conjured a ball of light that hung in the air ahead of them as they set off.

"As far as I know, this tunnel remains a secret from Dahlia, but we must be cautious."

They crept along with Edwina's guard on constant alert. There were signs of recent activity in the tunnel. Footprints running in both directions packed the dirt firmly under their feet. Wall sconces hung on the walls at regular intervals— some held the shaft of a burnt-out torch. A broken arrow, and filthy cape that someone threw on the ground, provided further evidence of fairy use.

Lina could not tell the time of day underground but felt as though she walked for hours. In the cover of two rocks which pushed through the floor like gruesome fangs, they finally stopped. After a quick meal, the enchantress ordered Lina to rest. She tried to find a comfortable position against the stones. It hardly mattered, so immense was her exhaustion, she fell right to sleep. Far too soon, Edwina shook her awake, and the girl rubbed the sleep from her eyes.

"Come, it is morning. If we make good time, we will reach the stronghold by mid-day, and we will reunite with your fellow Hirundo and the rest of the Resistors," her companion said.

Down the dark tunnel, Lina walked, the mantle of her destiny becoming heavier with each step.

CHAPTER 30

"The entrance to the Resistors stronghold is just ahead," Edwina informed the girl after a long morning of walking.

They stopped before a nondescript place in the tunnel. Lina's eyes searched for anything that resembled a door but saw nothing besides dirt interspersed with plants and the rare moss-covered rock.

The enchantress put her hand on a scraggly cluster of vines that clung listlessly to the wall. With the whisper of a few words, the spell activated, and the outline of a round-topped door frame appeared, its golden rowan wood gleaming against the dark earth of the tunnel.

"Who goes there?" a baritone voice bellowed from the other side.

"It is I, Edwina."

The door swung open, and the two stepped across the threshold. When the sentry shut the door, its outline disappeared on the outside wall rendering it invisible again. Inside, the room was spacious and bright, a pleasant contrast to the dark tunnel. High above, a few small shafts of light entered the chamber. These rays were redirected by a series of precisely placed mirrors to expand the light outward throughout the room. Lina had never seen something so ingenious.

Her gaze fell back to the sentry who allowed them entry. He stared at her with the same wonder she felt for the mirrors. Color rose in her cheeks.

"Lina, this is Lorcan," Edwina introduced.

He swept into a low bow, his fair hair flowing around his shoulders. "Your Highness."

Startled, Lina bobbed down in a curtsey. "It's nice to meet you, Lorcan."

"Come," the enchantress ordered.

Edwina strode purposefully down the long corridor in front of them. Several times they met armed guards, who jumped to attention as they passed. The mirrors lit the way to large double doors which stood open. They crossed the threshold, and a large circular chamber spread out before them, a bustle of activity within. Many other hallways ran off like spokes from a wheel hub. Fairies passed through the room from one corridor to another. Light poured in from crystals set in the ceiling above. A sizable table sat on a pedestal in the center of the room where several fairies studied something on its top. One of them noticed Edwina and pointed out their arrival to the others.

The entire room stopped; a deafening silence replaced the hum of affairs. Edwina continued toward the table, but Lina's feet dragged like lead in the suffocating hush, the weight of dozens of eyes scrutinizing her. A tall, handsome fairy stepped off the platform and hurried to greet them.

"Welcome, Your Highness." He swept into a grand bow. His blond hair fell across his brow while his wings folded around him. When he rose, a pair of jade green eyes stared unnervingly into hers. "I am Cornelius."

If she could have conjured him up from pure imagination, she could have done no better. From his striking face to his elegant bearing, he epitomized the words *fairy prince.*

"I need you to take her from here," Edwina told him. "I have to gather reports from the swallows and the scouts. I leave you in good hands, Lina."

Without another word, she briskly left the chamber down one of the myriads of passageways, leaving the Lina alone in this unfamiliar place. These fairies had waited for her, believed in her eventual arrival to defeat the evil queen. Likely, they expected her to be more of a warrior and less a meek girl. While whispers began around her, she knew she should act assertively. Yet, even though she was their princess and future queen, she felt woefully out of place.

"I'm Lina," she muttered, not exactly the self-assured demeanor she wished to show.

"Come." Cornelius took her arm, and she allowed him to awkwardly lead her to the table. "The other leaders of the Resistors are anxious to meet you."

Three females and one male waited around the table, all dressed in practical outfits in shades of green and brown. Under their expectant eyes, she tried not to cower. Would they assume she would have all the answers to defeat Dahlia? She ascended the pedestal, her meekness magnified under their gaze.

"Welcome," greeted a girl with flowing black hair, and they all bowed as one.

"Thank you," was Lina's only reply.

"This must be very overwhelming for you," said the boy, his voice lilting like chimes. His mop of brown hair bounced above his kind eyes when he spoke. "I am Dunlin."

"Yes, Dunlin, it is quite overwhelming for me," Lina said, thankful someone had spoken the obvious. She felt her stomach loosen a bit.

"We are so happy you are here. Now we truly have hope," the first girl said, her hair glinting like dark water in the moonlight. "I am Aelin, and this is Blythe and Renna."

Blythe, her hair as light as Aelin's was black, graced her with a wide smile. Renna's, however, appeared forced. Profound hurt seemed to settle in the girl's turquoise eyes, leaving Lina uncomfortable. Perhaps not every fairy looked forward to her return.

"Does she have the amulet?" Renna asked, her tone almost accusatory.

"I'm sure she does, yet she has nothing to prove to us," Cornelius admonished.

"It's all right," Lina said, pulling the necklace from underneath her shirt.

It glowed brightly, and all eyes turned in its direction. The fairies stared at it with awe. Lina took it from her neck, and they each held it in turn, fascinated by its sheer presence. In her youth, she considered it a pretty necklace, but their captivation reminded her of its importance.

"All right," Blythe said and handed it back to Lina. "Now back to business. Let's show the princess where we stand."

On the table sat a large map, certain positions circled in red or yellow with annotations scribbled next to them. Roshall Grove stood in bold black type along the bottom edge. Lina eyed the forests, streams, hills, and parts of a homeland she never knew. The main city was already crossed out, entirely under the grip of her aunt.

"The red circles are regions Dahlia controls. The yellow we know she has infiltrated," Aelin explained. These areas took up most of the map.

"Does she know where your hideout is?" Lina asked.

"Not this one. We've moved around a few times," Aelin volunteered, her voice soft as light rainfall.

"Thanks to Renna. She keeps us one step ahead of Dahlia. Her acumen and skill are an asset to the Resistors," Blythe beamed at Renna, who looked down shyly at the compliment.

"Yes," agreed Aelin. "It is a challenge trying to avoid Dahlia's notice."

"But none of that should matter now, right?" inquired Dunlin. "You two just need to *kiss,* and the evil queen will be defeated."

Lina froze in fear at the mention of the kiss, but Cornelius burst into laughter. "Easy there, Dun, it may not be that simple. We must consult with Edwina first. Besides, poor Lina just got here. Let her settle in before you throw the weight of the whole war on her shoulders. In fact," he turned to her, "you must be tired from your journey."

"Yes, I am," she replied, flooded with relief at his handling of the situation.

"Naya," he called. "Please take Lina to rest and refresh. We shall see you at dinner."

A fairy with long blond hair and silver-tipped wings sprang across the room and bade Lina follow her. With a nod and goodbyes, she followed Naya down one of the corridors. Along the way, fairies stopped and stared at Lina, whispering to one another after she passed. She prayed their destination was close so she could hide from all the scrutiny. They turned a few corners before stopping in front of a bright green door.

"Here is your room, my princess," Naya announced.

"My room?"

"We always kept one prepared for you in hopes you would come home. I am so happy you are finally here with us, Your Highness, and even happier to be your personal maid." She bowed, then opened the door.

Inside was a small but finely appointed chamber. Rich satins lined the walls while ethereal silks draped the ceiling. A sumptuous bed bursting with a colorful garden of pillows stood in the middle. There was an overstuffed chair next to a small table on one side. An elegant bronze vanity and a large wardrobe filled out the room. Compared to the simple bedroom she had grown up in, this was paradise.

"Let me know if you need anything. I will be right next door."

"Thank you, Naya," Lina said, still processing the elegance of her room.

With a quick curtsey, the maid left, the door clicking shut behind her. Only seconds later, a knock brought a boy with a tray of food. He set it on the table and scrambled away after a series of nervous bows.

The smell of steaming broth made Lina's stomach grumble. She sat and ate her fill along with some pieces of diced dates. Exhausted, physically and mentally, she climbed onto the luxurious bed amid all the pillows and stared up at the soothing array of fabric above. If only she could hide in here until she felt more like a leader. A tap at the door roused her, and she sat up as Edwina entered the room.

"Getting settled all right, dear?" The enchantress shut the door behind her.

"Yes, I guess. Though, I'm not quite sure what to do now." Lina plopped back on the bed.

"Word has spread throughout the camp of your arrival. Tonight there will be a banquet for all to gather. There you and Cornelius will finally kiss."

Lina's heart sank to her toes. "And will this… *kiss* mend the Primal Crystal?"

"That I cannot say, but it is the first step. One we must take. The prophecy is quite clear on the kiss of true love producing your wings. You are not a true Volant without them. Most are born with them and unfurl over time, but since you were hidden in the mortal world, that process never occurred. Once you have them, I can reassess the situation and decide how to proceed."

Lina nodded, but inside her thoughts tangled in a jumble of doubts. Though Cornelius was handsome and kind, *true love* was a generous description for her feelings toward him—a complete stranger. Yet, it was not her place to argue with a prophecy. Perhaps it meant overtime love would develop between them. In any case, tonight, she must kiss Cornelius whether she was ready or not.

"Now then," said Edwina, "let's get Naya and find you something to wear that is worthy of a princess."

CHAPTER 31

The barren ground around Dahlia shook, soil and stone vibrating. A deep fissure appeared, and the earth split apart. She felt the creatures she summoned stirring and ready to answer her call. With a quick wave of her arm, the quaking ceased. The earth suddenly bound itself back together, a faint line in the soil the only remnant of the spell.

She closed her eyes and exhaled. Each time she practiced, she grew stronger. When the time for battle came, she would be ready, as would her army. She glanced to where the castle stood, a dark menacing presence on the grey horizon. Deep plumes of black smoke rose from behind the walls where her forges worked around the clock crafting the necessary armor and weapons.

The dry ground around her was littered with decomposed tree trunks and jagged rocks. It amazed her, what her hatred had done, how the devastation inside of her spread across the land. Is this what Priya had hoped for? She would never know.

The old enchantress worked adamantly to give Dahlia a claim to the throne, but the recently crowned Ivy would hear nothing of it. She would not look at the precedent they found or agree to govern with her twin. In the end, all her promises of them ruling together were forgotten. Priya blamed Edwina, claiming she whispered lies about Dahlia's evilness to Ivy at every opportunity. When this rumor reached Ivy's ears, the new queen forbade her sister and Priya from mentioning it ever again. Anger and hate for her twin built inside Dahlia by the day.

Tired of biding her time, the old enchantress concocted a plan to bring soldiers from her allies in Elderbreach to help execute a secret plot to overthrow Ivy and Theros. Once they were removed, she would put Dahlia on the throne. She threw the scheme together with such haste, caution fell by the wayside. One of the rebels brought in found his fortunes much improved by betraying the old enchantress. The night her small force made their move, Ivy and Theros awaited them with many more of their own soldiers.

Dahlia remembered the moment as if it were yesterday. She was summoned from her chambers to the throne room where her sister sat, hands across her already rounding belly. The Primal Stone glowed brightly in its place atop the regal seat. Priya stood bound in chains of silver which not only burned her skin but left her powerless. Still, eight men surrounded her.

"How could you?" Ivy asked the old enchantress, a look of pure betrayal on her face.

"I merely want what is best for the kingdom," the accused answered calmly. "And you would not listen to reason."

"And you involved Dahlia?" the queen ventured, a gaze of fury leveled at her sister.

"No. Dahlia had no knowledge of this," Priya answered for her with a reassuring glance despite the chains that bound her. "I alone contrived this coup to put the proper heir on the throne."

"Take her away. Her fate is sealed. Everyone else, leave me with my sister." There was no room for argument in her tone.

The soldiers dragged Priya away with a hesitant Theros in their wake. He gave a wary glance back to his new wife, who nodded for him to depart.

"Did you know of her plan?" Ivy bluntly asked the moment they were alone.

"I knew she was unhappy, that she wanted me on the throne. But I did not know her exact plan." In truth, Priya had only told her something was planned, not the details. Though Dahlia would have agreed to any means to remove her sister from the throne at this point. "What will you do with her?"

"There is no choice in the matter. Priya will be executed."

"How can you? We have known her since childhood. She was our mother's enchantress," Dahlia pled.

"She has betrayed me, the throne, and the kingdom. Her thirst for power and dabbling in the dark arts have gone too far." She rose from her seat and descended to take her sister's hands, looking deeply into her eyes. "Dahlia, surely you see this. Surely you know she was behind our parents' death, that her allies in Elderbreach were involved. Come back to me, sister. Let us be as we once were."

Anger rose in Dahlia intertwined with panic. Her instincts had warned her Priya was complicit in her parents' death. Now the certainty of that betrayal was laid bare before her. Priya had been pulling the strings for a long time to get Dahlia more power and more power for herself. Even the bee all those years ago was no accident, but the start of her manipulation between the sisters. For a brief moment, the treachery shook her resolve. However, without Priya, Dahlia would lose her only ally, the one fairy who had supported her when no one else had. The *only* one who could help her avenge her baby's death. She pushed past Ivy and mounted the dais.

"What are you doing?" her sister exclaimed, stumbling to the side.

"Taking what should rightfully be mine," Dahlia declared, snatching the Primal Stone from its resting place.

Ivy ran to her and tried to grab the stone back. "Put it back. Stop this madness, Dahlia."

"Madness?" The word incensed her beyond reason. "You killed my daughter, and you speak to me of madness?"

"Dahlia, no! How could you think such a thing? That is not what happened!" Ivy cried. "Priya has blinded you. She is evil. There is a prophecy. She will seek to overthrow the kingdom."

"That is not what you fear. You fear *I* will overthrow the kingdom. Do not speak to me of sisterhood.

Your betrayal of our bond will be your downfall. The stone is mine."

Ivy pried her hands onto the stone, and each tried to wrest it from the other. In their struggle, they lost footing and toppled off the dais to the floor below. The Primal Stone crashed on the rhodium floor and spun away. Dahlia pushed off her sister and retrieved it as the door burst open. Edwina surveyed the situation.

"Return the stone at once," the new enchantress ordered.

"Never." Dahlia's wings lifted her off the ground where she hovered a few feet above them.

"I know of the prophecy. It came to me. I know it is about you, Dahlia," Edwina shouted. "And Ivy's child will be your downfall."

At that moment, Dahlia realized how she craved the power to fill the hole left by her baby's death—to take vengeance for her daughter. Ivy, Edwina, even her parents had spurned her at every opportunity. They all tried to deny her an equal inheritance in her own kingdom. Her sister did not deserve to rule after ostracizing her twin, after treating her as an outcast. Power would be hers.

Edwina uttered a spell, and the stone pulled out of Dahlia's hands. But, after months of training with Priya, she resisted, whispering a counterspell. Theros rushed in, followed by guards, but they were thrown back by the powerful magic which engulfed the room.

The Primal Stone hovered just outside of Dahlia's reach, two forces pulling in opposite directions. When it was slowly drawing back towards Dahlia, Edwina changed course and cast a new spell. With a thunderous crack, a tiny shard broke off. It sailed across the room, landing next to Ivy, still prostrate on the floor. Edwina flew to the queen's side.

Dahlia clutched the rest of the stone triumphantly against her chest. "I will return, and I will rule the Fairy World."

"You can try, but without this shard, you will not succeed." Edwina picked the small piece up and brandished it at her foe. "There is a spell on this now, a spell protected by the ancient wisdom that shields not only this piece of stone but the daughter Ivy carries in her womb. She will be protected by love, an emotion you have no connection with. She will be our redemption with the kiss of *true love* and she will unite the stone and take her rightful place in this kingdom. This prophecy will guide our people until such time."

"We shall see about that," Dahlia sneered before vanishing in a cloud of dark smoke.

All manner of hidden ways out of the kingdom were known to her. After a quick stop in Priya's chambers, she had all she needed to escape, except the old enchantress herself. Once freed, they would flee with the Primal Stone's power and amass an army to overthrow the kingdom. Ivy would pay for what she had done.

Now, after many years, on the barren fields of *Dahlia's* kingdom, she readied for the final battle, the one that would defeat her sister's offspring once and for all. She whistled to the sky, and Cotswold descended to her side. "Bring me back to the castle. There is much to prepare."

CHAPTER 32

"Ah, yes, I think this is the one. What do you think, ladies?" Edwina asked.

Lina stood before Aelin, Blythe, and Naya, in a pale green gown with gold-threaded trimmings draping her small frame. The front of the bodice scooped gracefully across her shoulders while the back dipped nearly to her waist. Unused to such fancy attire, a self-conscious Lina would have preferred a bit more fabric in several places. Nervously, she twisted the amulet in her hand.

"Beautiful," agreed Aelin, and the others nodded their approval. "What do you think, Lina?"

She stared at their eager faces and did not have the heart to tell the truth. "It's lovely. They all have been."

She glanced at her bed, now covered with unchosen dresses, scarves, and capes—the wardrobe supply seemed endless. The mountain of garments could clothe her forever, but none she would ever feel comfortable wearing. Hopefully, life as the inheritor to the throne would not require formal dress at *all* times.

"Now for her hair and makeup." Blythe clapped her hands in excitement.

Naya motioned Lina to a seat at the vanity. Deftly, she separated the girl's hair into sections which she twisted up and secured with pins. Once satisfied, she applied powder and some balm to enhance Lina's features. After the finishing touches, she stepped aside, and Lina gasped at her reflection in the mirror. Never had she looked so beautiful; she didn't think it was possible.

"The perfect look for such a special night," Edwina declared. "And with little time to spare. You ladies, go ready yourselves. I will get Lina to the banquet."

While the others bustled out, Lina fussed with the neckline of her dress. "I just wish it was a bit more... *modest*."

The enchantress laughed but put an arm gently around her. "You will get used to dressing as a fairy soon enough. Showing some shoulders is hardly immodest, and the fairies will want to see the amulet. Remember, it is proof of who you are. And you will need the back open for your wings. Please try not to worry. You look stunning."

"Thank you. I hope my actions can match the grace of my dress this evening. I've never been kissed and to have so much riding on it…"

"It is only natural for you to be nervous, but we must trust the prophecy."

All too soon, Edwina guided her from the room into the labyrinth of tunnels that lay outside her door. The underground refuge was enormous, and Lina thought they would never reach their destination. Soon enough, she heard the buzz of a crowd and light poured from a chamber up ahead. When they reached the entrance, the fairies parted to make way, necks craned to get a good look at the newly returned princess. The assembly was mainly Volant fairies, but Lina noticed Groundlings mixed among them, additional citizens who came to join the cause.

The vaulted ceiling was high, crystal circles embedded there allowed in the moonlight from the night sky, and hundreds of candles lined the walls, their flames dancing like dappled rainbows on the floor. Long tables ringed the room all circling a raised dais where a smaller table stood in the center of it all. In one of the two chairs that flanked it sat Cornelius, looking as handsome as ever. He waved Lina to join him the moment their eyes met.

"Go," Edwina urged. "Take your rightful place."

Lina crossed the room with all eyes on her, the amulet warm against her skin, and mounted the steps. Cornelius held out a hand, the white lace cuff of his shirt bright against his dark green doublet. He gently brought her hand to his lips for a kiss, and the crowd sighed in delight at the gesture. Lina's heart began to beat fast, and she was thankful when he pulled out the chair. She sat down with shaky knees.

Cornelius took the seat next to her. "You look lovely tonight."

"So do you," Lina answered, then bit her tongue. "I mean... you look very... handsome. Not lovely." She giggled nervously.

"Lovely is a fine word," he said with a disarming smile. "From you, I consider it a grand compliment."

His ease made her relax a bit. She surveyed the crowd where hundreds of fairies milled about the room. Some sat at the tables, some walked around admiring the splendor, and others hovered slightly above the crowd in private conversation. Every one of them stole the occasional glance at the two of them, waiting for the big moment.

Edwina spoke with the group Lina met upon her arrival. They listened to her intently. Perhaps Lina imagined it, but Renna's eyes looked red and swollen, as though she had been crying. Renna was the only lady who did not show up to dress her. Did she not like the idea of the princess returning? Lina's skin prickled with a sense of disquiet.

"Were you able to rest and refresh? Cornelius asked, filling two glasses for them with mead.

"Yes. Until the long procedure of dressing me. Apparently, that was a multi-fairy task," Lina commented, smoothing her skirt to cover the anxiety.

"Well, the result was more than worth it, in my opinion."

His admiration only made Lina more nervous, and her stomach somersaulted. Perhaps this is what love felt like. She would have hoped for something that did not involve nausea, but what did she know of matters of the heart?

"Thank you," she replied softly.

"To us, on this special night," he said, raising his mead. They toasted, and she took a small sip, its warmth joining the tumult in her belly.

Edwina fluttered over. "After the meal, you two will kiss."

"And that will end Dahlia's reign?" Lina asked.

"I don't think so. I think you will get your wings, which you will need when you face her in battle. If all the signs are correct, the Primal Crystal and your amulet must be in the same place for her undoing. Prophecies are not always straightforward. We shall see how things unfold." She fluttered off to speak with another group waiting for her.

None of this information made Lina feel any better. When she imagined the kiss, it had been in private, not for all to witness. Not to mention, she had no idea what to expect when her wings grew. Was it messy? Did it hurt? Again, she wished for solitude.

"Please don't look so worried. Try to enjoy yourself. I will be at your side the whole time," Cornelius assured, his jade-green eyes sparkling in the candlelight.

Lina took a deep breath, and he took her hand. Music began, the soft tinkling of bells and the gentle lilt of a flute combining into a calm melody. The food was served on delicate plates and laid in front of them. Lina was unfamiliar with most of the dishes, but they were all delicious, just the same. Course after course was brought out, and the mead flowed freely among the fairies.

When all had eaten their fill, Edwina returned to the dais. An expectant hush filled the crowd. Lina and Cornelius rose.

"My dear fairies," the enchantress began. "We have long awaited this day. The day *hope* of defeating our enemy would return to us. The prophecy which speaks of our success begins with a kiss. So without further ado…" She motioned to Cornelius and Lina at her side.

Cornelius stood confidently. An expectant hush filled the room, every fairy eye fixed on them. Lina rose on wooden legs, hoping not to faint from fear, her heart pounding against her ribcage.

He raised his glass. "To the start of a new era."

Lina obliged, lifting her own. The clink of glass echoed in the room, like a lock shutting on her former life, a daunting reminder of her new life ahead. Cornelius placed his glass on the table and turned to her. Robotically, she followed. Taking her cheeks in his hands, he gently placed a long, tender kiss on her lips. She returned it as best she could, having no experience in this area. The crowd broke into applause.

A sharp tingling radiated across Lina's back. When she staggered, Cornelius quickly steadied her, his hands cupping her elbows. Two prongs emerged between her shoulder blades and pushed outward from her frame. Just when the pressure became unbearable, it stopped. The projections opened into two shimmery wings. Lina stared back at them in wonder. The fairies, who had momentarily fell silent, cheered once more.

Cornelius grabbed his glass and shouted, "To Lina, our true fairy queen, long may she rule after Dahlia's defeat!"

He fell to a knee along with everyone else while a bewildered Lina looked on. Growing wings was one thing, defeating her evil aunt another. Still, with her back tingling, she took her glass in a faltering hand and raised it. The crowd answered with a rousing cheer.

Once the couple was seated again, fairies came forward to congratulate their newly winged princess. Cornelius presided over many introductions, each stacking weight onto the yoke of responsibility resting on her shoulders. At first, she tried to remember names and titles but soon gave up. She was too exhausted from the evening's expenditures.

A commotion at the entrance caught everyone's attention. A young fairy, his clothes dirty and tattered, darted in on silver wings. He stopped in front of the dais. When he spotted Lina, fear set in his eyes.

"What is it, Alaric?" Cornelius asked.

"It's Dahlia. She knows her niece has returned. She has gathered all her forces to march on us and destroy the Resistors once and for all."

CHAPTER 33

Two days had passed since the banquet. The same planning group from Lina's first day sat in a private room around a long table. For several hours, they had debated strategy for the imminent battle. Lina felt entirely out of her depth. She was raised as a simple farm girl, not a warrior, yet they expected her to take a lead role.

"What if we recall all of our troops from the outlands?" Cornelius asked.

"They will still outnumber us," Aelin replied, twisting the ends of her long dark hair. The scouts brought discouraging information regarding the size of Dahlia's army. Clearly, the evil queen had strategized and prepared ages for this moment.

"We need more fighters," stated Dunlin, a sentiment he had repeated many times. His golden eyes flickered with determination.

"There are none," Blythe shot back, tired of making the point yet again.

"It's true," Renna conceded. She had introduced several good fighting tactics but admitted they needed more manpower. Lina was impressed with her overall knowledge of battles. The group relied on her opinion the most when plotting a course forward.

"I'm open to any suggestions," Cornelius ventured with a sigh. He tapped a quill lightly on the table while they all thought. In his tailored doublet, he looked every part the king.

"On my travels," Lina said tentatively, so far, she had offered little input. "I met several fairies and creatures who have no love for Dahlia. There are many of them out there. Perhaps we could enlist their help."

"Unfortunately, many have chosen to sit out this fight. Those who haven't are already here with us," Cornelius pointed out.

"Cowards, in my opinion," scowled Blythe. "Dahlia poisons the land. With no one to stop her, it will spread everywhere eventually, despite what those in denial tell themselves."

"Let me go and try to persuade them," Lina urged. "Some did not know my true identity when I was with them. Perhaps they would be brave enough to fight now that I have returned."

"I think it would be too dangerous to have you out in the open land," Cornelius protested. "Especially now that Dahlia is sure of your return."

Blythe, Dunlin, and Aelin nodded in agreement with the prince.

"No, I think Lina has a good idea," Renna said, much to Lina's surprise. "She is the one fairy who could unite us. Let them see her face to face. Let them hear her plea for help."

"But Dahlia—" Cornelius began before she cut him off.

"I will go with Edwina to help protect her. Plus, we will take a swallow who can easily return to warn you if there is any trouble," Renna insisted. "That is, if this is all right with you, Your Highness."

"Yes. Thank you, Renna," Lina said, grateful someone had confidence in her plan. "I would like Knox to accompany us."

With more persuasion from Renna about the positive aspects of the idea, the others relented. It was decided the three fairies and Knox would leave the day after next. Edwina was summoned and informed of the plan. She bustled off to tell Knox. Lina was thrilled at the thought of seeing him again. Since she was not yet an experienced flyer, he could carry her. She always felt safe in his company.

The meeting broke, and Aelin pulled Lina aside. "Come down to the armory first thing tomorrow. We need to fit you with your battle gear. By the way, how are those wings feeling? Still sore?"

"Where they broke through feels a little better. The wings feel fine, but they've been an adjustment, especially sleeping. And, I can't even imagine flying!"

"Well, it was quite a quick transition for you. Most of us had wings grow over the years," Aelin acknowledged. "Don't worry, soon you will be soaring among the clouds, Your Highness."

"I hope so," Lina replied as they parted ways at an intersection of tunnels.

On the way back to her room, she spotted Renna and Cornelius together in the hallway and went over to thank the fairy for backing her plan, but instantly regretted intruding. The two were obviously in the middle of a heated discussion but fell silent when they saw her.

"Forgive me," Lina said. "I only wanted to thank you, Renna, for your support."

"Yes, of course, Your Highness." Her words hardly matched the distraught look on her face.

After a moment of awkward silence, Cornelius said, "I, for one, am quite hungry. Shall we go to the hall for some dinner, Lina? No need to dine alone in your room again." He offered his arm.

"Yes, that would be nice," she replied, taking it. "Won't you join us, Renna?"

"Thank you, but I have much to attend to before tomorrow's journey." With a dip of her head, she scurried away, leaving Lina somewhat confused.

"I don't think she likes me very much," she confided to the prince.

"Nonsense. She just has a lot on her mind these days." He stared at the fairy's retreating form. "Renna is a wonderful fairy. She will come around."

He quietly escorted her to the main hall to dine, and Lina noticed he was not his ordinarily chatty self. When they entered the chamber, his brooding expression had not changed. Around different tables, fairies sat in groups eating, chatting, and laughing. To Lina's relief, the room was spacious, but not fancy like where they dined the evening of the kiss. More practical than extravagant, it served the needs of the Resistors. Some fairies watched the couple cross the room to a table set apart from the others. Blythe and another blonde fairy rose to greet them. Lina recognized him as Lorcan, the sentry.

"Mind if we join you," Cornelius asked, guiding Lina to the head of the table. Once she was settled, he took his place across from her at the foot.

"Of course not. I mean, it is your table after all." Lorcan's laugh sounded like chimes. "Showing all your manners now that Lina is here?"

"You will refer to her as Your Highness," Cornelius rebuked, and the sparkle in Lorcan's eyes was snuffed.

"I apologize to you both. I will leave you. " Crestfallen, he bowed to them and departed.

"I feel bad for him," Lina said. Servants laid the food out in front of them and filled their glasses with mead. "I didn't want him to leave, and I don't mind if he doesn't call me *Your Highness*."

"But that is your title," Cornelius remarked with none of his usual kindness. "The fairies must address you as such. If you allow them to be lax in this area, how can you expect to lead them?"

"I agree," Blythe assented, "but go easy on him. All his youthful energy and drive to fight Dahlia are pent up in this bunker. He misses flying. We all do."

"True. These last few years have been tedious for everyone. But, there is an end in sight now. How is the training going, Blythe?" Cornelius asked between bites of bread.

"As well as can be expected without much opportunity to be above ground coupled with the shortage of weapons. Thankfully, we know where to find them now, thanks to Her Highness." She nodded at Lina respectfully.

While the fairy explained some other issues, Cornelius peppered her with a few questions. Lina remained silent and absorbed as much of the information as possible. Even with the recovered weapons from Mr. Tyson and the possibility of convincing more fairies to join them, Dahlia's force still sounded impossible to conquer. A page rushed in with a message for Blythe, and she excused herself. Lina and Cornelius were alone at opposite ends of the table. So thick was the ensuing silence; Lina could have sliced it with her knife.

"How are you adjusting to things around here? Feeling any more at home?" he finally asked, coming to sit next to her.

"Not yet. But technically, this isn't home. I suppose, if we defeat Dahlia, then we can truly go home."

"Do me a favor. Please do not let anyone hear you say *if* we defeat Dahlia," he scolded. "You must say *when*. You must lead with total confidence in our success. Otherwise, we are doomed."

"Yes, of course, you are right," she stammered, tears stinging the back of her eyes. Knox had called Cornelius fickle, and perhaps this is what he meant.

Immediately, he sighed and took her hand. "I am sorry, Lina. I should not have spoken to you so."

"Don't apologize. I need you to help me lead, to have your example to follow. My arrival has been an upheaval for you as well. You have carried the burden all this time only to have me show up and need instructions like a child." She dabbed the corners of her eyes with her napkin,

"It is my honor to support you. Forgive me. I was distracted by some selfish notions tonight. But you have my word; I will be with you every minute until Dahlia is destroyed. Then, at your side when you lead our kingdom back to greatness."

"Thank you," she managed, relieved the positive version of Cornelius had returned.

He called on the servants to bring out dessert. While they enjoyed a sweet berry tart, Lina wondered what *selfish notions* had caused his foul mood.

CHAPTER 34

The following morning, Lina met Aelin and Dunlin at the armory, a complex of chambers at the stronghold's eastern edge. First, they gave their new princess a tour to update her on the Resistor's weaponry status. They passed several rooms housing breastplates, helmets, shields, and the like. Though the doors stood open, they were each mounted with a massive lock.

"We learned a hard lesson about locking up our stockpile. Several times we fled hideouts, and when we returned to retrieve our weapons, they were gone," Aelin explained.

"It seems you have Mr. Tyson in Maizeridge to thank for that. He had your supplies hidden underground and expected to make a tidy profit from it," Lina said, skirting around a pile of boots.

"We thought it was someone working for Dahlia, not that pompous idiot. I think Edwina is most eager to discuss the matter of *profit* with him." The fairy laughed.

At the end of the complex, a tall room stood open to the sky. The clink of a hammer against metal rang out in the air. Inside, the heat from the forges enveloped Lina like a stifling summer day. Fairies stoked fires, melted steel, and pounded out swords in a swirl of activity around her.

"Can I show you something up there, Your Highness?" Dunlin asked. "I can carry you."

With her nod of assent, he held her waist and soared up to the top of the chamber. While they rose, the roaring sound of water grew louder. The strong fairy landed on a rock ledge and set Lina down. Aelin landed next to her. Above them streamed the underneath of a waterfall. The smoke from the furnaces below met the cool vapor of the cascade and dissipated.

"Ingenious," Lina admired. "It disguises any presence of a forge from the world above."

"It was Renna's idea. Her incredible resourcefulness helps us tremendously," Aelin praised, shaking some water droplets from her wings.

Back on the ground, they left the clamor of the chamber and entered a well-lit room. Three tables were situated around its walls, stacks of drawings and notations cluttered their surfaces. Excited by the prospect of preparing a princess for battle, Aelin called for assistance. Several workers flew around, stacking a few breastplates, swords, and shields nearby, while another took Lina's measurements. A last one brought a large mirror which she propped against the wall.

Aelin inspected all the breastplates with care before she chose one. She laid it across Lina's chest and turned her towards the mirror while she worked on adjusting the straps. The metal shone a lustrous silvery-white, unlike the armor from the storerooms.

"What is this made of?" Lina asked.

"Rhodium. It's the armor of the queen. Beautiful, isn't it?" Dunlin said, parrying around with a sword he found.

"Yes. It is so bright. Like sunlight," Lina marveled.

"It will be a nice contrast to all of Dahlia's black obsidian," Aelin said, finally satisfied with the fit. "You there... I want a quill and paper to discuss the design."

A worker flew off hastily at the order. Aelin and Dunlin were held in high esteem here, clearly respected leaders. When he returned, she drew some intricate lines, like letters, but none Lina had ever seen. "These are symbols to ward off evil. They will engrave them on your breastplate. Your shield will have the crest of Roshall Grove."

Lina slipped the heavy breastplate off and studied the elaborate drawing. "You are putting so much thought into my armor. I hope it helps against my aunt."

"You will be the spearhead of the fight," Aelin said as she tossed her black hair across her shoulder and continued adding to her picture. "All fairies will look to you for inspiration. I want them to see a powerful warrior."

"Your mission tomorrow is important," said Dunlin, "It will be imperative to convince more fairies to join us. And, animals too," he added, putting the sword down to join them. "Dahlia will have her spiders and snakes, so whatever we can counter with would help."

"I saw her snakes," Lina whispered with a shiver. She did not think the rabbits or mice she knew would stand a chance against them.

"Yes, they are frightening to behold. And her spiders aren't much better." He wriggled his fingers at her and smiled.

"I don't know how you can make jokes about it," Aelin said, looking up from her sketching, exasperation clear in her tone.

"Aw, c'mon, Ae, there is time enough to be serious. Let us have a few laughs while we still can," her friend implored.

"Please don't be angry," Lina said. "Renna was upset yesterday. I don't want anyone else in a bad mood."

The two others shared a knowing look which Lina took to heart.

"Is there a particular reason Renna doesn't like me?"

"Of course not," Dunlin said. "She will come around."

"Yes, that seems to be a general opinion," Lina sulked. She wanted to ask more, but both fairies clammed up on the matter.

"Aelin always yells at me for not being serious enough. But would you rather be stuffy like her all the time?" Dunlin pulled a face at his friend, whose only reaction was a slight shake of her head. He grabbed a sword and poked at her.

Quick as a flash, she picked up another, and with two fast moves, had Dunlin pinned on the floor, the point touching his chest. "I may be stuffy, but I can outmatch you every time."

For a moment, they stared at each other. Then Aelin's face broke into a grin. While they chuckled, she offered her hand to help him up and went back to her sketching.

"She's right," Dunlin told Lina, putting the weapons aside. "She beats me every time. But if we can't remember how to laugh and enjoy life, what are we even fighting for?"

"There. This is the design." Aelin held up her paper, thereby changing the subject. "This will go on the breastplate. Now let's fit you for a shield. I don't know about a helmet. I think Dahlia should see your face, but I'm concerned about the lack of protection."

"I think whatever Dahlia has in store for me, the helmet won't make much difference," Lina surmised. "Let her look me in the eye."

"Spoken like a true princess," Dunlin said.

Hours later, Lina tossed and turned in her large bed. Dunlin's words played over and over in her mind. *A true princess.* Could she ever live up to that title? Many tasks lay in front of her, one more arduous than the next. If she could enlist help from those she met on her journey, and that was a big *if*, would it be enough to make any difference? Her aunt was skilled in black magic and would never fight fair. The thought of her fate and the fate of the entire Fairy World exhausted her, yet sleep would not come.

In the wee hours of the night, she dressed for the morning's journey in the simple travel clothes she arrived in. Leaving her room, she wandered around the nearly empty halls. The few fairies awake gave her way and said nothing. She came to a small circular room that opened up to the sky above. The few visible stars that glinted against the fading darkness were suddenly covered as a figure descended to the floor.

"Hello, Lina."

"Knox, I've missed you." She hugged her friend. "How did you know I was here?"

"I can't explain it. When I saw someone moving down below, I just knew it was you. Can't sleep?"

"No, try as I might; I can't fall asleep," she replied sadly.

"Here, hop on."

He flew up and out the chamber hole, straight up to the boughs of a tall rowan tree. She hopped off into his nest and stretched out against Knox's side. They spoke of the upcoming journey and reckoning with Queen Dahlia. Knox offered no false hope or magic solutions. Instead, he listened while his wing wrapped her in safety. To the steady beat of his heart, she drifted into a dreamless sleep.

CHAPTER 35

A brief panic ensued the next morning when Naya did not find the princess in her bed. Lina returned to her chambers to see the entire hallway in chaos. Scattered fairies rushed about yelling. Only when the maid spotted her, did the scene calm down, and a bewildered Lina explained where she spent the night.

"You should not wander around without telling anyone," Edwina reprimanded as she barged into the room.

"I was with Knox. I don't think I could be any safer," Lina said. *He is the only one who I feel at home with*, she thought to herself.

With her supplies packed, she and the enchantress met up with Renna and the swallow above ground. A blue sky filled with clouds as fluffy as cotton candy would provide easy travel for the group. Several fairies gathered to watch the preparations. A small Groundling crept forward and bowed before them. Something about her was familiar though Lina could not place it.

"If you by chance go to Maizeridge, would you tell my mother that I am all right?" she asked shyly.

"Delphine?" Lina exclaimed, now the resemblance to her mother obvious.

"Yes," the girl whispered, wringing her hands.

"Your mother, Cora, showed me extraordinary kindness. I will be sure to let her know you are here and how proud she should be of your efforts with the Resistors."

"Thank you," Delphine beamed and, with a quick curtsey, rejoined the crowd.

Aelin, Blythe, and Dunlin flew over, with Cornelius in the lead. They landed by the group to exchange last minute thoughts and plans.

"Good luck to you all," Cornelius said, "I look forward to your return." He raised Lina's hand to his lips and kissed it. She smiled at him warmly. They shared a lovely dinner the evening before, and Lina was happy to part with him on a friendly note.

"Hopefully, this will be a quick and productive trip," Edwina remarked, taking off into the sky.

The princess hopped onto Knox's back, who ascended after the enchantress, followed by Renna. The ground fell away beneath them, and a soft breeze wafted across Lina's face. She looked down at the waving fairies below. Aelin and Dunlin shoved each other playfully while Blythe laughed at their antics. Cornelius, however, had his eyes fixed on the sky, but it was not Lina he stared at.

"We shall see the Ephemera first, and then the Rodentia," the enchantress called back to Lina. She and Renna led the way.

"You are flying so well," Lina said to Knox. "I am glad you are better."

"Yes, Edwina was kind enough to mend my tail feathers. I'm good as new now."

To prove his point, he swooped high in the sky before dropping back behind the others. Lina, who clung to him for dear life, cried, "At least warn me if you are going to do something crazy like that!"

They stopped once in mid-afternoon to rest and refresh. Renna, well educated in flora, found them plenty to eat. She brought an assortment of food to them, including seeds for Knox. Edwina settled down in a sheltered ring of stones and laid out the food. Lina sat beside the enchantress, but the other fairy flew off and sat alone atop one of the rocks.

"Come and join us, won't you, Renna?" Lina asked, determined to win her over.

Hesitantly, the fairy flew over to settle next to the others. Edwina peppered Lina with questions about her encounter with the Ephemera. The enchantress measured what tactic would be best to use upon their arrival. Knox and Lina added their opinions at intervals, but Renna remained silent. Try as she might, Lina was unable to draw the taciturn fairy into the conversation before they were off again.

Late in the evening, they arrived in the Ephemera's territory, and Lina guided them to the large tree which stood near the stream bank. They landed in the boughs hoping to find someone. The lower branches were empty of fairies, so they began to ascend the tree limb by limb. Just when Lina thought they would find no one, an Ephemera landed in front of them, a shimmery outline against the darkness.

"Greetings, fellow fairies, what brings you to our humble realm so late in the day?" The voice, though friendly, was guarded.

"It is I, Princess Lina, rightful heir to the throne in Roshall Grove. I come seeking your assistance." She had practiced this line in her head all afternoon, hoping to sound authoritative.

"One moment," he said and disappeared. Two more fairies joined him upon his return. One held a torchlight up to the visitors' faces, and three identical fairies stared at them over the flames, which rustled in the wind.

"Hazel?" said one of them in disbelief, this voice familiar to Lina.

"Yes, Kai. I could not tell you my true identity when I was here before. Now, I return on a most urgent mission and need to speak with your queen."

The other two fairies relaxed when their companion recognized Lina was not a threat. They conversed quietly amongst themselves for a moment. Kai stepped forward. "Follow me."

High into the sky, they flew to the very top of the tree. Here, within the highest branches, an elaborate edifice stood of sticks bound with a silken thread. Lanterns with blue flames hung outside the doorway and glowed within. Kai flew over to the sentries who guarded the entrance. After a quick word, they parted and motioned the group forward.

"I will wait out here," Knox whispered, and Lina nodded.

Edwina confidently led them through the doorway into a grand chamber with polished rowan wood floors. A high slatted ceiling opened to the sky; tiny bells hung down, tinkling in the gentle breeze. The blue lighted lanterns glowed brighter inside, giving the silken walls an iridescent sparkle. Fairies lined the walls, one indistinguishable from the next, watching the guests intently. At the room's far end, on a dais, sat a beautiful fairy in an ornately carved chair. Her dark hair shimmered in the moonlight. When the three fairies reached her, they bowed respectfully.

"I am Bryla, Queen of the Ephemera. What can I do for you, Lina of Roshall Grove?" Her voice flowed as smooth as water.

"I am Edwina, enchantress of the late Queen Ivy. The true heir has returned. We have come to entreat you for help in the fight against Dahlia, who plans her final battle to seize all the Fairy World into her evil grip."

Queen Bryla rose, her large wings opening wide around her small frame. Lina could not help but stare at her beauty, magnified in the company of her identical subjects. The queen walked down to their level. "Long have we stayed out of this conflict, content to keep to ourselves and see to our own business."

"Are you not part of this world?" Edwina asked; impatience dripped from her tone.

"Yes, but I must protect the Ephemera, not endanger them in a conflict which does not involve us." She hovered slightly above the ground, her movements graceful and fluid. Against her clone-like followers, she was a powerful presence.

"And once Dahlia has defeated us, she will eventually come for you. How long do you suppose you could stand against her?" the enchantress questioned.

For a long moment, the leader was silent; deliberations clouded her eyes. "I need to discuss this matter with my council. For now, take some food and some rest. I will let you know my decision in the morning."

The guests bowed, and Kai led them out. He took them to a comfortable chamber lower in the tree, Knox perched just outside the door. Several fairies followed soon after bearing trays of food, which they set on a large table in the middle of the room. They were about to sit when a messenger entered. "The council wishes to speak with the enchantress regarding the prophecy."

Edwina headed out with him at once. Lina stood in awkward silence with Renna, who would not meet her eyes. She must find some way to earn the fairy's friendship, if not that, at least her trust. Renna held an essential role with the Resistors and would be crucial for both the battle strategy and whatever followed.

"I, for one, am famished," said Lina, sitting down at the table. "Please, join me."

To her surprise, the fairy took a seat across from her. They spent a few moments surveying the fare and filling their plates before the uncomfortable quiet resumed. Lina tried to think of something to say, but the other girl spoke first.

"I suppose this has all been very disorienting for you, thrown into this world, expected to fight your aunt and ascend to the throne." The words slipped out quietly while the girl stared at her plate.

"Yes, it has been," Lina admitted, happy to have Renna show some interest in her. "I grew up in the mortal world and knew nothing of this until quite recently."

"You have done well considering, especially once separated from Edwina. We were worried for your safety." The fairy pushed her food around the plate but ate none.

"It was a harrowing journey. There was danger along the way, but I was fortunate to meet up with many kind fairies and creatures, ones who helped me without even knowing who I was. Lucky for me, since there is so much about the Fairy World I still do not know." Lina took a small bite of fruit.

"I'm surprised no one ever told you anything. You would think they would have wanted to prepare you," Renna ventured, with a side-long glance at her companion.

"It was not until my adoptive parents passed that Edwina finally told me. Then, I learned about Roshall Grove, Dahlia, the prophecy, and Cornelius," Lina said, pleased that the conversation between them progressed.

"And how do you like him?" Renna whispered, the words stuck in her throat.

"Well, he is smart and undeniably handsome. He has been nothing but kind to me, yet..." She noticed how Renna anxiously waited for the rest. "I hardly know him, and the talk of true love seems rushed to me. But, according to the prophecy, it is meant to be, so I must trust it."

"Yes," the fairy agreed, the sadness in her voice palpable.

Renna tried to hold back tears. Confused, Lina did not know what to say. She thought of the fairy's cold greeting, of Cornelius and Renna, arguing in the hallway, of Cornelius' gaze centered on Renna, not her, when they departed—and it all made sense.

"You love each other," Lina blurted out, the thought hitting her like a bolt of lightning.

Renna froze for a moment, then nodded. Her eyes filled with so many tears; they spilled over and ran down her cheeks, leaving tiny wet trails in their wake. While happy to understand the source of the girl's sadness finally, Lina's own heart grew heavy at the situation's reality.

"Oh, Renna, I'm so sorry, I never meant to…"

"Please, Your Highness, don't apologize to me. It is I who should be sorry. Cornelius was a match for you since birth. I had no right to develop any feelings for him."

Touched, Lina took her hand. "I don't know much about love, but I do know the heart has a will of its own. You couldn't control it anymore than you could control the sun rising and setting."

"Thank you for your understanding," Renna replied, dabbing away her tears with a napkin. "I hope you don't think any less of me now."

"Of course not, I respect you. I hope we can work together. I will need you by my side if I am to defeat my aunt. If you find it too difficult to be friends, I hope we can work for the common good of the Fairy World together."

"Honestly, Lina, I wanted you to be selfish and awful. I wanted a reason to hate you. But there isn't one. I am proud to serve you, and I do hope we can be friends. She rose to go around the table and embraced Lina.

Once seated again, she said, "Now let's talk about the rest of our journey and how we can enlist even more help against Dahlia."

The two fairies sat for a long time discussing events of the past and the future. The air between them was amicable. Perhaps they would not be best friends, but they could trust and respect one another with no unspoken resentments between them. Lina felt a knot of tension disappear from her heart.

CHAPTER 36

Dahlia tapped an impatient finger on the armrest of her throne; a slithering sound grew louder in the hallway outside. Kafir and Purus entered, undulating across the floor in complete unison as though they were one being. They halted a respectable distance away and bowed their heads.

"You have returned. Finally." Her voice dripped with displeasure.

"Yes, My Queen," their voices mingled. "With news. We tracked Lina to Maizeridge."

"But you were not able to capture her." A statement, not a question.

"No. We watched a failed escape attempt by Lina and a swallow. He made it out; she did not," Kafir explained, his scales twitching with trepidation.

"Escape attempt?" Though Maizeridge was no surprise to her, this was a new twist. She sat forward to listen.

"Yes, My Queen," Purus responded. "Tyson held her against her will. The bird attempted to rescue her, but the fairy thwarted him and locked her up. Until…"

"Until *what*?"

"The s…s…swallow returned with Edwina. She rescued the girl, and they flew off. I assume to… join the Resistors." The last words, a sibilant whisper, echoed off the obsidian walls.

Silence fell heavily on the room; the tapping of the queen's fingernails echoing menacingly off the stone. Dahlia knew Tyson recognized an object of value when it came into his midst. Naturally, the fool would try to leverage her. Unless Cotswold and his crew overtook Edwina, Lina likely made it to the rebel hideout.

"We have failed you. Please show us mercy, My Queen," Kafir cried, unable to stand the monarch's menacing quiet. Both snakes lay their heads on the floor.

"Yes, you have failed me," she boomed at the two prostrate forms. "However, in the end, I decided Lina being with the Resistors was best. That will spare you— *this* time. Now leave me and see that you are better prepared the next time I need your assistance."

"Yes, My Queen, you are ever merciful," they quailed, slinking backward out of the room.

Sighing, she rose and exited through a door behind the dais. Up the circular stairs, she wound until she entered her chambers, continued to the spell room and sat before the ball of crystal. With the conjuring words, the orb clouded, then focused to reveal a young fairy standing amongst a group of Resistors. At the sight of the girl, Dahlia gasped. Had she not known better, she would swear her *dead* sister stood alive before her eyes. For a long moment, she stared at the face before a wave of her hand cleared the ball.

Deep within her, something stirred—a wistful longing buried for so many years by anger, she hardly recognized it. If only things had been different, and she and Ivy had ruled together as they planned in their youth. But life, with its unyielding cruelty, had thwarted that idea long ago.

She remembered that last night when she and Ivy struggled, the hasty trip to this very room with the Primal Stone tucked in the crook of her arm. She threw it in a bag with some important books and vials. Through secret tunnels, she made her way to the dungeon where she found Priya's cell. It was guarded, but Dahlia loosened a brick near the floor in the chamber's far corner. She pried it off, lowered her head, and whispered to Priya, "I am here to help you escape."

The old enchantress leaned down the opening, her wrists an angry red against her silver bonds. "Edwina put an enchantment on this cell. It will alert her to any magic performed here. This is beyond your skill. There will be too many of them for us to escape."

"What should I do?" she wailed desperately.

"Take my raven, Cotswold. He will bring you to the army I have gathered for us. Safeguard the stone, then return to save me."

Dahlia knew it was unsafe to return to Priya's tower, so she crept up another set of stairs where her daughter's nursery sat unused. Crossing the room, her eyes fell on the cradle. Her heart ached at the sight of it, but she cut the feeling off and focused on her mission. On the balcony, she whistled for the raven who circled down to the railing.

"I need you to take me to Priya's allies in Elderbreach. Ivy holds her prisoner. We must rescue her," she commanded, a sense of power flowing through her veins.

The bird took off at once and flew with haste to their destination, clearly familiar with the way. At last, he circled down to the ground into a clearing among elder trees. Three fairies, one older than the other two, stepped out of the shadows to meet them.

"Who are you? Where is Priya?" demanded one of the younger fairies.

"I am Dahlia. Priya is being held captive by my sister, Queen Ivy. We must rescue her and claim the kingdom for ourselves."

The old fairy stepped forward and bowed, his white beard so long it swept the ground. "Welcome, my princess, I am Icas Sepitus, and these are my sons, Nyx and Lexx. I take it our contingent did not make out well?"

"No, there was a traitor amongst them. He warned the queen and king who slaughtered them all, including the turncoat himself." She noticed how they bristled at the information.

"Well, we will not make the mistake of showing up in small numbers again. Come with us, and we will muster our forces," Nyx growled, his red hair sweeping across his eyes. Dahlia could hardly take her eyes off of him, the only other red-haired fairy she had ever seen.

They led her to a large rock with an opening at its base. Once inside, they followed a dusty tunnel, the heat inside growing with each step. Up ahead, Dahlia saw a red glow against the walls. At length, it opened to a rock shelf overlooking a large cavern. Fairies swarmed below—some training, some working the forges, some sorting gear. She marveled at the size of the army assembled there. Priya must have been planning to overthrow her parents for many years. But it was too late to regret their deaths now. They had been narrow-minded about magic and needed to be eliminated.

"We can have them ready to go before the night is over," Icas assured her, absently stroking his beard.

"There is one other thing," Dahlia said, reaching to retrieve the bag under her cloak. "I have the Primal Stone. It must be left here and kept safe."

The sons gaped at the sight of the crystal, but the father nodded his head solemnly. "My son, Lexx, will arrange for its protection while Nyx and I discuss battle strategy."

"I know the perfect spot. Follow me." Lexx leaped off the ledge, his raven black hair flowing around his shoulders. He flew down into the cavern with Dahlia in his wake.

He summoned over a group of twenty fairies on the floor, and they all followed him into a labyrinth of tunnels deep underground. When she was sure they would never find their way out again, Lexx stopped at a door of dark metal. With the murmur of a spell, it opened, revealing a small, dark chamber. A flick of his hand lit the sconces on the wall, his dark hair gleaming in their glow.

"The stone will be safe here," he said to Dahlia, who handed it over to him. He laid it gently on the floor, then sealed the door with more words. "You men will take shifts in groups of four protecting this door against any who try to enter."

"Yes, sir," they said as one.

Lexx led her back through the maze and down a final tunnel which eventually opened to the sky. He flew out with her right behind. They landed in a broad field near a large hole in the rock.

"We will wait here for the army to marshal. It won't be long now. My brother, though young, commands with the acumen of a seasoned warrior." His eyes shone with pride when he spoke of his sibling. Dahlia never had such admiration from Ivy.

In a short time, the sound of armor and marching footsteps filled the air. The soldiers filed out with Nyx at their lead. Dahlia remembered his powerful presence that day. He was a young version of the general who served her so well over the years. Row after row paraded out of the hideout; more than Dahlia could ever hope to count. Watching the legion in front of her, she realized how much faith Priya must have in her. She would not let her down.

So full of righteousness and hope she had been that day. Now in the gloomy spell room, she awaited a battle that would solidify her rule once and for all. Yet the sense of justice and faith for the future, which had buoyed her then, were emotions now long erased from her heart.

CHAPTER 31

Lina woke early to an azure blue sky filled with wispy clouds. Edwina had come in late and left early, still in talks with Queen Bryla. Whether this was good or bad, Lina could only guess. An Ephemera brought her and Renna breakfast, unrecognizable fare, but delicious nonetheless. Afterward, the two went outside to join Knox on the branch where he had slept.

"Do you know how much longer Edwina will be?" the swallow asked.

"No," Lina remarked, a gentle breeze rustling the leaves. "I guess we should just wait here."

"How about we get you flying?" Renna suggested. "It will help you in battle."

Knox flew Lina down to a slight rise. Set higher than the surrounding land, it remained dry amongst the swampy terrain. Renna gave Lina some basic flight instruction with the swallow, adding his thoughts here and there. Despite her nerves, the blue sky beckoned Lina to try. Flying was a fairy rite of passage she needed to master.

"You're flapping them a little too fast," Knox said at one of Lina's many attempts to stay aloft.

"Why is it so easy for everyone else?" she panted through the exertion.

"You got your wings later than most. They need time to strengthen. You'll get the hang of it. Be patient," Renna urged as Lina sunk back to the grass. "Watch us. Even strokes to take off, then trust the air to help you glide."

Once again, Lina took off fine. Getting up was not the problem; staying there was. Her attempts at gliding felt more like falling. In a panic, she beat her wings furiously, which tired her out. She clumsily flapped back to the earth and stood bent, hands-on-hips while sweat poured off of her forehead. Her two friends wheeled around and landed down beside her.

"It's no use. I'm awful at flying," Lina sulked.

"Get on my back," Knox instructed. Lina complied, and Knox swooped high in the air. "Now watch how I use my wings."

She noted the confident pumps followed by long, outstretched wings to glide. At his side, Renna imitated his movements to a lesser degree with her smaller wings. "The trick is to stay relaxed."

"Try it now while we are up here. Don't worry. I won't let you fall," Knox insisted at Lina's worried frown.

Her first attempts were wobbly as she tried to master the sensation with Renna there to grab her hand if she became unnerved. Little by little, she trusted the air to carry her wings along. It took a while, but Lina could soon glide with her friends for more than a few seconds at a time. The feel of the wind in her hair and the sheer thrill of being so high induced a sense of freedom Lina had never felt before. Edwina appeared on a branch in their tree and motioned them over. They flew to her and alighted on the limb.

"Come, Lina. Queen Bryla wishes to speak to you," the enchantress told her. She took Lina by the shoulders and looked into her eyes. "And don't forget, you are the rightful heir of this entire realm. She is below you in the grand hierarchy. Speak to her as such," Edwina instructed.

On the way up to the Ephemera throne room, Lina steeled her resolve. If she wanted others to follow her, she had to lead. Edwina was a tremendous asset, but Lina could not always look to her when negotiations were required. It was time for her to accept the mantle of her rank and win back her kingdom. Dozens of identical fairies lined the sides of the room when they entered. Queen Bryla awaited them, her beauty magnified in the sunlight which shone into the room. Lina strode over to her with purpose in every step. When the princess did not bow, the queen inclined her head in deference.

"I appreciate the severity of your situation," the Ephemera ruler said. "Long did our kind live in peace and prosperity under the rule of your grandparents. However, I wonder at your actual chances of defeating Queen Dahlia, who has a strong command of dark magic."

"My power lies with this," Lina held up her amulet. She noticed every eye fixed on it and continued, "And with the prophecy. The restoration of the Primal Stone is the key to Dahlia's defeat."

"A fact I am sure the evil queen is aware of. I suspect she will be ready for any attempt you make to repair the stone. Do you understand the legions of followers she has at her disposal?" A murmur of agreement flowed around the room.

"Yes, I know of her numerous followers. That is why I seek more assistance from those who oppose her." Queen Bryla's skepticism, though justified, annoyed Lina.

She looked at the fairies lining the walls, but none would meet her gaze.

"As I said yesterday, my primary responsibility is protecting my subjects from harm. The thought of charging headlong into battle against a seemingly unbeatable foe does not seem a prudent course." With these words, the Ephemera queen crossed her arms as though the matter was settled.

"You say you lived under the reign of my grandparents. How different was the Fairy World then? Were you forced to hide and shrink your realm into the space of a few trees? If Dahlia conquers me, which you assume is a given, you will not be able to keep your territory or your subjects safe any longer. She is a scourge on the land. Her desire for power is insatiable. Plight will come to you and all who did not stand with me on the heels of my defeat. There will be nowhere for any of you to hide, and you will face her *alone*. Join me now. Fight with me. Help me return the world to what it was meant to be, what it was all those years ago when my grandparents ruled." The words poured from a deep source within Lina, one she did not know existed until now. It was an earnest appeal.

Whispers flitted around the edges of the room, the Ephemera exchanging opinions. A raised hand from Bryla silenced them. For a long moment, she regarded the young princess. Her eyes, filled with years of wisdom, gave no indication if Lina's plea was successful. Edwin returned to the girl's side, placing a hand on her shoulder, while they waited expectantly for an answer.

"You speak the truth, young princess. One way or another, Dahlia will confront all. In the end, I would rather face her with you than alone. I will alert my two sisters and we will all join you."

Lina felt a bit of weight tumble from her shoulders. This outcome gave her hope for the rest of their journey. The thought of returning with little to no aid had plagued her since they set out. The Ephemera's addition would bolster their chances, and she expected more would follow their example.

"Thank you, Queen Bryla. If all of us rise as one, we can challenge my aunt."

"Your aunt… yes… somehow I had forgotten that, a sad legacy for you to carry. I knew your mother. She would have made an exceptional queen. Not only do you resemble her in looks, but you also carry her bright spirit and understanding of sacrifice. It will serve you well."

With a gracious nod of her head, Lina turned and left the room. Once outside, Edwina hugged her. "I could not be more proud of you. Well done."

"I only hope others will agree to help as well. We need every creature on our side that we can find." Lina expected the Ephemera were like a drop in the bucket next to the masses Dahlia could conjure.

They returned to the lower branch. Renna paced up and down the limb while Knox flew in small circles. When the swallow saw the pair, he landed next to Lina. Renna stopped and looked wide-eyed. "Well?"

"Queen Bryla has agreed to send fairies to our aid. She will also send word to her sisters who reign over kingdoms in the north and south, asking them to provide troops as well," the enchantress informed them with a tone of relief.

"That's wonderful news," Renna said. "You were right, Lina. Others do want to help."

"It's a good start," Lina agreed. She absently patted Knox's feathers and leaned against his side.

"You should have seen her," Edwina praised, causing Lina to blush. "Every bit the rightful queen she truly is."

"I don't doubt it," Renna said with a wide smile. "What is our next move?"

"Now we will head over to Maizeridge," the enchantress said, a wry smile on her lips. "It is time to let Mr. Tyson know what we expect him to *contribute* to the effort."

CHAPTER 38

Lina's good mood faded into dismay at the thought of seeing Mr. Tyson again. Although he could not imprison her, knowing his character, he would not want to give them any help without what he considered fair compensation. He planned to profit from this moment for so long. The thought of his cowering form in front of the enchantress gave her hope. If anyone could get him to cooperate, it was Edwina.

Queen Bryla sent Kai and Ezlyn to restock their packs. It excited both fairies that their queen opted to join Lina. According to the two Ephemera, the general sentiment supported facing Dahlia now. Stuck in the tree for so long, they yearned for their freedom. Kai gave Lina a warm embrace before parting.

They set off in the early afternoon, the sky a patchwork of hazy clouds. Lina practiced flying for brief spurts, resting on Knox's back when needed. With each attempt, her confidence grew. Renna gave her constant encouragement, which strengthened the bond between the fairies. Lina tried not to think about how things might be once they returned to Cornelius. He obviously had not wanted her to know about his relationship with Renna, though he seemed ready to walk away from it. The situation would be problematic for all of them. She clung tighter to Knox, wishing she could always have the peace she found with him.

Late in the day, they arrived at the cornfield where Edwina called out for Mr. Tyson. As expected, he was less than happy to see the enchantress, though his usual bluster had returned since their last visit. The mayor did not intend to cower this time. He regarded Lina with the contempt a fisherman bestows on the one that got away. While Tyson stood arrogantly in front of Edwina, Cora and Teagan came above ground. They greeted the princess with hugs and excitedly inspected her new wings. Lina introduced them to Knox and Renna.

"To what do we owe the very great pleasure of your company?" Tyson drawled, sarcasm overlying the politeness of his words. They stood on the same field where Cora discovered Lina on that cold winter afternoon. The withered brown stalks were now pierced with the heads of new green shoots.

"The final battle with Dahlia is at hand, and I know you have stored armor which you stole from the Resistors. We need it for the fight," Edwina said matter-of-factly.

The glint of greed filled the large fairy's eyes. "But of course. How much is it all worth to you? I am willing to give you an excellent deal."

"I will not be paying for what is not rightfully yours. Think of it as your contribution to the war effort." Though she spoke the words courteously, her intention to retrieve the weapons was clear.

"Now, Edwina, I am a reasonable fairy, but asking me to part with all my merchandise for nothing? That is too much for even you to ask." Everyone's heads bobbed back and forth between the two fairies, interested to see how the situation played out.

"You rapacious fool," Edwina barked, drawing herself up, "either you give me the equipment or I will make sure Queen Dahlia knows it is here. If you would rather work out a deal with her, be my guest." Edwina shrugged her shoulders.

Mr. Tyson stood tall, but the arrogance left his face. The threat was effective. Dahlia would take much more than just his weapons and armor. "Very well. But how do you propose to transport all of it?"

"That is my concern. Not yours," Edwina informed him, a note of triumph in her voice.

With one last scowl, he turned on a heel and stomped off. Lina hoped that was the extent of his protests. Yet, he brought up a good point. The four of them could not get the gear back to the Resistors. Edwina must have something up her sleeve, though what it was, Lina could not guess. The enchantress took Knox aside, and he hastily flew away an errand.

That evening they dined at Cora's. She was delighted to cook for her company and proudly served up heaping bowls of stew to the three visiting fairies and was happier still at the message Lina brought from her daughter. Edwina used the opportunity to glean as much information as possible from their hostess, trying to determine how many fairies still resided in the underground city. As Lina knew, there were few who remained.

"There are some things I need to attend," the enchantress announced once her dinner was finished. After profusely thanking a blushing Cora, she left with no indication of where she was going or when she would return.

The other two offered to help with the cleanup, but their hostess flatly refused. "You are my honored guests. I would not have you doing such labor. Take Renna for a tour of the city while I get things in order."

Honored guest? Quite a switch from the woman who would have let Mr. Tyson marry Lina against her will. Even so, it was hard to hold a grudge against Cora. The fairy spent her whole life deferring to whoever was in charge. She was sincerely happy for Lina and glad to see her. To her, Mr. Tyson remained a symbol of the greatness Maizeride embodied all those years ago. Cora chose not to look any deeper at the man to keep that memory alive.

They walked down the sconce-lit hallways, Renna remarked on the cheeriness of the brightly colored doors. The main thoroughfare was empty, but a light shone over the shop of the seamstress. Teagan dropped the mending she worked on to greet Lina with another hug before showing her small store to Renna. She fussed over Lina's new wings, even offered to make her a special new cloak to accommodate them. "I can have it ready by morning."

The seamstress was so excited by the prospect, Lina did not have the heart to refuse. After a quick measuring session, the two fairies were back in the main square amongst the empty benches and shuttered shops. Their steps echoed off the empty buildings, fading into the rafters high above. No other sound was heard.

"It must have been something to see when it was full of fairies," Renna commented, a thought Lina had many times.

They walked up the hill to the park; the star-studded sky opened overhead. The night air was crisp but without the nasty bite of winter. Unlike her first few times, Lina knew the exact tunnel to take out of the dozens which exited the area. They wandered down the chosen one and soon came to the small alcove where she and Knox spent so much time. A sense of calm settled over Lina, and she sat on a large pebble that had been one of her favorite seats.

"This place must be very special to you," Renna noted. "I can see it in your eyes."

"Yes, Knox was ill when I found him in the tunnel. I brought him here to heal. We spent a lot of time together and became very close." Her months here with the swallow were the most she felt like herself since leaving the mortal world. Though she loved Hazel and Felix, they were her parents. Knox was her companion, her friend.

"I can see that when you two are together."

They headed back to Cora's house, where they shared the bed Lina used to sleep in. It was large enough to fit them both easily. Edwina had not yet returned, but such was her nature, so they did not worry. In the morning, after a hearty breakfast from Cora, the two fairies went back above ground to see if there was any news. To Lina's delight, she spotted Knox atop a nearby bush at the edge of the cornfield. She flew up to him, waving for Renna to join her.

"Where were you?" she asked after a quick hug.

"I went to gather animals who were willing to join our fight. Rabbits, mice, deer, and the like, even a lynx from the mountains, agreed to come. They are all on their way here." A happy but weary look graced his face.

"That should help our fight," Lina declared.

"Dahlia has snakes, scorpions, and other poisonous creatures at her disposal. She has long been breeding them for this purpose," Renna pointed out. "She also has a number of the Herptile and Reptilia fairies on her side. They think she will give them more authority in her new order, but I doubt that. They will remain her minions."

The enemy's side was strong. Lina did not know how they would stand against her, especially since her kiss with Cornelius had done very little to bring more power to their side. Perhaps if they kissed in the presence of the Primal Stone, something more significant would happen to aid them in this daunting battle. She toyed with the amulet around her neck. Knox sensed her uneasiness and leaned closer. She laid her head against his soft feathers and felt some of the tension melt away.

"Lina! Lina! We heard you were here!"

She turned to see Madame Mouse and her pinkies scurrying across the field in their direction. The three flew down to meet them. After hugs all around, Lina introduced them to Renna. "These are the mice who saved me from captivity."

"We heard you are back to find volunteers for fighting the evil queen. My brothers and I are ready for the fight," Ari exclaimed.

"Now don't go getting ahead of yourselves, boys," admonished Madame Mouse, "Lina needs more experienced fighters."

At their crestfallen faces, Lina said, "But don't worry, when I am queen, you three have an open invitation to join my guard as soon as you are old enough."

This proclamation pleased the youngsters, and they scampered about in a playful game of war.

"I truly hope many will answer your call to aid," their mother said quietly to Lina.

"More join us every day," Lina replied, hugging Madame Mouse close. "I will never be able to repay you for rescuing me."

"Yes, you can. Defeat Queen Dahlia and restore the land," the mouse answered.

A rumble like far off thunder caught their attention. Over a distant ridge, a great mass of animals crested, Edwina flying overhead directing them. Though not a ferocious mix of creatures, there were many more than Lina expected. They marched quickly toward the field, faces full of determination. Several large stags and a lithe grey lynx brought up the rear. Even from afar on the horizon, they were massive next to their companions.

Teagan and Cora poked their head above ground, their mouths dropping open at the spectacle, and came out to stand with the others. Edwina broke away from the army and flew over to them. They stood together while the head of the animal army marched up, led by a group of giant badgers, and stopped just before the enchantress. Lina marveled at the sight. The entire forest must be emptied.

"Mr. Tyson," the enchantress yelled. His head popped out of a nearby hole, shading his eyes from the sun. "These animals will transport the armor and weapons to the Resistors. You will show them where your store is located."

The large fairy nodded, a reluctant but defeated look on his face. One badger walked over to him and waited for instructions, and Mr. Tyson led the way to his stockpile. Cora, Teagan, and Madame Mouse disappeared underground, having had their fill of excitement for the morning. The pinkies stayed to watch while they brought up from its hidden chamber and made ready for transport.

"How did you get so many to come?" Lina inquired while she, Renna and Knox studied the vast array of creatures who answered their call for assistance. "The animals want the flourishing land of the Fairy World back. They suffer as much as we do in its destruction," Edwina said, as the last of the new arrivals passed by. Voicing the sentiment of all, she added, "I only hope this will be enough to sway things in our favor,"

CHAPTER 39

The rest of the morning was a flurry of activity. The smaller animals loaded the weapons and armor into sacks for the larger animals to carry. It was an efficient operation, which Renna devised, dividing the animals into several groups for optimal speed. The other fairies spread out among the groups to oversee and troubleshoot any problems, except for Mr. Tyson, who withered a bit more while they carried each item out of the hole.

"Lina, is that you?" the girl heard a voice call as she stood in the middle of a group of squirrels stowing helmets into bags, Knox by her side.

"Zander! Zavier!" she exclaimed. The rabbits hopped over to her side. "Knox, these are the rabbits who helped me when I was lost in Cedar Knoll."

"I'm so glad to meet you. Thank you so much for keeping Lina safe on her journey," the swallow said.

"How are you?" Lina interjected. "I was so worried when I saw the snakes invaded your burrow."

"Yes, they came upon us quickly. Somehow they knew you were with us," Zander explained. "We only just managed to escape. I take it the Cyanos were not as lucky."

"No, sadly they were not. But, thank goodness you are all right," Lina said before an unsettling thought entered her mind. "Where is Zara?"

"She didn't make it," Zavier whispered, eyes on the ground. "She blocked their path so that we could escape."

"I am so very sorry to hear that," Lina cried, a lump in her throat. She hugged the rabbits in turn.

"She was the bravest of us all," Zander declared, tears in his large black eyes. "We are here to fight against Dahlia, to avenge our sister's death. We are proud to follow your command."

"And I am proud to have you at my side." Lina was responsible for their sister's death, yet they still chose to fight with her. The burden of that debt rested heavily upon her.

By late afternoon, the stockpile was transferred and ready to go. Lina made her goodbyes to Madame Mouse and the boys, who were as serious as she had ever seen them, understanding the severity of the circumstances. She gave them each a solemn embrace. Cora wept at their parting, wishing Lina all the best, and handed out basketfuls of food for the journey. When she got to Lina she said, "Your rowan box is in there too. I know it means a lot to you."

"Thank you," Lina answered, touched by the gesture.

A handful of fairies from Maizeridge joined their ranks, the younger ones who were up for the fight. Teagan was among them. She proudly presented the newly made cloak to Lina, who admired its craftsmanship. Mr. Tyson begged to be left behind to defend the city if need be, but Lina had no doubt he would flee at the first sign of Dahlia.

Renna organized the caravan for the march west, putting Edwina at the head. A determined mood radiated from the entire group as they set off. Lina, Renna, and Knox followed the animals in the sky, with Lina flying parts of the way on her own. A large number of swallows, blue jays, and even several eagles flew just behind them. In the evening, they made camp in a grove hidden by some large pines. The cargo was placed in a large pile at the center. Some animals stayed on the ground, while others climbed the pines to find their more typical habitat. The lynx paced the perimeter of the camp, a menacing sentry. Knox flew off to search the nearby area for any additional animals or fairies who may want to join their cause.

Lina and Renna sat on a bough near the top of a tree, sharing the food from one of Cora's baskets. All around them, the crowd of followers gathered food and settled in for the night. A few branches below, a group of squirrels, chipmunks, and a few fairies found a knothole big enough to accommodate them all. They entered with seeds, nuts, and some water. Soon laughing could be heard among them.

"It's nice to see all these creatures willing to help us," Lina said, happy to be on more friendly terms with Renna.

"Edwina was right. It's in their best interest. The land dies under Dahlia's grip. Barrenness spreads across the east like a plague, and it advances west even as we speak. Soon there will be no place left for them to go." Renna bit into a honey cake, the crumbs dusting her lap.

"It must have been hard. Living under Dahlia's reign," Lina said, imagining the bleak picture her friend painted. Most in the Fairy World understood this was the harsh reality of their situation.

"I never knew anything else. Since I was a small child, I trained to help defeat her. We all have," Renna stated.

Lina knew that *we* meant Renna and Cornelius. They had grown up together, bonded by this common goal—until she had arrived. Had they secretly harbored ideas Lina would never return? Would she forever feel like the interloper in her own kingdom? Was she even prepared to lead an army against her aunt's evil forces?

"I was blessed with a quiet childhood," Lina said after a small bite of cheese. "But it does not seem *that* will serve me well in the days to come."

"On one hand, perhaps not. But on the other, you understand what peace and a life without tyranny and evil feel like. You know how precious it is and have the passion for fighting and leading others in that fight," Renna asserted, her black hair aglow in the moonlight. A gust of wind carried the crumbs from her lap.

"I never thought of it like that before. That gives me some courage, but the mission at hand is so enormous…"

"Don't worry," Renna said, taking her hand. "There are plenty of us ready to assist you in any way we can."

"Honestly, I think you are more up to the task than I could ever hope to be. I just can't help feeling like there is more my presence should have accomplished. I got my wings, but nothing really came from that. I suppose it was unrealistic to think a mere kiss could bring down a powerful enemy." Lina cringed as soon as the word *kiss* left her mouth. Surely Renna did not want to be reminded of it.

"Prophecies are tricky. Sometimes their meaning is not what we expect it to be," the other girl said, choosing to ignore the kiss reference. "But, word of your return alone has rallied everyone. Look at this army we bring back with us. For the first time, many believe we have a chance to defeat Dahlia. That alone is a huge benefit."

"Renna, thank you so much. I would be lost without all your knowledge. You have been so kind and helpful, even though it would be understandable if you hated me." She squeezed the fairy's hand.

"Stop right there. I already told you I don't hate you," Renna reassured. "Even if I wanted to, you are too sweet. Look, we are all in this together. Right now, our sole focus is to bring down the evil queen and restore the lands to what they once were. You have my loyalty one hundred percent."

"And if we are successful? What then? I will always know I came between you and Cornelius." In a way, it seemed trivial to worry about that when the monumental undertaking of defeating Dahlia remained undecided. Yet, the thought lodged itself into Lina's mind from the moment Renna admitted the truth of her and Cornelius' feelings for each other.

"If we are successful, you will be My Queen with Cornelius at *your* side. This was decided long ago, and we must act as the law dictates. Life will be different in many ways, but I promise to try as hard as I can to let nothing come between you and me."

"I am lucky to have you by my side."
Lina was not sure she could be as gracious in the same situation. She embraced Renna, who hugged her back in kind. It was always a blessing to find grace where animosity might have existed. The wind swept gently across the bough, caressing the two friends as they sat together in harmony.

CHAPTER 40

The group's return to the Resistors was met with enthusiasm. With the badly needed armor and supplies, their arrival was a significant morale boost for the troops. Fairies were shown to their new quarters inside the hideout, while the animals found relatively concealed spots in the nearby woods, a copse whose edges were already withering from the blight of Dahlia. The equipment was moved to the armory for inspection and repair.

After making sure all were settled in, Lina went to her chambers. She put her rowan box in her armoire while Naya drew her a bath. There she soaked off the grime from the journey. After lighting the fire, the maid helped her into a nightgown and robe, then excused herself for the night. Lina sat alone, staring across the room. A breastplate of armor hung on a stand, the symbols Aelin had drawn etched into the bright rhodium. Tall leather boots stood on the ground in front of a shield bearing the insignia of the family. It was the attire of a warrior, but to her, it seemed like a costume. What did she know of armor and battle? Yet, all would look to her to lead the coming war.

A sharp rap on the door broke her musings. When she opened it, Cornelius smiled from the other side.

"May I?" He gestured toward the room.

"Of course," she replied, stepping aside. They had only spoken a few brief directives since her return.

She offered him the lone chair, but he declined, insisting she take it. Instead, he leaned against a low chest of drawers. Drapes of silk hung down behind him, the perfect setting for a portrait of his *handsome* likeness—flames from the fireplace cast dancing shadows on the wall behind him. Lina's stomach knotted. They had never been alone in her room before. She pulled the robe closer around her. Thoughts of Renna filled her head, of her and Cornelius together. The pair had been together before Lina showed up to disrupt their relationship.

"I would like to take you tomorrow to show you where we plan to make our stand against Dahlia. I think it is important for you to see it beforehand."

"All right," she replied, wondering why this request required a special trip to see her. Surely, it would be discussed at the meeting planned for tomorrow morning.

    The fairy was silent, looking at his feet. Lina sensed he was uncomfortable. That made *two* of them. He usually exuded confidence and smoothed over any awkwardness. Unsure what to say, she remained quiet, though the silence hung heavily in the room. When it became unbearable, she blurted, "Was there anything else?"

    "Yes, actually," he paused, searching for the right words. "Renna told me you figured out we were a couple, but please know that is in the past and will have no bearing on our ability to rule the kingdom together. My place is at your side."

    "I am truly sorry to have come between you. After all, how could you have known if I would ever return? I am sure it is hard for both of you." She was happy he chose to speak openly with her about it.

    "Ah, but that is our duty. Since birth, I was destined to rule by the queen's side." He crossed the space and put his hands on her shoulders. "We must see our destiny through, you and I. It will all work out in the end."

After a quick kiss on her forehead, his grip released. At the door, he turned and said, "We will leave tomorrow at dawn. Until then."

With a bow, he was gone. Lina sank back into the chair, her mind awhirl with thoughts. Lina never asked for this predestined fate, and the simple farm existence in her mortal life was all that she expected. Cornelius bore it all with such dignity, such unquestioning faith. He had been nothing but kind to her, but could she grow to love him? If Edwina had brought her back when they were younger, perhaps love would have developed naturally. Now, it was forced, rushed, and somewhat of a lie if she was honest. How could she ever look into Renna's eyes, knowing what she deprived her friend of? Anger rose inside her at the fairy's supposed ironclad rules. In her whole mortal life, anger had barely played a part, but it was regularly roused here in the Fairy World. She was a homesick girl with no place to call her home.

For a long while, she sat in the chair, twisting her amulet around her fingers. The fireplace sputtered and died out long before she dragged herself to bed.

***

"Just a little way more," Dunlin called back to her.

It seemed forever they navigated a tunnel full of twists and turns. Twice it became so narrow, they had to squeeze through sideways. Guards situated at strategic posts gave them updates before stepping out of the way for them to pass. Lina walked with Renna at her side. Cornelius and Lorcan brought up the rear. The mission was purely for reconnaissance, so no larger force was needed.

"Here we are," Dunlin declared, stopping in front of a small offshoot to the main corridor.

Lina peered down the tunnel. A shaft of muted light drizzled into the space from a small hole in the ceiling. Tall pointy rocks stood in a haphazard formation, like dozens of crooked teeth pushing out of the dirt. Passageways broke off in all directions.

"They form a natural maze," Lorcan explained, "an extra layer of protection for this portal. If you choose the wrong course, you could wander lost for days."

He strode in with the confidence of someone who knew how to find his way. The others followed behind. As they progressed, larger holes opened above, allowing the light to strengthen. Lina glimpsed a sky not full of sunlight, but grey clouds streaked with red and black smoke. A smell increased as well, not the fresh scent of nature but something sulfuric, almost rotten. Lorcan wound his way amid the labyrinth, with paths breaking off in all directions until the rocks in the ground tapered in both size and denseness. The party halted where they ended.

"See what Dahlia has done to our land," Cornelius said. He stepped out and stretched his arm for Lina to join him.

She took his hand and moved forward; before her laid a barren wasteland. No vibrant colors of flourishing forests or lush fields met her eyes, only blacks, browns, and grays. Were it not for the wasted remains of a few dead trees interspersed with charred clumps of grass, one would never know a thriving kingdom ever stood here. She ventured out a few paces, her companions in her wake. The rotting decay stretched on endlessly in all directions, swallowing everything in its path.

"Follow me," Cornelius said, flying up to the blackened branch of a nearby tree.

They stood together and surveyed the area. To the west, toward the castle of Roshall Grove, ash and smoke grew heavier, a red tinge on the edge of the sky. Low rumbles of thunder sounded in the distance, where the horizon converged in blackness. Behind them, far to the east, the devastation diminished a spot of green land against a blue sky barely visible to them.

"This is somewhat of a mid-point between the castle and our hideout," Cornelius informed her.

"So much destruction," was all Lina could murmur at her surroundings.

"Yes," he agreed sadly. He gazed around for a moment before returning to the matter at hand. "From a tactical standpoint, it will not be possible to sneak up on her in any direction. She will see us coming from far off. This will probably be as close to the castle as we get before she intercepts us. But, fear not, your armies are ready. We have long prepared for this battle."

Lina nodded at his assessment, never taking her eyes off the darkness in the west. The black turrets of the castle stretched into the grey sky like the menacing horns of a monster. *Once*, this unimaginable wasteland was home to her family and their subjects. *Once*, fairies lived in peace and prosperity. *Once*, the verdant land flourished in beauty. But no more. Now, hatred took root, leaving an ever-growing trail of devastation that would eventually swallow all the Fairy World in its gloom.

From somewhere deep inside Lina, a resolve grew. Her parents' people, *her* people, deserved better than this cruel queen. Darkness would not prevail if she could do anything to stop it. She was ready to claim her destiny and return the kingdom to what it should be for everyone and all who came after her.

"It is time for me to face my aunt once and for all."

The words had barely left her lips when a deafening clap of thunder roared through the air.

CHAPTER 41

"There, My Queen," the servant said, securing the last buckle. "You are ready."

A window in the throne room served as her mirror. Dahlia had not thought armor necessary—the battle would be so uneven, an easy victory—but watching the engraved snakes swirl across the dark background of her breastplate, she conceded it added a menacing touch. She should look the part, after all.

"The General will alert you when he sees their approach," the servant informed. He polished her helmet one final time and set it down at the base of her throne. "I'll leave it here in case you change your mind."

"Go," she mumbled with the wave of a hand, and he scurried from the room.

The helmet would not be necessary. Dahlia wanted Lina to see her face and know who the *true* queen was before killing her niece.

The latest news that the Resistors planned to march on her was still fresh in her mind. The sheer audacity of it still had her fuming, though strategically, she could not have asked for a better development. Flushing them out of their lair would have been far more complex than facing them on open land. When Dahlia was younger, she might have admired their bravery, but time had taught her foolish courage was, more often than not, tantamount to suicide. Perhaps they were as weary as Dahlia with the many years of waiting and wished for a swift conclusion.

On a nearby table, the Primal Stone glowed under the edges of its protective cloth. *Today*, it would finally be restored, its full power available to her. *Today*, the entire Fairy World would be forced to bow down before her. *Today*, she would have her final vengeance on her sister.

And what of this prophecy Edwina spoon-fed to everyone all these years? That through the power of true love, the girl would defeat her? If Dahlia's life had taught her anything, it was love would never conquer strength. Her magic was potent, cultivated through years of focusing her malice and the will to dominate. Nothing could rival such power.

She strode to the window where she viewed her army amassing. Most of her soldiers operated like well-oiled machines with years of training for this *very* day.

They would be bolstered by the newcomers who worked hard these last months. This massive unit did not include the number of creatures she could summon through long practiced spells. They would overwhelm the enemy in a matter of moments.

So unlike the last battle fought here at the palace. Dahlia could recall the exact feel of the wind on her face the day she marched Priya's army to the gate. Peace had graced the kingdom for so long, Ivy and Theros were ill-prepared to deal with such an attack. Their troops were not ready for the battle against seasoned fighters. The ground shook as Dahlia's legion broke through the gate. Her men burst through their first line of defense like a child sweeping away toy soldiers with his fist. Her minions swarmed across the grounds in all directions, a seething mass of bodies chopping and hacking as they went. Dahlia felt the panic ripple through the kingdom at that moment, and she savored it.

The slaughter through the streets was swift and precise, cutting a direct line to the palace. Try as they might, Ivy's army was no match for the evil attackers. Well-versed in fire spells, they had the city aflame in a short time. The smell of smoke mixed with the splatter of blood and cries for mercy. There would be none from her.

Too long had the citizens shunned Dahlia, whispered of her evil nature. They turned her into what she was, and now they would pay.

Dahlia smiled at how easy it was. First, she would make her sister surrender the throne, and then she would free Priya. Together they would establish her reign. She marched up the stairs to the main palace entrance, a field of bodies strewn in her path, bright red splotches staining the pure white walls. Triumph rose in her with every step... until she saw it. At the front of the entrance, a long spike was impaled in the ground, a gruesome detached head stuck to its end. It was Priya. She was too late.

Her anger crystallized as she crossed the threshold into the castle. Nyx and Sepitus came to give her a report. "King Theros is barricaded in the throne room, but we have word that Queen Ivy and her enchantress have fled."

"You deal with Theros and whatever rabble remains. Leave none alive who will not pledge absolute loyalty to me. I will take a division with me to find my sister." She needed to retrieve the shard from the Primal Stone, confident her army would prevail in her absence.

Astride Cotswold's back, she took to the skies with a small detachment of soldiers. Her prey could not have gotten far. Ivy, now heavy with child, would slow their progress. There was nowhere for them to hide. Soon they were spotted below, near the entrance of a tunnel. Dahlia and her troops circled to the ground. Only a few guards accompanied the enchantress and queen. Edwina signaled them to continue on with Ivy while she turned to block access to the path.

"Give her up," Dahlia ordered, alighting from the raven's back.

"Never," the enchantress replied, squaring her shoulders against the oncoming threat.

"It is pointless now. There is no kingdom for Ivy to return to. Accept your defeat. Hope is lost."

"No, Dahlia, hope remains with her daughter. Ivy has the enchanted shard of Primal Stone. It will go to her daughter. She will be your downfall. All fairies will know of this prophecy. They will loyally await her return." Edwina held herself tall, despite her shaky voice.

"Do you think I fear one child? Do you think she alone could conquer me?" She thought of Priya's army, who at this moment overthrew the palace.

"She will not be a child forever. She will grow, and she will learn to love. It will fill her heart. *Love* will be your undoing. With the kiss of true love, you will fall."

Dahlia scoffed, yet inside, a tiny seed of doubt formed. Defeated by love? The image of Priya's severed head, her mouth lolling open, eyes wide with terror, flashed across her mind. She had loved the enchantress, and that love had gotten her nothing. Hate was where her power was spawned, what made it thrive.

"Enough talk. Get her," Dahlia commanded.

Her guards advanced, but Edwina threw up her hands. An explosion of bright light sent them all staggering back. By the time they recovered, Edwina was gone, and the entrance covered in fallen rocks. Dahlia removed them one by one using magic, a slower process than she hoped. Once the tunnel came into view again, she stepped in. "After them," she commanded.

Eventually, they had caught up with their quarry. Dahlia made short work of her sister, but Edwina had delivered her sister's child and escaped, the ring of dust a remnant of the portal to another world. Though she did not know when, Dahlia was sure Edwina would bring the girl back one day—a day she would be ready for. She returned to her new throne, secure that eventually, vengeance would be hers.

"Excuse me, My Queen," a voice interrupted her thoughts. "The enemy has been spotted on the horizon."

Dahlia turned to the door. After all these years, it was time to finish this girl and her enchantress once and for all.

CHAPTER 42

Mustering the troops did not require much time. As Cornelius said, the fairies had trained for this war for many years. They received an additional boost when Queen Bryla and her two sisters arrived with a sizable army behind them, the Ephemera eager to stand with their Hirundo brothers. The queens had spread word far and wide, and only one day behind them, a multitude of other fairies and animals responded to their call.

"Those over there with the colorful wings are the Lepidae," Renna informed Lina, pointing to a group whose wings resembled butterflies. "And those are the Columbidae." Lina admired a group of grey-bodied fairies accompanied by hundreds of doves.

Besides the Volants and a large group of Cyanos, just as many Groundlings answered the call. Rodentia and Arboreas also arrived from far-flung corners of the realm. In all, the new arrivals nearly doubled their forces. The Hirundo dispensed armor and equipment to all who needed it, and the extensive stock provided by Mr. Tyson was invaluable. Knox and his fellow swallows saw to all the animals' needs. Organizing the army was an enormous undertaking that Cornelius and Renna pulled off effortlessly. All Lina could do was stand and watch. She was no match for the couple's battle savvy. The morning before they left, Lina sat high on a tree branch, watching the army assembled in a large open field. A rush of wind touched her cheek as Knox roosted on the branch beside her.

"It is quite a sight," he said, of the orderly groupings of fairy and creature.

"Yes, Renna and Cornelius are amazing. They included me in all decisions, but we all know they could do it without me." She hung her head.

"It is your presence that will be important, Lina. You are the lightning rod for this army," Knox reminded her. He edged closer to nudge her with his forehead.

"I know and I will lead with all my heart, but if we survive this, can I be a *true* leader to all these fairies? It was never something I wanted or asked for. Sometimes I wish you, and I could just fly away from here and live together in peace." Tears stung the back of her eyes. The security of the childhood cottage from the mortal world flitted through her mind, then slipped away.

"Many must rise to become what they never asked to be. You are kind and honorable, exactly the qualities a good leader needs. And, I will be here to help and comfort you in times of trouble."

"Thank you, Knox." She hugged him close while a soft breeze blew through the bough.

A bright sun dawned in the pink sky, a clear, unspoiled morning that belied the magnitude of the day. Today the war would be decided one way or the other—troops assembled for the march to the palace, the entire encampment somber and determined. Lina stood in her room while Naya secured the breastplate across her back to not inhibit her wings. The buckle tightened shut against her fluttering heart.

"There you go," the girl said, pleased with her efforts. "You look every inch a queen."

"Thank you, Naya. Now go make yourself ready."

"Yes, Your Highness." With a quick curtsey, she left, her cheeks aglow with the excitement of the impending battle.

Lina turned to the mirror, her finger anxiously toying with her amulet. The fairy in the reflection looked dressed for battle, but her face lacked the color and enthusiasm displayed by her maid. Whether Naya was naturally naïve or happy to finally have the battle fought, Lina could not say. The weight of expectation pitted in her stomach. Somehow she must find the conviction to lead this army, even if it were to doom. She must exude all the confidence they needed from her. After a few deep breaths, she tucked the amulet under her breastplate and went to join the others.

Cornelius and Renna escorted her to the front of the troops where Edwina awaited. Together, the two experienced fairies situated everyone into the agreed-upon formation. The fairies would lead with the birds above them and the remaining animals to follow behind, pulling catapults and other such heavy weaponry. It would be one long, straight march. Lina watched the pair work with such unison and precision. It was like they were of one mind. Her role at the moment was to be the figurehead, nothing more. Knox flew to her side, and Lina's heart swelled at the sight of him. She placed her head against his warm feathers.

"Edgar and I will be among the swallows flying just above you when we make our approach," he informed her.

"Good. It will be a comfort to know you are there." When the fighting was done, if they were lucky enough to prevail, she knew he would support her as she navigated the unfamiliar terrain of leading the Fairy World. The slim hope of success was all she had to hold on to.

    The troops set out just after sunrise; pink clouds still clung to the horizon. Their pace was not fast but orderly and efficient enough to make good progress. Most of the Volants chose to fly overhead of the Groundlings and animals. Queen Bryla offered her best Ephemera scouts for surveillance, and they flew up ahead of the leading group. Lina's spirit bolstered at the sight of many different fairy orders mixed together in the air and ground. Slowly, grass and plants gave way to the lifeless tones of dirt and stone as the verdant land faded to shades of yellow, then brown. The trees loomed leafless overhead, spindly branches reaching for the sky. The horizon ahead was dark, thick with black clouds which swallowed up the sunlight with every passing step, and hot gusts of wind burst across the barren ground. Except for a black speck circling high above in the grey sky, Lina's army had yet to meet or be challenged by their enemy. Though Dahlia had not confronted them, Lina surmised she was keenly aware of their approach.

After what seemed like miles of nothing to Lina, a solid form started taking shape—at first only a smudge on the horizon—the walls around the castle of Roshall Grove. It grew more menacing as they neared, a massive structure of pure black obsidian glimmering in the flashes of lightning which increased as they advanced closer. Intermittent bolts cracked down around it. A wide black gate, with two giant metal snakes coiling around each other across the front, stood firmly closed in the center. Lina had trouble reconciling this edifice with the beauty and splendor of the white palace in the picture of Cora's book.

Across a wide-open plain, littered with dead tree stumps and broken rocks, Lina's army marched, the air becoming heavy with dust. The sound of footsteps and armor echoed off the dark fortification like beats of a drum, fusing with the rolling thunder. The heat increased with every stride they took. And still, they met no resistance.

Twenty meters before the wall, they halted. Lina finally glimpsed the enemy and knew she could not waver. Fairies armored in black manned the parapet, swords at the ready. Above them, more fairies hovered with crossbows which they aimed but did not discharge.

While Lina's fighters were a diverse group, all of Dahlia's fighters had the same disfigured look. If not for the wings, it would be impossible to tell Groundling from Volant as they stared down at their foes with glowing yellow eyes.

Both sides stood for long moments in the tense silence, only the ever rumbling thunder to be heard. As planned, Cornelius flew out slightly ahead of their army. With a commanding voice, he declared, "Dahlia, we come to take back what is ours. Surrender to the rightful heir of the Hirundo."

A menacing laugh filled the air from somewhere behind the wall. The metal snakes on the entry slowly unwound from one another, and with a loud groan, the gates opened. In the void where they stood, a dark figure came into view.

CHAPTER 43

She was smaller than Lina imagined. Her black breastplate scrolled with snakes that slithered in endless circles around its front. Long hair, the red of deep blood, flowed around her face before cascading down her back. Here it joined a raven-colored cape that pooled on the ground around her. Her eyes were the same eerie yellow of her followers, unnerving against her pale face. Though she was small, she cast a significant presence.

Two large snakes flanked her, diamond-marked heads raised from their slithering bodies, tongues flicking in and out with each step their master took. Lina recognized them as the snakes who had waylaid Edwina and attacked the rabbits. Kaffir and Purus, she would never forget their names. Behind them, a large army assembled but halted before setting a foot outside the gate.

Dahlia continued on, stopping a few meters in front of them. Her eyes passed over Renna and Cornelius, lingered on Edwina who held her stare, before coming to rest on Lina, who felt her aunt's gaze like a physical touch. Up and down, Dahlia regarded her niece. Lina felt warmth under her breastplate as the queen's eyes fixed on the spot where the amulet lay. The stone pulsated against her chest, which elicited an enigmatic smile from her aunt, who lifted one arm. An object floated out from beneath the folds of her cape. The broken Primal Crystal hovered at Dahlia's shoulder.

    The chain around Lina's neck strained as the shard pulled toward its larger self. She stumbled forward. Cornelius grabbed Lina's arm while Edwina flew to her side. Together they held her firmly in place.

    "You look much like her. Your mother, that is," Dahlia said, her voice a deep hum in the echoing thunder.

    "You mean your sister? Your twin? The woman you killed without mercy?" Lina shot back, anger flaring inside of her at the mention of the mother she never knew.

    "Ivy was weak, as you are, I suspect. In the end, you will die as pitifully as she did." She crossed her arms as though bored with the entire conversation, her certainty of victory visible.

    Edwina, unable to bear another word against her dearest friend, exclaimed, "It is you who are pitiful, Dahlia. Usurping a crown not meant for you, killing the land, leading your kingdom into darkness. Was it worth the life of your sister? Your own flesh and blood?"

The evil queen waved her hand dismissively, her merciless laugh again piercing the air. "Edwina, by hiding this girl, all you did was to prolong the inevitable. You thought a silly prophecy would help defeat me, but she has been kissed, she has her wings, and yet, here I stand."

At these words, Cornelius swung Lina toward him. He took her face in his hands and kissed her passionately. She kissed back, panicked; desperation threatening her mind. Lina willed something to change inside her, for love to grow for Cornelius, for her to become the warrior needed to defeat her aunt. Nothing happened. Hope faded from Lina's heart as Cornelius released her.

"Please tell me you don't still believe in that *silly* prophecy, Edwina?" the enemy taunted. "Even now when your defeat is imminent?"

"We have goodness and right on our side," the enchantress proclaimed. "We will prevail."

The queen raised a hand and whispered some words. The pull of Lina's amulet ripped her from Cornelius' side, dragging her close to her aunt. Dahlia muttered under her breath, and with another sweep of her arm, the Primal Crystal formed a circle of light around them. Lina heard a click as the glowing light closed like a cage, rendering her immobile inside the light with her aunt. "Oh, really? And your ragtag little army—will they stand against this?" Dahlia sneered.

She held out her arms, incantations of mysterious words tumbling from her lips. The ground behind her cracked in numerous places, and from the fissures, many spiders and scorpions swarmed. An audible gasp ran through the Resistor's army. From the sky, a dark cloud emerged, racing closer and closer until they could see it was not a cloud at all, but hundreds of bats, their fangs bared and ready.

The attack was as fast as it was ruthless. Lina's fairies fought valiantly but were no match for the host of evil creatures. Dahlia's fairies assailed them from atop the wall with their crossbows. All around her, fairies fell. Some were pulled into the sky by the bats, who devoured them in flight. The swallows swooped down against them to no avail. On the ground, those not stung or maimed by scorpions and spiders were locked in combat with Dahlia's soldiers, who marched through the gate in the wake of the evil creatures.

Renna and Cornelius battled back to back, their swords thick with black blood as the enemy surrounded them. Edwina flew overhead, casting spells to aid their fighters while trying to stay out of the grip of the bats. Lina frantically attempted to join the fight, but she could not escape Dahlia's circle of light. All around them, the battle raged. The Resistors had been naïve when it came to assessing Dahlia's true powers. It would be their doom.

"Stop," Lina called out in sheer desperation. "Fight me, Dahlia. Fight me *one on one* for the title of Queen."

Her aunt raised a hand and all her servants froze. "You challenge me to a fight? And the conqueror wins the kingdom?"

"Yes," Lina said. "If you win, the kingdom is yours. All I ask is that you spare the lives of my people." She knew her aunt would win either way, but hoped facing her in battle *alone* would be too enticing to pass up—a final show of Dahlia's power against her sister.

For a long moment, Dahlia stared at her niece; calculations raced across her face.

"Agreed."

CHAPTER 44

The circle of light extinguished. Dahlia's army of fairies and creatures drew back behind their queen. Edwina grabbed Lina's arm and tried to pull her back. Lina took a few steps and then explained the agreement she and Dahlia made.

"No, Lina! She will kill you," the enchantress cried.

Renna and Cornelius, dripping in sweat and blood, flew to her side. Queen Bryla and her sisters joined them. Lina surveyed the carnage surrounding her. Lorcan lay dead nearby, a sword wound in his chest still gushing. He was one of many whose corpses littered the field around them. But it was the sight of Naya, a scorpion sting on her neck, with lifeless eyes still looking at the sky that set Lina's resolve the most.

"We can't let you do this," Cornelius echoed the enchantress. "You cannot defeat her."

"I must do this, or she will kill all of you down to the last fairy. This is the only way to ensure any of us survive."

"There must be another way," Edwina insisted.

"There is no other way."

The silence this statement met proved they all knew the truth.

"The prophecy may still hold some truth," Lina told the distraught group. "Perhaps it gives me a protection we cannot see."

"You are a brave woman," Queen Bryla said. "My sisters and I are honored to have called you *our* queen."

They each kissed Lina on the forehead.

Renna's eyes filled with tears. She embraced Lina. "You are a true queen and a true friend."

Cornelius hugged her tightly. "I only wish there was more I could have done."

"You must look after our people when I am gone. Find a safe land for them to settle in," Lina whispered.

"As you wish, My Queen," he choked out, then held a sobbing Renna in his arms.

Edwina enfolded Lina in her arms. She had no words, but her body was wracked with silent tears. The enchantress was loath to let her go, but Lina finally pulled herself away.

She took up her shield to face her aunt. Dahlia removed her cape and laid it on the ground behind her—the Primal Crystal moved to hover just above it. With a deep breath, Lina took a step toward her. Every fairy, every creature, even the land itself, was completely still, waiting as Lina raised her weapons.

Dahlia hurled a lightning bolt. Lina jumped from its path. She deflected the next two with her shield, moving closer to her aunt each time. Lina reached for the dagger strapped at her waist. Her hand gripped the hilt in anticipation of the strike she would make on the evil queen's neck, one of her only exposed parts. When she was only a step away, Dahlia shot another bolt. This time Lina deflected it right back at its originator. Her aunt buckled as the bolt rebounded off of her. Lina saw her chance. She lowered her shield and raised the dagger.

Her opponent spun, holding up her hand. Lina froze in place. The amulet around her neck slid out of her armor, the chain pulling toward the Primal Stone. She wanted to grab it, secure it back under her breastplate, but her body was numb to any command. Dahlia raised her other hand with a triumphant smile and shot a full force bolt at her niece's chest. The chain broke. The stone fell to the ground in front of where a mortally wounded Lina collapsed. With the last of her life force, she prayed her people would remain safe. Then her eyes went dark.

For a moment, no one moved, frozen in shock, until, quick as a flash, Renna ran forward and grabbed the necklace.

"Get me that stone!" Dahlia yelled as Renna sprinted back to Cornelius.

The brave fairy's action roused the Resistors, who tried to aid her escape while all of Dahlia's servants descended on them. Fighting renewed all around. Fairy fought fairy, rabbit and mouse fought snake and scorpion, birds fought bats. The large deer trampled forward with the lynx at their flank to rescue Renna and the amulet.

Away from the battle, in the black sand, Lina lay alone, still as a shadow. No one had time to notice her, nor did they see the broken-hearted Knox. He flew to Lina's side, laid his head against her, the same way she mourned him in the tunnel all those months ago. "Rest well, my beautiful Lina. I will love you always." He kissed her soft cheek, still rosy even in death. A tear dropped from his eye and fell onto her face.

A loud rush of wind raced through the air. The Primal Stone flew across the sky, stopping over the spot where Lina lay on the ground. At the exact moment, the shard of stone from the amulet burst from Renna's hand—with a gasp, she tried to grab it, but it soared out of reach. The fighting ceased as all eyes followed it in mesmerized silence. The amulet shard broke from its bindings and sailed to its counterpart, where it snugly locked itself into place.

Bright prisms of light shone down from the Primal Crystal onto Lina. Her body twitched, and Knox hopped backward in amazement. Lina lifted off the ground amid the blinding rays, and her fairy wings suddenly grew large as blue feathers sprouted from her head and back. Her breastplate dissolved, only to be replaced with red feathers. Lina's nose and mouth morphed into the shape of a beak while her legs shrunk to thin stems, with her feet morphing into long talons. When the bright light faded, she floated to the ground, the Primal Stone landing at her side. Lina's eyes fluttered open, her sight the same yet somehow different, and her body felt foreign. In confusion, she looked around, her gaze landing on Knox.

"Lina?" he half-whispered.

"Yes, Knox. It's me," she replied, the act of speech strange in her throat.

"Lina… you're a swallow."

CHAPTER 45

And so the prophecy was fulfilled, though not in the way anyone imagined. With the kiss of true love, Lina grew her wings, and the Primal Crystal was restored. The moment it became whole again, the evil spell was broken, and Dahlia's powers disappeared.

The obsidian walls transformed to shining ivory, a gleaming rhodium gate with Lina's family crest at its center. Inside, darkness melted from the castle, revealing pure white marble now glowing in the sunlight, where the smoke had evaporated into an azure sky. All around the battle carnage, the earth sprung to life. Grass grew, trees burst into leaf, flowers bloomed, and a clear stream wound its way across the field.

Dahlia's fairies scattered, frightened, and confused by the burst of energy. With a groan, the cracks in the ground sucked all the spiders, scorpions, and bats into its gaping abyss before sealing shut. Kaffir and Purus turned to stone, which crumbled to dust. The evil queen watched her army disappear, a look of disbelief on her face at the turn of events. She tried to cast a counterspell, to no avail.

Lina's army was slow to react, watching the transformation in amazement. When they finally processed everything, Dunlin yelled, "All hail, Queen Lina!"

The surviving fairies and animals rejoiced at their victory. Edwina flew to Lina's side, Renna and Cornelius right behind, eyes full of wonder. The enchantress reached out and touched Lina's new wings. "Well, I'll be," was all Edwina managed to say.

"Lina, do you feel all right?" Renna questioned, concern filling her face.

"Yes," she replied, the sensation of speech through a beak still new to her.

"You have vanquished Queen Dahlia," Cornelius, ever the soldier, said. "We await your orders on how to proceed and what to do with her."

All heads turned to their defeated enemy. She stood alone in a field now rife with the nature she had held at bay, bewilderment etched on her face. Her dominating aura faded with the crystal's repair, and Lina noted how small and fragile she looked. Dahlia's gaze fell on the small group, her expression hardened to hatred. The moment had come for Lina to avenge her mother's death, to show no mercy to the one who had mercilessly killed her parents and usurped her kingdom. Yet, this seed of revenge died before it could bloom in her heart. She flew to the top of a high stone and addressed the assembly.

"Today, we celebrate our victory," she began to rousing cheers. "But it has not been without sacrifice. Bring our wounded inside the castle where they can be tended and see to our dead. Make sure they are buried with the honor they deserve," she announced

"As for Dahlia, there has already been too much killing, too much evil. I will not start my reign with bloodshed. Take her to the highest tower. There she will remain imprisoned, her magic now nullified by the Primal Stone's reunification. Guard her against any chance of escape." After the proclamation, she flew back to the group.

"All will be as you wish," Cornelius replied. He and Renna flew off to fulfill the request. At their orders, fairies sprang to life to complete their tasks.

"We have much to discuss, Edwina," Lina said, taking the enchantress aside. "But first, please go retrieve my mother's body. I saw her remains in that tunnel the day we arrived, and I will not have her rest there alone forever."

"Of course, Lina. It would be my honor."

"And now, Knox, I think I may need another flying lesson."

While the enchantress flew off, Lina spread out her new bird wings. They certainly seemed more substantial than the fairy wings she had just learned to use. Knox urged her into the sky, where she was happy to discover how easy it was to fly. They soared up and down across the great expanse of blue, landing at last on a high turret of the castle far above the healed land.

"So, this was unexpected…" she said.

"Yes," he agreed. "Though I cannot say I am unhappy about it."

"Nor I. It makes sense and feels right to me. You are the one I truly love."

"And I love you, Lina."

The sun shone brightly, a cool breeze wafted the newly altered flag over the castle. Lina felt a freedom she never experienced before. She reveled for a moment in the exhilaration before the weight of her responsibilities landed squarely on her shoulders. The fairies who bustled below were her subjects. The re-establishment of the kingdom was her priority, her fate, and she must see it through.

"I did not know how I could ever be the leader these fairies need, but now, it's even more complicated. Am I still supposed to be their queen now that I am a swallow? It is unprecedented." She looked down at her new feathers in wonder.

"I have no doubt you will be a fair and just ruler whatever form you take." As always, Knox believed in her more than she believed in herself.

"And Cornelius, what of him? He was to rule at my side. This is probably not what he had in mind."

"Be patient, Lina. You have only just transformed. Perhaps the answers will become clearer with the passing of a little time."

"Thank you, Knox. You always make my heart feel better." They laid their heads together.

He was right. Now was not the time for hasty decisions. Clarity would come. The next few weeks were spent establishing order in the kingdom, now freed from her aunt's evil grip. Those who perished during the battle were buried together. A special memorial was constructed over the gravesite so their sacrifice would be remembered. Troops led by Renna routed out any remaining creatures with loyalty to Dahlia. The few they captured were imprisoned. Edwina led a council formed by Lina to institute leaders for each fairy order throughout the kingdom. Everyone was to gather in Roshall Grove for Lina's coronation.

One day, after a morning of activity, Lina flew into the throne room. Perched in the rafters high above, she looked down at the chamber of white marble, sunlight shining off its walls. Her newly crafted throne of rhodium had the Primal Stone embedded at the top of its high back. Sunlight shone right through it, casting a myriad of rainbows on the floor. And though she knew her heart should be whole at this sight, instead, an empty sensation filled it. There was a whisper of air, and Knox landed next to her.

"Impressive," he noted, eyes scanning the room.

"Yes, I suppose it is."

"But you are not happy." It was a statement, not a question.

"I don't know. I should be, but I am still confused about how to proceed, how to best rule the fairies. None of this feels right to me. I'm too big to even fit on that throne. Look at me. I hardly fit in with my own subjects."

"Granted, this is a unique outcome, but you have Edwina to guide you," he said. "She knows this kingdom and its histories better than anyone."

"True. But, there are pieces of my aunt's story I need to understand to move forward. Does that make sense?" The questions ate at her insides every day.

"Yes, it does. Dahlia took much from you, and you deserve answers. But, realize that she may not be willing to give them to you."

With those words, Lina flew out of the throne room into the sky. She circled the highest turret, soaring all the way to its peak. There she landed on the railing of a small balcony, the only outside access her aunt had from her prison. The lone doorway was too small for Lina to fit through, her bird form dwarfing the small terrace. While she debated whether to call out, the door opened, and Dahlia emerged.

"I thought you might pay me a visit," the ex-queen announced, stopping in front of her niece. Once again, Lina marveled at how tiny she was, given the reign of fear she had imposed for so many years. "Come to gloat over your victory?"

"No," Lina answered truthfully, the thought of reveling in glory the farthest thing from her mind. "I came to ask you *why?*"

"Why what?" her aunt retorted, eyes narrowed in suspicion.

"Why you betrayed your sister, your people, and your kingdom? Was it worth it?"

"Well, clearly not since I am now your prisoner," she replied blithely.

"That is not what I meant. I want to know what happened inside your heart? What hurt you so badly that evil seemed your only option?"

For a moment, Dahlia stood speechless, a flood of emotions playing over her face that she managed to distill down to one—anger. When she found the words, they tumbled out in a torrent.
"Because I was mistreated at every turn. Not just by my parents, but by life. Three minutes. That is all that separated Ivy and me at birth, but she inherited it all, and I nothing. My parents saw to her future, but not mine. Then I found Priya and showed an aptitude for her arts, and again, I was disregarded… swept aside."

"But Priya was evil," Lina interjected, remembering the lessons in fairy history she had received since arriving here.

"No. That is what they would have you believe, but spells are not good or bad by nature. Only the fairy casting them can choose their purpose. Many could have been used to great benefit, but no one would listen. Then, Ivy was betrothed to Theros, who further tried to drive a wedge between us. My sister! We could have ruled together to the advantage of all, but no one would listen. They would only honor the days-old laws without acknowledging another way that may be better suited to rule. At every turn, fate conspired against me. Alone and abandoned by all I believed in, I forged my own path." She finished her tirade, a grim determination set on her tiny face as she awaited a response.

"I'm sorry," Lina said softly.

"What?" Dahlia barely whispered.

"I'm sorry that you felt so forsaken and alone. It must have been difficult."

Dahlia's eyes narrowed further. The years had taught her not to trust kind words, as they were usually followed by cruelty. She waited for the blow from her niece, but it never came.

"I was fortunate in my childhood," Lina continued. "My mortal parents were nurturing and thoughtful. I never felt alone in the world. Until I got here…"

"Your mother and I were so close once—her the light, me the fire. You looked so like her as a fairy. Simply beautiful." The words tumbled out of Dahlia's mouth before she realized she even thought them.

"Not so much now," Lina remarked and observed the ruffle of her new feathers.

"No, I suppose not," Dahlia conceded. "Not the ending either of us foresaw."

They both sat silently, absorbing the emptiness of unmet expectations.

"And what of me, Niece? Execution? You are the queen now. It is your decision." She expected no less of a fate from this pitiless world.

"I'm not sure. You are the only link to my past, my own flesh and blood. This weighs heavily on me. Killing you does not feel right to me. Does not every creature deserve a chance to change and make amends?"

"You would show me mercy? Even after everything?" After all the years forging her way alone, the thought of such kindness was foreign to Dahlia.

"It seems mercy is something which was lacking from your life. Perhaps in time, you could find peace with your lot, use your vast knowledge for good. It is what I wish for you."

Dahlia stared at Lina in disbelief. Anger slowly melted from her heart, exposing the emotion that anger and hatred protect her from… *grief*—grief for a young fairy who was always misunderstood, who always seemed on the short side of the odds, who only felt the sting of love, never the balm. So overwhelming was the emotion, she tried to summon back her anger to overpower it, but it vanished in the crushing tide. An abyss of despair opened before her for love she would never know.

"Think about it," Lina added. "I will come back to see you soon."

"Your kindness is appreciated but misplaced, Lina. I am too broken to fix. Life has already seen to that." She bowed her head and returned back inside her tower. Lina's eyes followed, her heart filled with an aching hollow.

CHAPTER 46

The following morning dawned bright, the sun a perfect yellow orb in the clear blue sky. The castle shined a brilliant white, the flag with Lina's family crest flapped high upon a turret. Only days ago, the land was grey and barren under the rule of darkness. Now grass grew, and flowers bloomed. Tonight the fairies would celebrate their victory at Lina's official coronation.

From the nest Lina and Knox shared, she looked down on the castle grounds, a bustle of activity preparing for the evening's event. The pit in Lina's stomach grew at the thought of her impending monarchy. The fairies dismissed her misgivings about ruling the kingdom by reminding Lina the law must be followed. Even Edwina would hear nothing of abandoning the rightful heir.

Suddenly below, fairies stopped what they were doing and congregated in small groups, talking and gesturing frantically. Many looked up to where the swallow couple sat. Something must have happened. Whatever it was, Lina would not have to wait long to hear. Renna flew up to their nest and, without delay, delivered the news, "Dahlia is dead. She threw herself from the tower balcony last night. She never even opened her wings to save herself."

"I'm very sorry to hear that. Please prepare her body for burial. I will address our people about her death tonight," Lina declared.

Renna nodded and left. Lina showed a brave face at the news, but it hit her hard. Knox saw it in her eyes. She spent the rest of the morning in the branches of a newly blooming tree, a vibrant spot of blue amongst its pink flowers. The death of her aunt further agitated her sense of unease about becoming queen. Her mind entertained a host of competing thoughts, but no option felt right in her heart.

"Thinking?" Knox asked, landing beside her after she had been there most of the afternoon. The bough shook slightly when he landed.

"Yes." Her quiet reply, nearly carried away by the wind.

"About Dahlia?"

"In a way. About the unfair turns life can take and what it can do to us over time. Think about it, most of this tragedy occurred over three minutes, a fraction of time that caused years of heartache."

Knox simply sighed at her statement. There were no words he could think to offer.

"What if Dahlia had been born first—three minutes ahead of Ivy? Or if my grandparents used their own judgment in choosing an heir rather than insisting on following a precedent? Many lives would have been different." She paused a long moment. "I have made some decisions. I will announce them at the coronation tonight."

"I will go check to make sure everything is in order," he said.

She cocked her head. "You're not even going to ask me what my decisions are?"

"No. I trust you to rule this kingdom in a way that is best for all." He nudged his head against hers before flying off.

When she arrived at the castle that evening, Cornelius awaited her at the entrance. He greeted her with a warm smile and an awkward hug. Dressed in his finest attire, she could not help but think how handsome he was, so elegant next to her ungainly bird form. They must look like an odd pair.

Outside animals, too large to enter, gathered by the door. Right in front were Lina's special guests, Zander and Zavier, along with Madame Mouse and her children. They marveled at Lina's transformation, the young mice viewing the dramatic change as something out of a magical legend. Their excitement was infectious, the crowd humming with anticipation.

Inside, Renna stood with Aelin and Dunlin. They approached her and bowed, each taking a moment to wish her well. She noticed the wistful looks passing between Renna and Cornelius, but he stayed by Lina's side as other fairies came to greet them, including Bryla and her sisters. Kai waved at her from a group of nearby Ephemera. It took several minutes to cross the room, everyone wanting their chance to see the new queen. Cora, now reunited with her daughter, and Delphine stood with Teagan. They bowed when she passed. Edwina waited at the bottom of the dais, packed in amongst the spectators. Lina took up so much space in the room, it was challenging to fit in the large crowd.

"Welcome, Queen Lina," the enchantress said. "Long have your people awaited this moment. Now take your rightful place."

"Thank you all for coming," Lina said, once perched high on the back of the small throne. Every eye in the kingdom was on her. Nerves built up in Lina. Would they accept what she had to say? She noticed Knox in the rafters and calmed at the sight of him. "As many of you know, Dahlia took her life this morning."

A murmur of approval rushed through the crowd.

"Though this may seem like a well-deserved fate given her history, the loss of any fairy life is tragic. While I do not condone her choices in life, I will not celebrate her death. The capricious nature of fate affects us all, some to a worse end than others, but none should rejoice in the ill fortunes of another."

The audience hushed, the impact of the words sinking in.

"I have given much thought to the future of this kingdom. While laws and precedents are conceived with all the best intentions, the unforeseen turns of life are not always best suited by following them blindly. With this in mind, I command a change. Renna and Cornelius, please step up here."

After exchanging surprised looks, the two mounted the dais.

"You have guided our people with both courage and heart. Without you, any hope for this kingdom would have perished long before my arrival," Lina spoke to them before turning to the crowd. "From this day forward, I decree that these two will rule as queen and king. They will be wed, and the new line of royalty will henceforth descend from Renna's daughters. The Primal Stone is now linked to her bloodline. As for myself, Knox and I will serve as High Advisors to the new queen and king on all matters for which they require guidance. Now, join me in congratulating Renna and Cornelius. Long may they rule."

A stunned silence filled the room until Edwina stepped forward and cried, "Long may they rule!"

The enchantress's approval sanctioned the news for the rest of the fairies.

"Long may they rule!" the crowd shouted in unison.

Lina glanced up at Knox, who nodded his approval. She flew down to the newly named monarchs, who stood bewildered on the dais. The crown was brought out, and Edwina placed it on Renna's head. Next, Cornelius received his circlet of gold. All around them, fairies cheered and applauded their new queen and king.

"You honor us, My Queen," Renna said to Lina with a curtsey.

"You are queen now with Cornelius by your side. I can think of no two people more deserving." The words could not be more true.

"We are humbled. Not only by being able to be together but by being asked to rule. How can we ever thank you for such a selfless act?" Cornelius asked.

"My act was more virtuous than selfless. After all the years of darkness, you will rule with fairness, wisdom, and, most importantly, love. The Fairy World will be filled with light and peace again."

She spread her wings, and they embraced her. As their tears of joy soaked her feathers, the wisdom of this decision solidified in her heart. Then, the two turned to take in the praise from a roomful of happy fairies.

Edwina flew to Lina's side, her eyes glistening. "You are the wisest of us all. Your judgment brings a better outcome than I could ever imagine. How proud your parents would be to see you now. Both the fairy and mortal ones."

The weight of expectations she carried since learning her new identity was finally lifted from Lina's shoulders. A clear future, one on her terms, lay before her with open arms.

***

"I thought I might find you here," Knox said. He landed next to Lina on the top of a slight rise.

The morning had seen Renna and Cornelius wed in a beautiful service befitting their love. They could not have asked for a fairer day with the warm sun cooled by a gentle breeze that sent fluffy white clouds sailing across the sky. The city was filled to near bursting with all who had come to witness the event. Fairies and animals from all over the land attended. After, Lina had craved some solitude.

The pair now stood on a hilltop before two graves, modestly installed under a rowan tree. Ivy and Dahlia. Lina chose to bury them together in this quiet place rather than with Theros in the royal tombs. Somehow it seemed fitting for the twins to be together once more.

"The ceremony was wonderful, don't you think?" Knox asked.

"Yes. Cornelius and Renna will be fair and just rulers. The kingdom will flourish for countless years to come. It gives me *hope*. Not just for the fairy world, but for them." She gestured to the resting places. "*Hope* that they are reunited, the bond between them mended just as the Primal Stone was restored. *Hope* they can be as happy as two young sisters once were."

And with hope in her heart, she and Knox settled into their lives. When not needed by the monarchs, they explored the skies and lands, relishing the beauty that returned to the entire kingdom. Occasionally, they even visited the mortal world where Lina looked happily upon her old house, now the home of a young family whose children filled the space with energy and laughter. At night in their nest high above the city, Lina would nestle next to Knox, her heart overflowing with love as she drifted to sleep. She had found the place where she belonged, after all. Despite all the twists and turns of Lina's journey, she finally found a home.

The End

ACKNOWLEDGEMENTS

Publishing a book takes a village and I have many who helped me on this journey to thank. To my incredible editor, Mellisa Higgins, thank you for strengthening my story in more ways than I thought possible. To Mulan Jiang of **Graphics by Mulan Jiang**, thank you for the breathtaking cover that you somehow plucked right from my imagination. To Angelique Bosman of **The Book Studio,** thank you for your formatting savvy and the care you took with my book. To my beta-readers, Barbara and Jill, thank you for your time and your honest input. To my fellow author, Krysten Hagar, thank you for your advice and mentoring. To my family, thank you for your unwavering support. To my sweet kitties, Zelda & Link, thank you for keeping me sane in a house full of boys. Finally, to you the readers, thank you for allowing my stories into your lives. If you enjoy reading them as much as I enjoy writing them, I am truly blessed.

ABOUT THE AUTHOR

Reading was always a big part of Jane's life. Creating her own stories developed out of this love. To date, she has published the *Not Every Girl* trilogy, a YA Fantasy/Adventure. Her latest work, *A Prophecy of Wings*, is a retelling of the classic fairy tale, *Thumbelina*. These books represent her goals as a writer—stories of adventure for teens with strong, yet relatable, female protagonists.

She lives in New Jersey with her husband, two sons and two extremely spoiled cats. When she is not running around with her family or writing, she can be found curled up with a good book and said cats.

You can visit her at: www.janemcgarrybooks.com.

Made in the USA
Middletown, DE
09 November 2021